The Chinese Mid-Autumn Festival: Foods and Folklore

William C. Hu

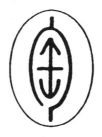

Ars Ceramica, Ltd.

Library of Congress Cataloging in Publication Data

Hu, William Chao-chung

The Chinese Mid-Autumn Festival: Foods and Folklore

p. illus. (Foods & Snacks of Chinese Festivals)
Includes: Glossary of Chinese Terms

1. Food Habits - - China   2. Cookery, Chinese
3. Confectionary - - China   4. Tales - - China
5. Diet Therapy   6. Dim Sum
I. Title

GT2853.C6H87   641.3'

ISBN:0-89344-036-1
LC 90-084107

Manufactured in the United States of America

Ars Ceramica, Ltd.
P.O. Box 7366
Ann Arbor, Michigan 48107-7366

Dedication

For My Sister

Mrs. Ellen Young

and her Daughters

Linda, Brenda, and Wanda

Contents

MID-AUTUMN FESTIVAL

Preface

Traditionally, China's agricultural system has enabled her to feed a large population with a relatively small area of arable land. China's agriculture depended mainly on highly productive crop varieties, recycling of nutrients, efficient use of water resources, and highly skilled intensive labor. In China's early history, the government was committed to giving agriculture a high priority in order that there was the availability of food, not just for the population, but also for military security.

From ancient times, the Chinese had a great fascination with food, cuisine, and elaborate dining and banquets. Ritual and ceremony help to institutionalize social codes and behavior surrounding recognition of honor and status. Respect for the old and for elite individuals was expressed in feasts. The gods also insisted on the best, they ate the essence of the foods sacrificed to them, while the human beings consumed the material portion. In addition, the Chinese, early in their history, had developed a medical science in which nutrition played a most important role. Many foods were grown and eaten solely for their medicinal and nutritional properties.

These beliefs led to demands on the food production system as even the poor wanted gourmet fare, for major festivals and also for their aged parents' birthdays. Moreover, the central government promoted through customs and traditions of festivals consciousness of nutrition and keeping healthy by eating the proper foods. As a vehicle for propaganda, many stories, legends and folk tales have been linked with these foods, serving two purposes — the promotion of eating the proper foods and the values of good citizenship.

However good the intention of the central government, there occurred in traditional Chinese society a great paradox. As the system of festival foods intensified in its promotion, the elite and well-to-do always had their chefs invent new dishes and varieties, and the peasants, trying to keep up with custom, found themselves in dire straits and marginal subsistence. Therefore it may be surmised that festival foods are not necessarily regional but reflect economic status differences. Nevertheless, whether it is gourmet food or not, festivals demand the eating of certain food items.

This study is not a comprehensive study of all the foods eaten during the Mid-Autumn or Moon Festival celebration, but a sampling of the more important food items in order to better understand this festival. The Moon Festival is not only observed by the Chinese but also by other Asians. The Japanese call it Jugoya, the Koreans,

Chuseok or Kawi and it is considered to be the 'Harvest Moon' and the occasion for thanksgiving and partying. The Japanese had adopted the Chinese custom of setting out melons, green soy beans, and fruits in the garden as offerings to the moon. Sprays of Susuki *(eulalia)* are displayed on the veranda and tiny skewered dumplings (Dango) and vegetables are offered to the moon. It is said that displaying Susuki, which resembles the rice plant, will ensure a good harvest. Sweet potatoes (Satsuma imo) and taro (Imo) are commonly offered so Jugoya is also known as Imo meigetsu (taro or sweet potato moon). Likewise, this festival is celebrated in Vietnam, Malaysia, Singapore, Hong Kong and other Southeast Asian countries as well as in Chinese communities in the United States and Europe.

The research and publication of this book has been generously supported by grants from the C.K. and Soo Yong Huang Foundation, Foodland Super Market, Ltd., and Hawaii Medical Library, Inc. and I am grateful to these institutions for their support. To Mrs. Thema Zen, William and Aileen Ho, Maurice and Joanna Sullivan, Mrs. Lily Sun Wong, and John A. Breinich, for their support and encouragement in urging this publication, I express my deepest and sincerest thanks and gratitude.

It is also a pleasure to express my thanks to my dearest friend, Libby and her brother Biddy of Hong Kong, Paris and San Francisco for allowing their family chefs to instruct me in the preparation of the many fesitval foods in this book. I extend my thanks and appreciation for assistance also to James Lee and C.H. Kwock of San Francisco, Drs. Ernest K.H. Lee, Leta Yang, Mun Chung Hu, Douglas and Jennie Mun, Jan Wah and Ella Chun, Melvin and Jeannette Miyata, Kalvin Ko, Dennis Wong, Wesley and Sandra Leong, Sharlene Chun, Joseph and Gloria Menor, Steven Chun, Christine Miyata, and Alan Mun of Honolulu and Dr. Carol M. Ways, of Ann Arbor. To Fred Bleicher, Marjorie E. Uren and Robert Soichet who read my complete manuscript and offered their expertise and suggestions, I am most deeply indebted. Finally I wish to thank the publishers, Ars Ceramica, Ltd. of Ann Arbor, Michigan for designing and publishing this beautiful book.

Ann Arbor, Michigan   *William C. Hu*

Summer, 1990

Introduction

The ancient Chinese, as an agricultural people had the advantage of watching the annual cycle of nature in the temperate zone. They could easily have seen that the vegetation, and to a lesser extent the animals living upon the vegetation, were always changing in accordance with the changing weather. Moreover, the weather changed in accordance with the solar and lunar motions. The success or failure of their crops always depended on diligent observation of the natural changes of the season. It is the inevitable conclusion that importance be placed on the orderliness of organic nature (harmony and cyclic periodicity) of all physical and biological phenomena.

The *I-ching* or *Book of Changes* bears good evidence of the 'orderly' or 'organic' characteristic of such a philosophy of nature. Since all plants obey the laws of nature, the success of a crop and farming depend on the harmony of the three cardinal factors (San-ts'ai) proper season, proper ground, and proper human effort. When human effort is applied properly with regard to space and time in accordance with the three factors, the highest degree of success is guaranteed of the union of nature and man.

Chia Ssu-hsieh in his *Ch'i-min yao-shu*, a 6th century agricultural encyclopaedia, noted that: "Following the appropriateness of the season, consider well the nature and condition of the soil, then and only then, the least amount of labor will reap the best success and results."

Just as plants must be planted and harvested at specific times, so it is with their consumption: foods should be eaten in the proper seasons. In addition to this, the Chinese from earliest recorded times have regarded food as one of the most important subjects for social regulation and symbolic structuring. This is shown by the incredibly detailed sections on food in ancient books of rites such as the *Chou-i* and *Li-chi*, the writings of Confucius, Mencius and other philosophers, and both folk and classical poetry.

In addition, there is also placed a great importance in traditional dietary lore. The Chinese have ancient and still widely followed nutritional practices, not always in accord with modern scientific findings but at least as sophisticated and accurate as any culture's traditional beliefs about food as medicine. In the *Pên-ts'ao kang-mu* or the Chinese Materia Medica by Li Shih-chên (1518-1593), there is even the codifying of this foodlore.

The most important concept in Chinese foodlore is the influence of energies and flavors of foods. The five energies of foods are categorized hot, warm, cold, cool or neutral. Hot or warm or the 'heating of the body' is the heat of spirit or energy rather than of temperature. Rich, high-calorie, spicy foods, and foods subjected to high heat in cooking, are the most heating. They may cause or aggravate, fevers, constipation, rashes and sores, and other symptoms of heat or tightness.

Low calorie, cool-colored, bland foods, notably vegetables, such as watercress or white radishes are cooling. These may lead to weakness, low body-temperature, pallor, shivering and other symptoms of cold or chill. Most other foods are neutral or balanced such as staple grains, many fish, many fruits and vegetables.

Part of the same system, less important but widely held, is the 'wet-dry' continuum. It is considered important to know the energies of foods, because different energies act upon the human body in different ways. This has important effects on good health. Therefore much home treatment of illness and prevention of disease is carried out by varying the diet according to this system.

This Chinese system is in many ways basically the same as the Galenic or Hippocratic humoral system of Europe. This Chinese *yin-yang* dichotomy, influential in the classification of energies and flavors of foods was instituted in China long before the arrival of the humoral theory.

In addition to the 'hot-cold,' 'wet-dry,' continuum, there is also a continuum from 'safe' to 'poisonous.' Many foods not poisonous in themselves are poisonous in some combinations and situations or to some individuals. Other foods are specific for clearing away 'wetness,' for cleaning, clearing and harmonizing the body, and for building strength or building blood. These foods tend to be either nourishing, digestible protein foods or, in the case of blood-builders, red-colored, a kind of sympathetic magic. For similar reasons of appearance, walnuts are thought to strengthen the brain. In these and other ways, medical beliefs have greatly influenced the diets of many Chinese.

However, another influence of food was and is its use to communicate social messages. Here the Chinese have taken the use of food and food language to a pitch of complexity probably unrivalled elsewhere. Foods are used to mark group affiliation, occasion, status, respect, and other social factors. Almost every occasion such as festivals, weddings, birthdays, religious rites and sacrifices, are marked by special foods and delicacies.

In an ancient and complex society, the use of food as a major mode of social communication, also served as a means for the central authority to promote, encourage and administer public health, as well as agricultural planning and economy.

In the *Yüeh-ling* or Monthly Ordinance section of the *Li-chi* or *Book of Rites*, we read that: "In the second month of autumn (8th lunar month), the sun is in the position of Spica and Virgo, . . . the number is nine, its taste is acrid and bitter, and its smell is 'Hsing' (the strong smell of newly-killed meat, especially the smell of sheep and goats, or fishy smell). . . . Sudden and violent winds come. The geese arrive, and the swallows return whence they came, while various birds store up provisions for the future. . . . In this month, there should be special care and nourishment to the weak and old. Distribution of (sitting) stools and (walking) canes or staves and supplies of congee for food are presented to them."

'Congee', called chou (Cantonese: chuk or commonly spelled as jook) by the Chinese, is a porridge made of either grains or cereals, beans and other legumes, fruits and nuts and even herbs, although most popular are that of rice. This versatile dish is usually eaten as breakfast and sometimes as a snack. It is eaten both by the wealthy and poor, depending on the richness of its ingredients. In figures of speech, the eating of congee means to be poor and unfortunate. It is also used as food for the sick or those with poor digestion and also as medicine. Chou or congee is widely used in famine relief and other natural disasters as a means of feeding the masses. As Congee or Chou, has bad connotations being associated with poor and sick, it is not used as a festival food. There is, however, a Buddhist memorial celebrated on the 8th day of the 12th lunar month, popularly called 'La-pa' which commemorates Sakyamuni's enlightenment and attainment of Buddhahood. At this time, temples and Buddhists prepare a sweet congee, called 'La-pa-chou' which is made from grains, fruits and nuts which is offered to Buddha and given as a gift to others and also eaten. To counteract the bad connotation, this special congee is given the appealing name 'Ch'i-pao-chou' or 'seven-jewelled porridge.'

In Hawaii, there is a tradition of serving raw fish and congee during the Mid-Autumn Festival celebration. This unique Hawaiian custom unfortunately is not a traditional Chinese custom. It may have been developed by the early Chinese contract laborers who did not have much money. In order to feed lots of people at a low cost, they resorted to serving Chou or Congee. It should also be pointed out that the most famous and expensive Chou served by the Cantonese had been 'Yü-shêng-chou' or Raw fish Congee. The fish in this dish is not eaten raw but dipped into the hot congee which contained enough heat to cook it. It may be surmised that the early Chinese in Hawaii had separated this famous dish to be eaten as two separate items. In Hawaii, there is quite a precedence for this as the native Hawaiians used to say, "Fish and Poi" which is similar to "Raw Fish and Congee."

It should also be pointed out that the Mid-Autumn Festival is celebrated at night and there is a Cantonese idiomatic expression, "Shik-ye-chuk" (literally, eating Congee at night) which means to work all night or to endure hardships. Therefore, it could well be understood why Congee is not eaten as a festive food during the Mid-Autumn Festival as it would be considered inauspicious.

As a point of interest, similar to the Japanese eating Sashimi during the New Year, raw fish is also eaten during the Chinese New Year celebration, more specifically on the 7th day of the 1st lunar month. A large platter with raw fish and condiments is placed in the middle of the dinner table and everyone helps to mix it. This communal mixing is called by the Cantonese slang as "Loh-shai-kaai" or "Making one's fortune." This dish is called 'Yü-shêng' (Cantonese: Ue-shaang), a homonym for 'abundance to be gotten.' However, when raw fish is eaten at other times in the year, it goes by another name, 'Yü-hua' (Cantonese: Ue-waat).

In the *Li-chi*, congee is used to strengthen the weak and old in order to fortify their bodies to withstand the coming cold weather. The ancient classic also recommended that the populace should eat foods tasting 'hsin' which has qualities of bitterness or acrid. Also foods being 'hsing' are suggested, such as lamb, goat, fish, geese or ducks. Certainly, there must be some reasons for these guidelines and the recommendations of specific foods.

In the *Nung-sang-i-shih tso-yao* by Lu Ming-shang, which is a *Yüeh-ling* or Monthly Ordinance for the Yüan dynasty (1260-1367), there is a sampling of recommendations of various agricultural chores, products as well as food-processing for the 8th lunar month. This accounts in part for why these foods have been used to celebrate the Mid-Autumn Festival.

It mentions that: "In autumn when the Water Caltrop have turned black, it should be harvested. Replanting some by scattering them in the ponds, which would naturally take root and sprout new plants. . . . During this month (8th lunar month), sprouting of the taro is exceptionally rigorous. Remove the soil around the plant and remove the smaller corms and sprouts. Replace it with new soil which should be richly manured and contain leaf mulch. This allows the tubers to grow healthy and large. If this process is omitted, the taro will suffer in being small." There are instructions for dividing up clumps of chives, reducing the size of ducks and geese flocks, harvesting persimmons, jujubes, ginger, garlic, etc.

In the 6th century agricultural classic, *Ch'i-min yao-shu*, we find mention of the preparation of various kinds of salted and plain pickles made of 18 different plants. It also spells out specific instructions of the storage of fresh grapes, pears and chestnuts for both current and later use in winter. As for animal husbandry, there is mention of culling the herd so that there would be enough forage to keep a good breeding and spring herd. Sheep, goats, ducks and geese are specifically mentioned to be slaughtered at this time. The animal flesh is to be consumed or dried into jerky or smoked. The ducks are made into La-ya (Cantonese: Lop-opp) to be sold later or eaten during the twelfth month.

Black Bean Sauce (Tou-shih)

There is also an important passage on making (tou) shih or prepared 'black beans sauce' which is used in a variety of dishes served during the Moon Festival. The following is a description for its preparation:

"[Tou] Shih is usually made in the 5th to 8th lunar month, as this is the timely season. Take 1 *shih* (approx. 22 liters) of beans, scour them well, and soak overnight. Steam it next morning. Rub a grain between fingers, if the skin slips out, it is well done. Spread on the ground to a thickness of 6 cm., or on a mat if the ground is bad. Allow it to remain there and cool down. Cover with rushes, also 5-6 cm. thick. After 3 days, see whether all have turned yellow. If so, take off the rushes and spread the beans to form a thinner layer. Make grooves with fingers among the layers, shape into 'plots.' Mix them up and spread them out again making 'plots' a few hours later. Repeat these three times a day for three more days. Cook another portion of beans to get a thick syrupy decoction. Take 5 *shĕng* (1 *shĕng* = 0.22 liter) smaller 'starters' (made of glutinous rice) and 5 *shĕng* good table salt, mix both into the yellowed beans, sprinkle with bean decoction. Knead with both hands, till some juice begins to run out between the fingers. Then place in a pottery jar until full, but don't press down! Any empty space left on top should be stuffed with wild mulberry leaves. Tightly seal on with mud. Place in the middle of the courtyard for 27 days. Then pour out, spread and dry in the sunshine. Steam, sprinkle with a decoction of mulberry-leaves. Steam as long as if to steam raw beans; when done, spread and sun again. After steaming and sunning thrice, the finished product is obtained."

There are also instructions for the utilization of lactic (acid) fermentation to prevent spoilage of fresh vegetables as the underlying principle of making pickles. The lactic acid micro-organisms convert soluble sugars, free or derived from amylolyses, present in plant juices to lactic acid. Although a rather weak acid, lactic acid when accumulated is 'antiseptic' in the sense that it retards and inhibits the growth and development of putrefying microbes. Its pleasant flavor and odor are both appealing and appetizing.

Thus the author of the 6th century classic, *Ch'i-min yao-shu*, notes that, "in teaching people (various agricultural arts and skills) . . . it will all provide for the people. . . and if various works are done in their proper and due time, it will enrich the state and benefit the people." Therefore, the various foods served and eaten during the Moon Festival, (and other festivals as well) were not only chosen to utilize the proper foods at the proper season, it was also to provide for the encouragement of public health and nutrition as well as promoting the storage of foods for the non-growing season. An additional economic function was served to insure that the yields of crops would be duly sold and the farmers were thus encouraged to improve their yields.

As to the special diet of certain vegetables, fish, meat, and grains eaten during the celebration of the Mid-Autumn or Moon Festival, there is a specific underlying reason — vitamin deficiency. The Chinese people have lived for centuries in conditions, if not of over population, of relatively high population density, subject to constantly recurring natural calamities, such as earthquakes, and especially, floods, with their concomitant destruction of harvest and widespread famine. Vitamin deficiencies have therefore been endemic in Chinese life. It should also be pointed out that in contrast with the milk-and-mutton diet of the Mongolian plateaus, the Chinese farmers were always exclusively agricultural, not pastoral, growing wheat in the North and rice in the South, and using oxen only for draught purposes, not for milk or (anciently) for flesh food. Of the vitamins, therefore, A and the B group were derived from cereals and oils, and C from herbs of all kinds, and sprouted and pickled vegetables. It may be pointed out that within the limits of the possible, the Chinese understood very well the choosing and cooking of a well-balanced diet. The intake of vitamin D was probably always on the borderline, sufficient in the South where there is plenty of sunshine, but not in the North.

By the end of the last century, it was clear that diseases like scurvy, beriberi and rickets, could be cured empirically by the addition of suitable foods to the diet, although there was no knowledge of the chemistry or the nature of the deficient substances. As to beriberi, a disease which we now know to be due to vitamin B1 deficiency, L. J. Harris in his *Vitamins and Vitamin Deficiencies* wrote that, "This disease, known in China as early as 2600 B.C., was first conclusively shown to have a dietary origin in 1880 by Takaki, the Director-General of the Medical Department of the Japanese Navy. By simply increasing slightly the allowance of vegetables, fish, meat and barley in a diet still consisting predominantly of rice, he was able to reduce the incidence of disease to virtually vanishing point."

Inasmuch as the recognition of beriberi is a disease of dietary origin and often attributed to the eminent Japanese naval officer, Takaki, it should be noted that in the 14th century, Hu-ssu-hui, who was an Imperial Dietitian wrote a book entitled *Yin-shan chêng-yao* or the 'Principles of Correct Diet.' In prefacing his work, he used the phrase, 'shih-liao chü-ping' that is, 'Food cures various diseases.' In this work, there are a number of recipes for diets suitable for curing beriberi, including the use of various meats and herbs.

For the cure of 'wet' beriberi, the following recipes are given:

1. Make a soup of rice and Ma-ch'ih-ts'ao, and let the patient drink it on an empty stomach early in the morning.

2. Cook 16 ounces of pork with one handful of onion, 3 ts'ao-kuo, pepper, fermented beans and rice (1/2 lb.) and let the patient eat it in the morning.

For the cure of 'dry' beriberi, the following recipes are given:

Cook 1 big carp with 1/2 lb. small red beans, 2/10 oz. of tangerine fruit peel, 2/10 oz. of small dried peppers, and 2/10 oz. of ts'ao-kuo. Let the patient eat it.

For cases with edema, the following recipe is suggested:

Stuff 1 lb. small red beans and 5 ts'ao-kuo into a duck, and make a soup. Let the patient eat it in the morning.

It can be seen from these recipes that a good intake of vitamin B1 was assured, but other vitamins would be present in addition, an important fact since many or most of the deficiency cases would be lacking in more than one vitamin.

Beriberi, a disease known in China as 'Chiao-ch'i' has been cured by dietary means for many centuries. We do not generally realize the antiquity of human knowledge concerning deficiency diseases. However, the existence of a knowledge of dietary treatment of various diseases in China can be traced back as early as the time of the Warring States. We find that in the early 12th century B.C. work, *Chou-li* or *Book of Rites*, there is mention that besides the Imperial Physician and Imperial Surgeon, there was also an Imperial Dietitian among the medical officers of the Chou court.

The official class of China, fundamentally an agricultural country, has always had an interest in the food of the people. In surveying of the early medical literature, including the *Pên-ts'ao* editions together with the older *Chin-kuei yao-lüeh*, we find that the latter work, gives an account of the causes of the diseases and a theory of therapy. It contains many vivid accounts of deficiency diseases in their various stages, and describes preparations which, we know today, would be rich in the various vitamins.

It is interesting that the famous writer Han Yü (762-824 A.D.) states in one of his essays that the disease beriberi was particularly prevalent south of the Yangtze River. This was still true in 1935 when Hou Hsiang-chuang in his study, *Nutrition Notes*, noted similar difference, and referred it to the difference in diet between the wheat-eating north and the rice-eating south. In the Sung dynasty, there appeared a monograph especially devoted to beriberi, the *Chiao-ch'i-shih-fa tsung-yao* by Tung Chi which appeared during the later half of the 11th century.

So deeply imbedded in the Chinese people was the ancient dietetic knowledge, that to this day the phrase 'grandmother's cures,' is used for traditional dieting, and even in present times, both groceries and drugs are sold in the same store. In China, it has been found that in the absence of flood and war, the country folk know by experience what to eat and how to eat to maintain a satisfactory state of well-being at low economic levels. The Chinese use a sort of food calendar to regulate their diet and certain foods are dictated as festive foods that everyone should eat.

However, the propaganda promoting the eating of these festive and seasonal foods, in order to gain wide popularity, took on various fascinating and interesting stories and tales to attract public attention and general awareness. The foods thus promoted later became traditions and part of annual custom and story tellers added more stories about them from time to time. In keeping with the agricultural tradition of the Chinese, besides the stories and some recipes of these festive foods and dishes, there is included also a selection on the preparation of various preserves, candies and sauces.

Chapter 1:
Mid-Autumn Festival

Festivals and celebrations have always been a most important aspect of daily life for the Chinese people. Food and nutrition are also valued highly by the Chinese. Thus it is not surprising that festival foods provide a rich, complex and intriguing area of study. The Chinese central authorities have instituted certain festival foods as a means of promoting public health and encouraging the consumption of proper foods throughout the year. The production cycles for food stuffs of the largely agrarian nation with such a large population required control of the delicate agricultural economy. Thus the seasonal cakes, pastries and sweet meats that have been associated with every major Chinese festival serve several purposes at once such as using seasonal harvest foods at their peak of supply and nutritive value, encouraging preservation methods for foods to be eaten out of season, aiding the selection of variety in the diet and so on. At the New Year celebration there is the Nien-kao or New Year Pudding, Chiao-tzu (dumplings), the Tzu (a glutinous rice cake) and the San-tzu or fried twists. During the Lantern Festival or Yüan-hsiao, which is the 15th day of the 1st month, T'ang-yüan, which are (glutinous rice dumplings) are eaten. At the Ch'ing-ming festival Pao-ping are consumed. At the Dragon Boat Festival, we find Tsung-tzu and Chu-sha-ping a pink-colored sugar cake, the featured delicacy. Yüan-sui-ping are eaten on the 8th day of the 4th month, and so on.

The Chinese term, 'Kao' is applied to cakes, puddings and the like. They are usually made of glutinous rice, glutinous millet, or common rice flour and steamed. Those made of glutinous rice are called 'Tzu,' and those of rice, beans, and sugar are called 'Erh.' Those made of the common rice are considered the most digestible while those made of common millet are thought to injure the spleen and should be forbidden to children. The former nourish the spleen, stomach, intestines, benefit the breath, and harmonize the centers. The latter benefit the breath, warm the centers, and assist in excretion. They are specially recommended in the diarrhea of the aged.

Used in close association with the term 'kao' is the term 'ping' or cakes in general, forming the compound term 'Kao-ping.' The 'Chêng-ping' or steamed cakes are usually made of wheat flour and are of many varieties. They are usually raised with leaven, and are eaten both hot and cold. They are considered peptic, nourishing, a hydrotic, and eliminative. They are recommended in chronic diarrhea, colligative sweating, etc.

Fried cakes called 'San-tzu,' 'Huan-ping' or 'Nien-t'ou,' are made of glutinous rice and flour, with a little salt, and are fried in sesame seed oil. They are said to tone up the excretory organs, lubricate the intestines, warm the centers, and benefit the breath. Chronic dysentery is treated with them.

Sweet meats are known by the names 'I-t'ang' and 'Hsing.' They are made of a variety of grains, fruits, nuts, and seeds. Often malted grain is used which much resembles glucose. Various confections including candied fruits generally termed,

'T'ang-kuo,' are also included as festival food items. They are regarded as tonic, cooling, strengthening, carminative and expectorant.

Inasmuch as festival foods were basically promoted by the central authority within the cultural behavior and rites, these foods are interpreted only by folklore and symbolism. This makes their development not only more complex but adds greater interest and color, allowing for newer creations and inventions.

As it was beyond the average citizen to extract the scientific or economic reasons for these festival foods, the general masses found great delight in the intriguing and mystifying stories woven by the professional storytellers. In time, these stories became the most important factor and aside from the aspect of symbolism, all other reasons and meanings for these festival foods were overlooked. However, as higher education and greater economic gains were achieved, many looked to find the real meaning and background to their cultural heritage. It is due to this interest along with the rise and fall of dynasties and the rise and fall of economic power that we should find numerous citations within Chinese literature relating to the various festival practices within each period of history. Yet, what is standard in Chinese culture is found in the rites and ceremonies that are recorded in various dynastic histories, local gazetteers, family records, etc. The problem is not that customs are lost but simply that sometimes they are not currently practised.

The foremost and best known food item connected with the Mid-Autumn or Moon Festival is, of course, the Moon Cake. Although this delicacy was known centuries ago, nevertheless, the popular stories and tales surrounding it date it to the mid-14th century. The following are some of the stories both serious and humorous about the Moon Cake popularly told by storytellers during the celebration of the Moon Festival.

Stories of the Moon Cakes

The Mongol emperors of the Yüan dynasty were the descendants of Genghis Khan, who had united the tribes of the steppes in 1206 and conquered a part of north China in 1215. The conquest of China as a whole was completed by his grandson Kubilai Khan in 1276-1280. After their conquest, there were a number of severe measures imposed on the Chinese to insure that there would not be any rebellion or organized resistance. Twenty households were formed into a unit called *Lü* and a Mongol soldier was appointed as its administrator. Only one chopping knife was to be used by every ten families. Moreover, a congregation of more than five persons meeting together was against the law.

The living expenses and maintenance for each Mongol administrator billeted was to be borne by all the members of each unit, which caused considerable hardships. The Mongol administrators were not only arrogant, they usually demanded the best in food, clothing and shelter. They ate expensive fish and meats and wore silks and brocades, while living in the best quarters within each unit. They were like household guests who had to be waited upon hand and foot. Wherever they went, it was either on horseback or by litter, the expenses of which were to be again furnished and maintained by the people of each unit.

With any dissatisfaction, floggings were dispensed freely as well as killings and executions on occasion. All this merely served to instill a hatred of the Mongols and the despised Mongol administrators were dubbed ironically 'Kuan-chia-kung' or "Mongol stewards."

After the extinction of the Sung dynasty, there were no organized loyalist movements fighting against the Mongol overlords as they had a strong strangle-hold on the Chinese. The population acquiesced to the the new regime. Loyalist feelings for the defunct Sung were, however, widespread among the intellectuals. Nostalgia for the past splendor of the Sung was frequently expressed in writings, which were seldom censored by the Mongol government.

However, during the first decades of the 14th century there occurred some minor local rebellions, all without lasting effect. Only under the last emperor did popular rebellions weaken Mongol rule, chiefly after the disastrous floods of the Yellow and Huai Rivers which displaced many peasants. The attempts of the government to repair the dams using forced labor created further unrest and discontent. At the same time local rebellions broke out in the densely populated regions of southeast China, some of them led by messianic Buddhist sects. In the 1350's large parts of China were fragmented into virtually independent local regimes and satrapies. A spirit of rebellion was in the air, induced by discrimination, unsound fiscal policy, political corruption and the increase of famine conditions in certain areas. This was a period of social and political upheaval, an era of lawlessness and disorder compounded by peasant uprisings and bandits amidst the breakdown of central authority. Rebel leaders one after another arose to challenge the Mandate of Heaven, inflicting unprecedented torment and privation on the people. Overwhelmed by an army of rebels, including Hsü Shih-ch'êng and Ch'ên Yu-liang in Hu-Kuang, Chang Shih-ch'êng in the Yangtze delta, Kuo Tzu-hsing and Chu Yüan-chang in the Huai regions, and Fang Kuo-chên in the Chekiang coast, the Mongols were too feeble to organize resistance. Of all the rebel leaders, Chu Yüan-chang, succeeded in eliminating rival movements and in conquering Ta-tu the capital. He was able to bring the Mongol rule to an end and institute the glorious Ming dynasty.

Liu Po-wên and the Moon Cake

It is said that once when Chu Yüan-chang, who was from peasant stock, was leading an army just about to attack Chin-hua, Ch'u-chou and Wên-chou, the people of those areas sent messengers to beg him to help rid themselves of the hated Kuan-chia-kung or Mongol stewards. Chu Yüan-chang was enraged when he heard of the descriptions of the injustice done to these people and wanted to move immediately with his army for an all out open attack. However, he had to consult with his chief military advisor, Liu Po-wên, on the best strategy.

Liu Po-wên, whose chosen name was Liu Chi, is an enigmatic figure in Chinese history. In traditional moralistic writings, he is described as an exemplary Confucian statesman and the chief architect in the founding of the Ming. In popular fiction, however, he appears as an ingenious tactician, efficacious prognosticator and a Taoist type of mysterious figure with occult powers.

When Chu Yüan-chang saw Liu Po-wên, and told him of the situation, the latter remarked, "Although there is the enemy before us, My Lord, the vast plains of the empire have not yet been conquered. With so many leaders contending for supremacy and occupying specific areas, if you were to divide your army, this would weaken your authority and recovery would be difficult. In this present situation, allow me to devise a scheme whereby all that you desire will be met without the use of a single soldier. This I promise can be accomplished in a fortnight. I hereby guarantee success in gaining victory over these three occupied areas and thereby ridding them of all 'Mongol stewards'."

Inasmuch as Chu Yüan-chang was perplexed as to what action would be taken, nevertheless, he had great faith in his minister and so gave him *carte blanche* without inquiring what remedies he had in mind. However, the curious Lord wanted to know what steps his adviser would be taking so he placed agents to spy on his chief counsellor, and to report back on his every movement. After a while, his spies returned with the observation that the chief counsellor had awakened early in the morning and left camp with several private secretaries. What they were up to, why, or where they were going remained uncertain.

Before long, it was the night of the Mid-Autumn Festival and there was jubilant celebration within the camp. Both officers and men joined together in drinking toasts to the moon and celebrated this occasion with great joy. As the soldiers were offering toasts to their Commander-in-chief, Chu Yüan-chang, suddenly there was an announcement that the chief counsellor had arrived at the banquet. Chu Yüan-chang was so glad to hear this announcement that he arose from his seat in order to greet Liu Po-wên personally.

"My trusted adviser," he said to Liu Po-wên, "I have not seen you for several days. Have you devised a good plan to eliminate the Mongol stewards yet? When will this plan commence?"

Liu Po-wên, smiling responded, "These are but trivial matters. Why should my Lord even bother with them? Tonight is the celebration of the Mid-Autumn Festival. Let's place aside these matters so that we may relax and enjoy these festivities in toasting each other with wine!"

After drinking three rounds of toasts, the excited Chu Yüan-chang again wanted to question his adviser, but Liu Po-wên interrupted him by suggesting that they go outside and play a game of chess in the bright moonlit night. Although Chu Yüan-chang complied, his mind was not on the game and he lost twice to his adviser. While the chess board was being cleared for another game, Chu Yüan-chang was now growing more impatient. He pulled Liu Po-wên's long sleeves and said, "My trusted adviser, should we not repair back to the military headquarters for some serious discussions in making military preparations?"

Laughing, Liu Po-wên replied, "Calm yourself, My Lord. I'm afraid that this is premature. Now is only *Tzu* (11 p.m.-1 a.m.) or the hour of the Rat in the third watch period. Let us wait until the end of the fifth watch and the beginning of *Mao* (5-7 a.m.) or the hour of the Hare."

Reluctantly, Chu Yüan-chang agreed and started to play a third game of chess with Liu Po-wên. Nevertheless, instead of concentrating and paying attention to the game, he was more mindful of the watchman tolling the hour on his wooden drum and gong. His curiosity and puzzlement were peaking as to what schemes his counsellor had conceived, but he was just too polite to inquire. Looking at Liu Po-wên he saw that he was calm, patient and stoic and that there seemed to be nothing that could move him from his leisurely and carefree pace in playing this game of chess.

The curious Chu Yüan-chang felt in his mind that his chief adviser was up to something and he just had to know its details. Not being able to contain this anxious feeling inside of himself any longer, Chu Yüan-chang was just about to burst out asking him again pointedly of the plan when they were rudely interrupted by one of the returning spies who elatedly reported, "Those Mongol stewards, they have all been slain! Completely killed and wiped out!"

Hearing this, Chu Yüan-chang was greatly surprised and shocked as he could not comprehend the turn of events since no troops had left camp or been dispatched. Just as he was about to ask some questions about this, couriers and forward guards from the western, southern and northern stations all came rushing in with similar urgent reports. All indicated that the Mongol soldiers stationed at each Lü unit were completely wiped out. The news was frightening as it was unknown who was committing this wholesale slaughter of the Mongols. Nevertheless, he was happy to hear of these reports and news. Just then the watchman started to beat the end of the fifth watch. It was now *Mao* or the hour of the Hare (5-7 a.m.). Realizing this, Chu Yüan-chang nodded his head with satisfaction and smiling remarked, "What my trusted counsellor had said earlier, 'Wait until the end of the fifth watch and the beginning of *Mao* or the hour of the Hare', is certainly a great prognostication which I now understand!"

What Chu Yüan-chang did not know earlier was that Liu Po-wên had fully utilized the practises of the Chinese celebration of the Mid-Autumn Festival in constructing his plans. Approximately seven days earlier, he had ordered some of his men into these three prefectures. There they sought out every baker and every cake peddler, cake store and bakery ordering them to bake several hundred thousands of moon cakes. In each of these moon cakes, they were to insert a small piece of paper with the filling. They also were to spread the word that everyone within the three prefectures should celebrate the Mid-Autumn Festival as the moon rose into the sky. The people were told that if everyone ate a moon cake during that time, all their problems and grief would dissipate and calamity and misfortune would be averted. The news spread rapidly and everyone followed these instructions.

On the night of the Mid-Autumn Festival as everyone was enjoying the brightness of the Harvest Moon, they each ate a moon cake as instructed. To their surprise, they each found a small piece of paper with a twenty character poem:

> The gods are secretly hidden
> Aiding the people to rid the icy cold
> The time of 'Tzu' is best
> Together slay the Mongol stewards.

As soon as each person saw this message, they became surprised and startled. They quickly returned to their homes and awaited the sounding of *Tzu*, the hour of the Rat which was the third watch of the night. They all sent out some members to scout out the situation in their own neighborhood. Knowing that everyone had received the same message, they proceeded to make preparations and to coordinate their actions. At the sound of the third drum beat, announcing *Tzu*, the hour of the Rat, they all rose up like an erupting volcano and breaking the chains to the chopping knives and with staves, clubs, pitch forks and anything that could be used as a weapon, they rose up in rebellion. In one night's time, they managed to kill every Mongol soldier within the three prefectures, leaving not a single enemy to escape alive. The result was an overwhelming and undisputed victory!

From that time onwards, it became a custom and a tradition that whenever moon cakes are given as gifts on the Mid-Autumn Festival, a piece of paper was always attached. Sometimes it was placed on the bottoms of each cake and other times it was placed on the package. That is why each box or bundle of moon cakes sold today, always has a piece of printed red paper covering it.

There is another version of this story that is often told by storytellers which should be presented here as there are details in the story that have become folk practises which are not found in the first version. This second version is given below.

Liu Po-wên Distributes Talismans

In 1280 Kubilai Khan, the grandson of Genghis Khan actually was seated on the throne of China and founded the Yüan or Mongol dynasty. Immediately there was a policy change in that the entire population was divided into four main categories. The highest category, of course, was the conquering Mongols followed by what was called *Sê-mu* literally 'colored eyes.' This second category was comprised mainly of Central Asians and border regions peoples who had earlier capitulated to Mongol rule. The third category called *Han-jên* were the Han-Chinese who lived north of the Yellow River and who had been subjugated and were under Mongol rule. The lowest category, *Nan-jên*, were the Han-Chinese living south of the Yellow River and who belonged to the Sung dynasty.

All high administrative positions were recruited from the first and second category of peoples. The lower and less important governmental positions were all that the third and fourth category of people could hope to attain.

Nevertheless, the power resided with the conquering Mongols who were cruel, savage and tyrannical. The Mongols were given preferential and special treatment at all times under the law. Even if a Mongol should violate the law and commit a serious capital crime, the courts could not beat him in order to extort a confession. If it was a minor offense, the courts were forbidden to even physically bind or restrain him. However, if a Mongol were to strike a Chinese, the most the Chinese could do was to file a complaint in the courts. On the other hand, should a Chinese strike back at a Mongol, he would be apprehended and charged with a serious crime and be severely punished. If a Chinese were to be killed by a Mongol in a drunken brawl, the only punishment would be conscription into the military or being required to pay the burial expenses. In the case that a Mongol should kill a *Sê-mu,* the Mongol just had to pay a sum of forty pieces of gold. But if the victim was a Chinese, all he had to forfeit was one donkey. With such preferential treatment condoned by laws and statutes, the Mongol was embolden in his actions especially towards the Chinese.

When the areas south of the Yellow River came under Mongol rule with the defeat of the Sung dynasty, every twenty families were organized as a unit called a 'chia.' This chia unit was headed by a *Sê-mu* or a Mongol. The entire living expenses were to be the responsibility of the people of each unit. The chia unit chiefs exercised absolute authority over the Chinese people under their rule and were guilty of all manner of willful oppression against the civilian population. In addition, all Chinese households were forbidden to have lights from 7 p.m. until 5 a.m. They were not allowed to be out of their homes during the curfew. The Chinese population was forbidden to bear arms, study, train or teach martial arts or military science. Should anyone even possess a suit of inherited antique armor or ten sets of bows and arrows, (one set consists of a bow and thirty arrows), they would receive capital punishment by beheading. The rule was so severe that even the ceremonial weapons in the temples could not be made of metal. In fact, no one was allowed to work in metal unless licensed and under strict supervision. The Chinese suffered greatly and were brutally treated by the Mongol conquerors as slaves.

During the first decades of the fourteenth century, there occurred some minor local rebellions all without any lasting effect. However, in the 5th month of the 11th year of the reign of

Shun-ti (1351), the last emperor of the Yüan dynasty, under the leadership of Liu Fu-t'ung, the White Lotus secret society initiated a rebellion in Ying-chou and managed to capture several hsien or districts. Their forces quickly grew to over one hundred thousand strong. Encouraged by this success, people elsewhere also followed suit.

At this time, Chu Yüan-chang, who later became the first Ming emperor, was a low-ranking military officer in the rebel army of Kuo Tzu-hsing, who had revolted in Hao-chou. By the 14th year of Shun-ti (1353), Chu Yüan-chang had independently struck out and became a leader of several thousand men. Having successfully taken the Ting-yüan district in Anhwei province, he then marched on to attack Ch'u-chou, a place in Anhwei near Nanking. How he was successful in taking such a well-fortified place as Ch'u-chou, makes a most interesting story.

It is said that at that time, Ch'u-chou was a great stronghold of the Mongols. Not only was the city fully fortified and manned, there were also ample food and water supplies. It could not only stand a frontal attack but could hold out for a long siege as well. To take Ch'u-chou was no simple task. However, Chu Yüan-chang had to attack and capture Ch'u-chou as it was a most strategic city guarding the approach to Nanking. Therefore, Chu Yüan-chang summoned his chief military adviser, Liu Po-wên for consultation.

When told of the desire to attack Ch'u-chou, Liu Po-wên started to furrow his forehead for a short moment as he was deep in thought. All of a sudden, he conceived of a plan and walked over to Chu Yüan-chang and secretly whispered the strategy in his ear. As Liu Po-wên whispered, Chu Yüan-chang's eyebrows started to rise and dance up and down as the plan pleased him greatly. He quickly cried out, "An excellent plan, a great idea! . . . I must beg you to quickly put it into action!"

Having received his superior's approval, Liu Po-wên disguised himself wearing a Taoist cap and robes, and entered Ch'u-chou as a travelling Taoist priest. In the city, Liu Po-wên quickly made contact with members of the secret society who had infiltrated the city earlier and ordered them to spread various propaganda amongst the people.

Throughout the city, a rumor quickly was spread that the Jade Emperor of Heaven in a rage had sent five plague gods to Ch'u-chou to afflict the people with plague and epidemic. However, there was a compassionate immortal who sent one of his disciples to Ch'u-chou to help protect and save the people. This disciple was, of course, Liu Po-wên. The people all came to him begging him for protection. Immediately Liu Po-wên ordered an altar and held Taoist rites for three days and three nights, reciting various incantations and paraded throughout the entire city. Then he informed the people that he had implored the five plague gods to spare the people of Ch'u-chou, provided the people followed his instructions precisely.

On the fifteen day of the eighth lunar month, at the first stroke of the third watch (11 p.m.-1 a.m.), every household was to raise a triangular flag with the design of the seven stars of the Great Dipper as well as lighted lanterns. They were also to beat on drums and gongs in order to be saved from the pestilence.

As part of the ritual to avoid evil, Liu Po-wên had distributed small cakes to every family within the city. He told them each cake contained a talisman inside. They were to cut and eat the cake only at the appointed hour. All these things must be done exactly as ordered at the first stroke of the third watch (11 p.m.) to guarantee salvation and deliverance from evil.

The populace had placed great trust in the disguised Taoist priest, Liu Po-wên, as he acted piously and sincerely. He neither demanded nor accepted any money or presents from them. Moreover his great concern for the salvation of the people, led to his distributing small cakes containing charms and talisman to each family without accepting any re-numeration. Truly, they believed in him and trusted him greatly. Observing that his plans were secured, Liu Po-wên hastened back to camp.

A few days later, it was the time of the Mid-Autumn Festival. Throughout the city of Ch'u-chou, after feasting and the usual festival activities, the people waited in their homes until the third watch. At that moment, every household raised flags, hung bright lanterns, and beat on drums and gongs. The entire city was lit up and roaring with the sounds of drums and gongs. Cutting open their small cakes, they found slips of paper with the message:

Tonight we shall raise a righteous revolt. Armies will be attacking the city. Everyone should rise up and help kill the 'Ta-tzu'!

Ta-tzu was what the Chinese called the hated Mongols and Sê-mu. The people came rushing out of their houses, armed with kitchen knives, wooden sticks and anything that could be used as a weapon.

Just at the same moment, Chu Yüan-chang's army was approaching the city. The soldiers carried torches and filled the air with deafening battle cries, drums and gongs as they marched forward.

Seeing all the lights and the deafening sounds, the Mongol soldiers, not knowing the strength or numbers of their attackers, fled in fear and confusion. Those who lingered were quickly killed. Without much actual fighting, Chu Yüan-chang was able to capture the strategically important city of Ch'u-chou.

Commemorating this event, people have raised triangular flags with the seven-star design of the Big Dipper and lanterns in celebrating the Mid-Autumn Festival. In addition, the beating of drums and gongs was to celebrate freedom and to usher in peace and tranquility. These became folk practises that were part of the Chung-ch'iu or Mid-Autumn Festival celebration.

Although these two stories are commonly told and oft repeated to explain the origin of the Moon Cake, there are several reasons to question their accuracy. It is true that Chu Yüan-chang did take Ch'u-chou in Chekiang province in December, 1359. However, it was without the aid of Liu Po-wên.

Ironically, Liu Po-wên had been a loyal Yüan dynasty official who served in a number of positions. He had received his *Chin-shih* degree in 1333 and three years later, in 1336, he was appointed assistant magistrate of Kao-an, Kiangsi, but was cashiered for disregarding the wishes of his seniors after only two years in office. Next, he served as chief clerk in the Kiangsi branch secretariat (1339-1340) and assistant inspector of public academies in Hangchow (1343), but resigned because of a dispute with his superiors.

During the following years, he assisted the authorities of Chekiang in fortifying several local sub-prefectures against bands of rebels, notably those from the west under Hsü Shou-hui and the pirates of the Chekiang coast under Fang Kuo-chên.

In 1352, he was appointed an assistant secretary by the provincial authorities to take part in the defense of the coastal region, and in 1353, he became an assistant secretary in the Chê-tung branch secretariat with headquarters in Hangchow. He criticized the government's deliberation on an attractive offer to the rebel, Fang Kuo-chên, to secure his surrender and was placed in confinement in Shao-hsing as an obstructionist.

Three years later, in March, 1356, he was reappointed as secretary and sent to the aid of Shih-mo I-sun, assistant prefect of Ch'u-chou, in the defense of the city. In the following year, Liu Po-wên raised a band of volunteers and conducted a successful campaign against the rebels. His success, however, did not win him any recognition from the Yüan authorities. In despair, he abandoned his official career and retired, withdrawing to live in his native Ch'ing-t'ien, Chekiang. Liu Po-wên was loyal to the Yüan regime but blamed its misrule on those officials who were self-seeking and unscrupulous. He showed no sympathy for the leaders of rebellion either, for in his eyes, they were no more than agents of destruction and disorder. Disillusioned by the political climate and powerless as an individual, he remained at home devoting himself to study and writing.

In his study, he developed his vision of an ideal government administered by men of caliber and virtue. He criticized the government for mismanagement and ineptness which had brought on misery and political collapse. It was not until after Chu Yüan-chang had seized Ch'u-chou in December, 1359, that he succeeded in acquiring the services of Liu Po-wên and other scholars who met with Chu Yüan-chang in April, 1360 in Nanking. Therefore, the popular tales must be in error due to the sequence of events. Still these stories are delightful even if historically inaccurate.

In an attempt to establish an earlier dating of the moon cake and to have a moon origin. There is another traditional tale that is related to the famous Tung Yung.

Weaver Maid and Moon Cake

Tung Yung, 2nd century A.D., a native of Kan-ch'êng in Hupeh, has been celebrated as one of the twenty-four examples of filial piety. It is said that when his father died, there was no money to pay for funeral expenses. Accordingly, he borrowed the necessary funds upon condition that if he could not repay it, he would become the bondsman of his creditor. On returning from the funeral, he met a young lady, who asked him to marry her, and they went together to his creditor to arrange about the debt. The latter said that he would require 300 pieces of silk; whereupon the young lady set to work, and within a month's time, she had completed the task. Then she turned to Tung Yung and said, "I am Chih-nü, the Weaver Maid (who was also called Seventh Sister). The Jade Emperor had sent me to help you as a reward for your filial piety." With that she soared up to heaven and disappeared.

Just before the goddess, Seventh Sister (Weaver Maid) had to return to heaven, she gave birth to a little boy but had to abandon her infant son to his mortal father, Tung Yung.

As the little boy grew up, there was one day on the fifteenth day of the eighth lunar month, when the youngster saw some of the village children playing under the large Cassia tree growing in front of the village. They seemed to be enjoying themselves and having so much fun that the young boy also wanted to join them in play. However, as he approached them, no one paid him any attention. They not only intentionally ignored him, they also rebuked and scolded him. "You don't even have a mother, a shameless little bastard child! Who would want to associate or play with you? Go away and leave us alone!"

Annoyed by what the children were saying, the youngster screamed at them and then turned and ran away. Sobbing and wiping his eyes, he ran outside of the village to a large shade tree. There where no one could see him, he sat down and openly cried his heart out. Every so often he would cry out, "Mother! Where have you gone? Come here quickly to your pitiful son! Are you not aware that he is sad and misses you? Mother, your son needs you!"

His wailing and most pitiful crying was heard by the celestial, Wu-kang who took pity and sympathized with him. Quickly he disguised himself as a villager and approached the little boy. Regardless of how he tried to comfort the youngster, it was of no avail. The little boy was crying his heart out and wanted his mother and refused to stop crying.

Wu-kang was afraid that all this crying may be injurious to the youngster's health and he had to do something constructive to help him. Listening to the pitiful crying, melted Wu-kang's heart and moved him so that he quickly sent word about this to his goddess mother, Seventh Sister.

Still trying to comfort the little boy, Wu-kang silently brought out a pair of magical shoes call 'Têng-yün' shoes to mount the clouds and ascend to heaven. Softly and comfortingly he spoke to the youngster. "If you wish to see your mother, then wear these magical shoes when the moon is fully round and shining brightly in the sky. However, you must stop this crying."

Hearing these words, the little boy quickly stopped his crying and took the pair of magical shoes, holding them tightly against his chest. After Wu-kang had disappeared, the little boy followed exactly every word that was relayed to him and he sat anxiously waiting for the sun to disappear behind the mountains and the moon to appear.

When the moon was shining brightly overhead, the little boy quickly put on the pair of magical shoes under the moonlit night. As soon as they were firmly on his feet, he started to soar and flew upwards until he reached heaven.

There he was greeted by his goddess mother, Seventh Sister, along with his six goddess aunts. His mother was so happy to see her own son that she began to cry as both mother and child held onto each other in a passionate and tight embrace. After the initial meeting, his six goddess aunts each presented the little boy with various delicious goodies, such as apples, persimmons, pomegranates, chestnuts, peanuts and walnuts. His mother, Seventh Sister, hurriedly took some of the sweet and fragrant cassia honey that she had received from the Moon Goddess, Ch'ang-O, and combined it with fruit and nut meats to make a filling. She placed this in little round cakes shaped like the moon. They were sweet, ever so fragrant, tasty and flavorful. He enjoyed these cakes immensely as he had never before tasted anything so delicious as these.

Their being together was so pleasant and comforting as they laughed and enjoyed themselves immensely. However, news of this unwarranted and illegal meeting reached the Jade Emperor who was so enraged that smoke could be seen coming out of his head as he fumed in great anger. He immediately had Wu-kang arrested as the main culprit who had violated the laws of Heaven and made possible this intrusion of a mortal into heaven's domain. He banished Wu-kang to the lonely moon with the stipulation that amnesty could be extended only when he had succeeded in felling the cassia tree. Yet each time Wu-kang struck with his axe, the tree healed the cut immediately, dooming him to eternal futility.

The Jade Emperor also ordered the heavenly soldiers to deprive the little boy of the magical 'Têng-yün' shoes. He was then carried back to earth on a Ch'i-lin (Kirin) or Chinese unicorn.

To the little boy all these miraculous and joyous events, seemed like a dream. And so it was made to be just that way by the gods. He later found himself awakening from sleep under the shade of the large tree just outside of the village. However, he did not know whether it was real or a dream and although most details of his trip to heaven were hazy, nevertheless, he vividly remembered every detail of his meeting with his mother and eating those delicious cakes she had made for him.

Many years later when he was grown up and became an official, he ordered that the people in each of the districts under his jurisdiction, should celebrate the fifteenth day of the eighth lunar month. They should make offerings of fruits and nuts and other delicacies out-of-doors to the moon. The most important item was to fashion round cakes with fillings of sugar, melon seeds, almonds, orange peel, sweetened cassia blossoms and other fruit and nut meats, an item to remember his mother. Since these round cakes resembled a full moon, people started to call them *Yüeh-ping* or moon cakes and so perpetuated this charming custom.

Aside from stories of the origin of the Moon Cake, there are a number of clever and amusing stories centering around various ways a young or naïve person is tricked out of their Moon Cake treat.

The Hsiu-ts'ai and the Moon Cake

There once was a 'Hsiu-ts'ai' or 'cultivated talent' which was an unofficial designation for men qualified to participate in provincial examination in the civil service recruitment examination sequence, having real or nominal status of a government student in Confucian schools at the prefectural or lower level. This Hsiu-ts'ai had spent most of his life reading the Confucian Classics in preparation for government service, however, he was unable to pass the higher examinations which he had taken numerous times. Unable to secure any other employment, he decided to open a school. Inasmuch as he was able to enroll several students, his teaching methods were somewhat chaotic. Being disorganized and not truly devoted to teaching, he would not repeat either his lessons or explanations. As if dreaming, he would give the lessons, reading and chanting for his own pleasure. Should anyone ask questions or interrupt him, he would be enraged and turn on the student accusing him of being lackadaisical, inattentive and stupid. Therefore, he was not a popular teacher and had but a few students, whose tuition fees were just enough for him to buy essentials and nothing more.

One day, he saw one of his students just about to eat a moon cake. His eyes widened and his mouth began to salivate as he had not had enough money to purchase any moon cakes for the Mid-Autumn Festival. Coveting his student's moon cake, he began to think of a scheme to deprive the student in order to secure it for himself.

Quickly, he waved at his student and asked him, "Come here, and bring what you are holding." The young student did as he was told and very politely came forward and bowed before his teacher.

His teacher then started to question him. "In your present studies, what Confucian Classic are you reading?"

"Responding to your enquiry, Teacher," replied the student, "I am now reading the text of the *I-ching* or the Book of Changes."

"Oh?" Looking seemingly surprised, his teacher then responded. "And do you comprehend and understand the text?"

"Teacher," replied the student, "the text of the *I-ching* is certainly not an easy text to either read or understand. Moreover, its meaning is quite difficult and it escapes my comprehensive abilities."

The teacher nodded his head in agreement and stroking his beard, he said. "It is true, the text of the *I-ching* is not easily read and even more difficult to derive an understanding of its meaning. I'm afraid that this is your teacher's fault of not giving you adequate attention in assisting you with the lessons. However, it is not too late for me to make up for this deficiency. It would be best if I had something to illustrate these ideas as I explain the meaning of the text." Then eyeing the moon cake, he said, "Give me that moon cake so that I may use it to illustrate my explanations."

Obediently, the student handed over his moon cake to his teacher who smilingly accepted it. With satisfaction and a smile on his face, the teacher began his lesson.

"It seems that from the beginning, within the cosmos there was a division. The heavy elements (Yin) sank and formed the earth and the light elements (Yang) rose up and formed the heavens. This concept is then referred to as the cosmological system of the Yin-yang dichotomy."

Breaking the moon cake into two halves, he said, "This is the way it was done!"

Then he continued his lesson. "There was a further division which brought forth the four directions, north, east, south and west." Having said this, he broke the two halves again into four little pieces. "Then the four divided to form the eight trigrams," and he proceeded to break it into eight smaller pieces.

Smiling, the teacher looked at the eight pieces of moon cake which were of a convenient size for him to place in his mouth to eat. However, he could not just eat them outright. Salivating and desiring to eat a piece of that moon cake, he nevertheless continued his lesson.

"There is no need for me to talk about the heavens or cosmology as it is rather complicated and beyond your youthful comprehension. However, I will turn to matters on earth as it best serves our interests." Then after a short pause, he continued. "From the time of P'an-ku, the Creator and the period of the Three Sovereigns and Five Rulers, there had always been peace on earth. Likewise with the Emperors Yao and Shun, there were no wars and the people were contented and happy. After Yü had abdicated in favor of his son K'un, there was established a dynastic rule called Hsia, which was perpetuated by hereditary lineage, from father to son. The Hsia dynasty lasted for 439 years. The last ruler, Chieh, was corrupt and degenerate and was overthrown by T'ang the Victorious, founder of the Shang dynasty (in 1766 B.C.). He had defeated and wiped out the Hsia like this!" As he said this he placed a piece of the moon cake into his mouth and ate it. Having finished off the first piece of moon cake, he continued his lesson.

"The virtuous Shang rule who later changed their dynastic title to Yin, had received Heaven's Mandate to overthrow the weakened Hsia dynasty. After 31 Shang emperors had occupied the throne, they in turn became dissolute, until the last ruler called Chou-hsin. Their Mandate was passed to the virtuous Chou. Wu-wang, the military king, conquered the Shang/Yin and killed Chou-hsin." Again illustrating his talk, he took another piece of the moon cake and ate it before continuing.

"Now the Mandate of Heaven was passed onto the virtuous Chou, which continued to rule until the reign of the ruler Yu-wang. He did not rule well and was given to corruption and debauchery. He was killed and his traditional western capital had been sacked by barbarians and dissidents and was no longer habitable." He then helped himself to another piece of moon cake and consumed it.

He then continued his story saying, "Afterwards, the kingdom was divided for 20 years, until the ruler P'ing-wang of the eastern portion re-united the regime and called the dynasty Eastern Chou. P'ing-wang and his descendants became pawns in the hands of powerful ministers or noble factions. These vassals fought amongst

themselves, and eventually formed into seven kingdoms. It was a case of big fish swallowing small fish." He then paused to eat a piece of the moon cake. Then smacking his lips again, he said, "Yes, and the small fish swallowed the tiny shrimp." Pausing, he took and ate another piece of the moon cake. "Then the shrimp swallowed the smaller micro-animals." With that he helped himself to yet another piece of the moon cake. Then looking up and thinking for a while, he said, "It is a case of you defeating me!" and he ate another piece of moon cake, "and I defeating you." With that statement, he ate the last piece of moon cake, before he noted that, "In this way, one dynasty succeeded another, one after the other."

Having eaten all eight pieces of the moon cake, there remained only some broken pieces and crumbs left on the table. Looking at them, he did not want to forego anything or be wasteful. He was not to be satisfied until he had consumed everything. Thinking a while, he cleared his throat and continued his lesson.

"There appeared in history a person called Chêng of the state of Ch'in. He succeeded in conquering and annexing the six states of Han, Wei, Ch'u, Chao, Yen and Ch'i and assumed sovereign rule over all these territories and called himself, 'Shih-huang-ti', or the 'First Emperor'. It was like this." He then was gathering up all the smaller pieces and crumbs off the table and sweeping them into his hands, he lifted his hand towards his mouth and ate them, and repeated the process until nothing was left of the moon cake.

The surprised student, looking at his teacher who now had a most satisfied expression on his face, remarked, "Thank you teacher for the lesson which I now fully understand. However, I will inform my father to make a large moon cake the size of a mill stone which I will bring to you tomorrow so that you will have sufficient material to illustrate your lectures on the twenty-four dynastic history of China!"

There is another similar story of a cunning older boy trying to trick a younger boy into relinquishing his moon cake.

The Moon Cake

A little boy had a moon cake that an older big boy coveted. Designing to get the cake without making the little boy cry so loud as to attract his mother's attention, the older boy remarked that the cake would be prettier if it were shaped more like the moon. The little boy thought that a cake like the moon must be desirable, and on being assured by the older big boy that he had experience making many such, he handed over his moon cake for manipulation.

The older big boy took out a mouthful, leaving a crescent with jagged edge. The little boy was not pleased by the change, and began to whimper; whereupon the big boy pacified him by saying that he would make the moon cake into a half-moon. So he nibbled off the horns of the crescent, and gnawed the edge smooth. But when the half-moon was made, the little boy perceived that there was hardly any cake left, and he again began to snivel.

The older big boy again diverted him by telling him that, if he did not like so small a moon, he should have one that was just the size of the real orb. He then took the cake and explained that, just before the new moon is seen, the old moon disappears. Then he swallowed the rest of the cake, and ran off, leaving the little boy waiting for the new moon.

Of the many stories told about the Moon Cake, there is one that gives greater credence to why people should consume them. This particular story is better known in Peking and throughout the province of Shantung than elsewhere. This interesting story is given below:

The Jade Rabbit and the Moon Cake

It is said that there is a particular kind of cake within the Moon Palace that cures all ailments and illness. It is believed that these cakes were made from the medical compounds that were pounded by the Jade Rabbit on the Moon. However, the Moon Maiden who has charge of these cakes is selfish and greedy. She only looked to those with wealth and snubbed and ignored the poor and helpless. Only those who could afford to give rich presents got these cakes. She would deny them to the sick and poor who were in great need of them. As far as this heartless Moon Maiden was concerned, she felt she was not a charity and whether these poor lived or died, was none of her business. To the poor, she was totally unapproachable and unavailable.

One year, there was some illness of epidemic proportions in the city of Ch'i-nan in Shantung province. A brave and determined young man named Jên Han had set out to get help. He managed to sneak into the Moon Palace, undetected and stole a supply of these miraculous cure-all cakes. However, his escape from the Moon Palace became a problem as he was weighted down with these cakes. In such a perilous time, the Jade Rabbit sacrificed himself so that Jên Han could use his hide and disguise himself in order to make his escape and return back to earth.

When Jên Han returned to his native Ch'i-nan, he visited all the 72 water springs where people gathered to obtain their water supply. He made a distribution of these cakes to the poor and general populace and became successful in saving the people from this dreaded epidemic.

In memory of the sacrifices of the Jade Rabbit in the Moon and Jên Han, the people called these cakes, Moon Cakes. Therefore, the Moon Cake fillings were all made with some sort of paste filling or nuts and sweetmeats all chopped fine to symbolize the Jade Rabbit's pounding his medical compound. Moreover, the traditional fillings were all dictated in using seasonal fruits, nuts, herbs and other seasonal products.

The honor given to the Jade Rabbit has caused so great a reverence among the people that his image is used as the central figure on the altar during the Moon Festival. He is represented either as a clay image or a votive printed on paper. However, he is never depicted as an ordinary hare but one dressed either as a martial hero or as a high civil official. In honor and reverence, they call him 'T'u-êrh-yeh' or 'T'u-tzu-wang,' names of great respect. Various string toys with movable parts of the rabbit pounding are also popularly sold at this festival time. Eating Moon Cakes is a pleasant manner to dispense medicine as public health.

Besides the Moon Cake with a variety of delicious fillings, there is also a special cake that is most popular in Peking which has an herbal filling. This is called 'Fu-ling chia-ping' is a compound of Jujube fruit paste and Fu-ling that is sandwiched between two crispy thin wafers. Fu-ling or China Root is a fungus-like substance found on the roots of the fir-tree and is eaten to strengthen the body and is considered 'Pu' or a health tonic. This cake is especially eaten during the fall and winter months.

Chapter 2:
All About Moon Cakes

There are a number of theories or explanations concerning the origins of the Moon Cake. In a quick survey, we find that the earliest theory maintains that the Moon Cake had evolved from the ancient 'Chü-ju' or honey cakes which are mentioned in the 3rd century B.C. work, *Ch'u-tz'u* in the section *Chao-hun* (Summons of the Soul). This essay was purported to have been written by Sung Yü to summon back the soul of Ch'ü Yüan, who was in exile at the time, and that his ulterior motive in writing it was to persuade King Huan to recall Ch'ü Yüan from exile. In enticing the soul, bribes were offered including food. It mentions, "Fried honey-cakes of rice flour and malt sugar sweetmeats."

Some scholars contend that the 'Chü-ju' (honey cakes) later evolved into the modern Moon Cakes. According to the 6th century agricultural encyclopedia, *Ch'i-min yao-shu* by Chia Ssu-hsieh, 'Chü-ju' were made with glutinous rice flour in a mixture of water and honey. This dough is somewhat dry and resembles noodle dough. It is rolled out by hand to approximately 8 inches in length then the ends are pinched together to resemble a ring of dough before it is fried in oil. The author also noted that in the 6th century, 'Chü-ju' was called Kao-huan or fried rings. From the descriptions, they resemble pretzels or crullers, which are eaten during the Chinese New Year and called 'San-tzu' (Cantonese: Tsuei-ma-faar). However, these cakes were not called 'Yüeh-ping' or Moon Cakes.

Some scholars have made a turn-about and instead of looking into ancient literature as a source, they have turned to the more recent Ch'ing dynasty (1644-1911) literature. A poem by Yang Kuang-fu, contained in his *Sung-nan yüeh-fu,* reads in part:

Sung-nan (Woosung, near Shanghai) is pleasant and beautiful
There is a seasonal delicacy offered
Of Moon Cakes filled with walnut meats
Or with sweet pastes like packed white sugared snow.

Inasmuch as there is such a vivid description of the Moon Cake, nevertheless, descriptions of round cakes resembling a moon with various delicious fillings had already been noticed in earlier literature even in the Northern Sung dynasty (960-1126). The famous poet, scholar and gourmet, Su Tung-po (1036-1101) in one of his poems, wrote:

Chewing small round cakes shaped like the moon
It is crisp and flaky and filled with sugar and sweetmeats

The term 'Yüeh-ping' or Moon Cakes is also found in the *Wu-lin chiu-shih* a record of contemporary institutions and customs at Hangchow during the Southern Sung dynasty (1127-1259) written by Chou Mi (1232-1308). However, it is after this period, in the mid-14th century that there emerged the ever-popular stories and tales, so frequently told, of the Moon Cakes associated with Ming dynasty Emperor, Chu Yüan-chang and his chief adviser, Liu Po-wên, in the overthrow of the despised Yüan or Mongol dynasty.

We know that during the Ming dynasty (1368-1643), the Moon Cakes were considered a festive delicacy used during the celebration of the Mid-Autumn or Moon Festival. The *Cho-chung-chih* by Liu Jo-yü (1584-ca. 1642), which gives an enlightening account of life in the Imperial palace, was written by a grand eunuch to record what he knew about the events of his day and life in the palace. He wrote that, "In the 8th lunar month, the palace is decorated throughout with blossoms of begonia and tuberose. From the first of the month onwards, Moon Cakes are being offered for sale in the market place . . . until the 15th of the month. At that time (15th day), every household would prepare sacrifice to the Moon with melons, fruits . . . and especially Moon Cakes. The entire family would gather together afterwards in a quiet and cool area and share these delicacies. Therefore, this (Moon Cake) was also called 'T'uan-yüan-ping' or 'Perfect circle cake,' meaning that the family is united together."

In the beginning of the Ch'ing dynasty, there is another vivid description worth mentioning which describes the decorations of the Moon Cake. This is found in the *Yu-chou t'u-fêng yin* a collection of poems by P'êng Yün-chang (1792-1862). Of the various decorations on the Moon Cakes, he wrote:

Moon Cakes with mansions and palaces
Or with a silvery toad against shadows of purple mansions
Even a pair of a toad and a rabbit are popular with many people
There is also Ch'ang-O, regretting for having stolen the elixir
Fleeing to the Moon to escape but finding no way to return
There is also the laboring of the chopping of the Cassia tree.

The decorations described, fully utilized the tales and folklore surrounding the Moon Festival. These depictions were either stamped onto the cakes or made from carved wooden molds. The designs were delicately and exquisitely executed which added greatly to the aesthetics of this festive delicacy.

It was also an attempt to link the Moon Cake with longevity and an elixir. With depictions of heavenly beings and other designs, the Moon Cake symbolized the heavenly blessings to be bestowed at this time. The sweet pastes, chopped sweetmeats and other fillings delicately prepared were reminders of the Jade Rabbit's pounding of the elixir of immortality. It was a means to promote not only good eating but also good health.

Later in the Ch'ing dynasty, the literary critic and essayist, Yüan Mei (1716-1798) in his famous discourse on cooking, *Sui-yüan shih-tan*, written in a vein of charming banter, noted that, "Flour from Shantung with high gluten content is used to make a flaky cake which contained pine nuts, walnut meats, melon seeds all chopped fine and combined in a sugar paste and lard as fillings. Yet when eating them, it is not overly sweet but exudes a fragrance, softness which gives a satisfying bite."

Yüan Mei was also attracted to the Moon Cakes made by the Ming-fu bakery which he considered to be comparable to those from Shantung's Liu Fang-po. A unique aspect of the Ming-fu Moon Cakes is that the baker was a woman. Yüan Mei describes these favored Moon Cakes as, "melting in one's mouth giving a pleasant sweetness without being greasy, oily. Its filling is soft yet not hard packed."

Yüan Mei's descriptions of Moon Cakes were repeated in Chapter 76 of the famous novel *Hung-lou-mêng* or *Dream of the Red Chamber*. However, in the novel, the Moon Cakes eaten by the Matriarch of the Chia family were made within their own kitchens of which the ingredients must have been more exquisite and delicately executed than those commercially bought.

During the Ch'ing dynasty, there seemed to be a proliferation of the varieties of Moon Cakes with regional differences, specialties and uniqueness. As the Mid-Autumn or Moon Festival was approaching, many of the bakeries were set up exclusively to produce Moon Cakes. This, of course, caused great excitement and added greatly to the festive mood. In the streets of old Peking there was a popular contemporary song that describes this festive mood and scene.

> In celebrating the Mid-Autumn Festival, stalls and structures of all sorts and colors are set up and constructed
> Cakes in the shape of a round moon reflects throughout and are honored with various beautiful names.
> New varieties of 'Fan-mao' Moon Cakes take on new forms
> And also the white and red varieties, they all fill the various stalls.

The red and white varieties are the famous 'Tzu-lai-hung' and 'Tzu-lai-pai' Moon Cakes of Peking. The many varieties of the Moon Cake have both evolved and developed so greatly that there are several hundred different kinds known.

It should be understood that the original Moon Cake was made at home but because Chinese households do not have ovens in their kitchens, these early Moon Cakes were simply fried or steamed like the New Year's pudding or 'Nien-kao' (Cantonese: Nin-ko), but containing some filling.

As a Moon Festival food item, Moon Cakes were eaten by the celebrants as well as being used as an offering to the Moon. The consumption of the Moon Cake is not only a reminder of various aspects of human virtue but also for health purposes. However, the Chinese, true to their gustatory predilections, were quick to proliferate the varieties of Moon Cakes, stuffing them with various delicacies and sweet meats.

Therefore, when professional bakers started to make them, they developed a huge variety of different styles. These styles are regionally categorized as Soochow, Peking, Ningpo, Yunnan, Swatow and Cantonese styles. Of these, the Cantonese and Swatow styles are usually categorized together as Kwangtung or Cantonese style and are found most commonly in bakeries and grocery stores in the United States. The next step naturally was to consume them throughout the year and not only during the Mid-Autumn Festival celebration.

Contrary to popular belief, the Moon Cake need not necessarily be round as they are of various shapes: square, triangular, crescent and even octagonal. They also vary in size from the size of large checkers to larger sizes of a foot or more in diameter. Moreover, they are not all sweet as they are made in a variety of flavors. They may be shaped in carved wooden molds or freely formed by hand. The color of the dough also varies from snow white to dark browns and greys.

Soochow-style Moon Cakes which date back over a thousand years, had been described in poems by the famous Sung dynasty scholar Su Tung-po. The most significant characteristics of Soochow-style Moon Cakes are that they are heavily larded and sugared, and the dough is flaky and in layers. They are hand formed and may contain fillings that are sweet, salty, meaty or vegetarian (fruits and nuts). There are over a dozen varieties, however, the most famous and representative of the Soochow Moon Cake is one called 'Ch'ing-shui Mei-kuei yüeh-ping.' This hand formed Moon Cake has a light and flaky dough with fruit and nut filling.

In the Peking-style, the Moon Cakes are basically of two varieties. One is called 'T'i-chiang' which was first made in Tientsin and was influenced by the Soochow variety. The term 'T'i-chiang' is a description of the dough which is a light meringue type. The egg whites are beaten with sugar until the soft point period, before flour is added. The other type is called 'Fan-mao' which has a crisp and flaky white dough. The two most unique types of fillings are Shan-cha or jellied Mountain hawthorn and T'êng-lo-hua or Wisteria blossom flavor. These Moon Cakes are delicately shaped and decorated and are very attractive and appealing. The Moon Cakes are either white or red so they were appropriately called Tzu-lai-pai (Spontaneous white) or Tzu-lai-hung (Spontaneous red.) These are homonyms to respectively mean, "hundreds (of dollars) spontaneous gotten" and "abundance (of money) spontaneous gotten."

The Ningpo-style of Moon Cakes is popular throughout Chekiang province. The dough is quite firm and hard, but most of the fillings are influenced by the Soochow varieties. However, two unique and outstanding varieties of Ningpo Moon Cakes are the 'T'ai-ts'ai yüeh-ping' with fillings of edible seaweed and 'Huo-t'ui yüeh-ping' with ham filling. The edible seaweed filling is made of a mixture of edible seaweed, sesame seed and sesame oil, melon seeds, and walnuts. The delicious flavoring is called 'chiao-yen' or a bit spicy or peppery with a salty taste.

The Yunnan-style of Moon Cakes are called 'T'o' by the natives. Although there are a number of different varieties, they are mostly sweet. The unique characteristics of Yunnan-style Moon Cakes is that they are made with a variety of different kinds of flour, such as wheat flour, glutinous rice flour, buckwheat flour, etc.

Of all the styles of Moon Cakes, the Cantonese-style, which incorporates also the Swatow-style has the greatest varieties. The chief characteristics of the Cantonese-style Moon Cake is that it utilizes a sweet floured dough formed in wooden mold and baked to a golden brown. There is a great amount of filling with a thin enclosed dough wrapping. Although it utilizes a lot of sugar, it is light in oil and the cakes are not easily broken nor do they fall apart. As for number of varieties, there are about 200 different kinds listed. Of these, the main types have fillings of melon seed paste, lotus seed paste, bean paste, black sugar, coconut, etc. Aside from these sweet flavored fillings, there are fillings with processed ham, chicken, duck, roast pork, mushrooms, thousand-year-old eggs, salted duck eggs, etc.

The Swatow-style, which is incorporated into the Cantonese-style closely resembles the Soochow-style in dough but strictly is Cantonese in its fillings. It uses a flaky white dough with egg wash and is formed by hand to resemble a small drum. The various fillings used are mostly pastes and jams and are quite soft. The most famous is the melon fillings.

In the Cantonese-style, there is still preserved a steamed variety of Moon Cake which is called 'chêng-ping' (steamed cakes) or 'ping-p'i' or iced or snow crust. These usually have a black sugar or bean or lotus seed paste as fillings.

Like so many things in Chinese life, the naming of the many varieties of Moon Cakes was governed by conventions and rules that have developed over the centuries. The names are not simply descriptive but also involve layers of meaning and clever allusions that are appropriate to special festive foods. The names of the various Moon Cakes, fall into five basic categories.

Although the Moon Cake is called 'Yüeh-ping,' this precise combination of words are never used together and are avoided in the names. This is due to the fact that these words are homonyms of 'transgressing into sickness (Yüeh-ping).' Fearing that calling the Moon Cake, 'Yüeh-ping' might be an invitation for inviting calamity, the Ch'ing Emperors began to give another more auspicious or literary appellation of 'Yüeh-hua' or 'beautiful and glorious moon.' This term is a homonym to mean 'greater glory or splendor.' The term, 'Yüeh-hua' was used only in the confines of the palace and by the literati along with the rich and powerful, but not by the general populace. Nevertheless, the superstitious public also avoided the use of the combination of the words, 'Yüeh-ping.' Instead, they used only the term 'yüeh' or avoided the word completely.

The term 'Yüeh' or moon was symbolized by the use of a whole duck's egg yolk in the filling. This is especially true and used extensively by the Cantonese in their fanciful names such as 'Yin-ho yeh-yüeh' literally 'the moon reflecting on the shining river's surface at night.' However, this name has another meaning as 'Yin-ho' refers to the Milky Way and 'Yeh-yüeh' in reverse order as a homonymn refers to the 'old man under the moon' a patron for lovers. This becomes very romantic and symbolizes the meeting of lovers. Moreover the filling of this variety of Moon Cake is a lotus seed paste called 'lien-jung,' a homonym for the 'uniting of a handsome (couple).' Such a name with such bountiful meanings is certainly good packaging and merchandizing of an otherwise common Moon Cake.

Another category of naming is based on the process by which the Moon Cake was made. The famous 'T'i-chang' Moon Cake of Peking is such an example. 'T'i-chang' refers to the beating of egg whites with sugar to form a meringue before flour is added to form a light and airy dough. The term is not only descriptive of a process, it is also a homonym to mean 'to bring forward and expand.' Therefore, when combined with the term 'Tzu-lai-pai,' it may sound like, 'to bring forward and expand the hundred (of dollars) spontaneous gotten.' Therefore the naming may be hopeful thinking or reflections of desired wishes.

A third category of naming is based on the type of filling contained in the Moon Cakes. In the Cantonese variety, there are the ever-popular 'Chin-t'ui' and 'Wu-jên' Moon Cakes. The term 'Chin-t'ui' is an abbreviation for Chin-hua huo-t'ui or Chin-hua ham. Chin-hua is in Chekiang province which is famous for the production of hams just as in the United States, Virginia is known for hams. Indeed Virginia's Smithfield's ham, closely resembles the Chinese ham. Although the term 'Chin-t'ui' is an abbreviation of something specific, it also sounds like another term, 'Chin-tui,' meaning 'heaping piles of gold.' Likewise, 'Wu-jên' although referring to the many different nut meats used in the fillings, literally means the blessings of the 'five virtues.'

The fourth category is of names derived from the decoration on the Moon Cakes. These may be reflective of the outer appearance of the cakes, such as a sprinkling of black sesame seeds or nuts on it. However, especially in the Cantonese variety, the names are derived from the exquisite designs of the carved wooden molds that formed the Moon Cakes. The depictions of Ch'ang-O fleeing to the Moon are called 'Ch'ang-O pên-yüeh' and the depictions of palaces on the moon are called 'Kuang-han yüeh-kung', etc.

The fifth category are the popular or common names, regionally used and sometimes even in dialects. These are usually derived from some interesting or fanciful stories or tales. A good example is the famous Swatow Moon Cakes filled with winter melon filling called 'Lao-p'o ping' literally 'old lady's cake,' the term 'Lao-p'o' being a commonly used term for a wife. In the *Ch'ing-pai lei-ch'ao*, a compilation of various institutions and customs of the Ch'ing dynasty by the author Hsü K'o, it is recorded that, "In the city of Canton in the province of Kwangtung, there is a type of (Moon) cake which the people curiously call 'Lao-p'o-ping.' It is said that formerly there was a person who was so greatly fond of eating this type of cake that he bankrupted his family's fortune. This led him to sell his wife in order to satisfy his appetite for these cakes. Of these cakes, the best is made by the bakery called Liang Kuang-ch'i."

Because the man sold his wife to obtain money to satisfy his appetite for these cakes, they became popularly known as 'Lao-p'o-ping.' Although it was originally a Moon Festival delicacy, its popularity caused it to become a bakery staple and so it was produced as a year round commodity and not restricted only to the Moon Festival.

Quite often, there are new varieties of Moon Cakes invented, but their naming basically follows the above conventions with some liberties and modifications. As an example, with greater prosperity, instead of using one duck's egg yolk in each Moon Cake, sometimes there are two used. However, if the egg yolk symbolized the moon, how would it be possible to have more than one moon? This is only possible if we were to live on another planet such as Jupiter with a multiple of moons. How would the use of two egg yolks in a Moon Cake be named? An ingenious twist is utilized by calling it 'Shuang-huang' literally 'double yolks,' but used as a homonym and an abbreviation meaning 'two reed-organs' referring to a love-song or another meaning of having great splendor and grand in appearance.

All the names for the Moon Cake reflect the joyous and wishful thinking and hopes for happy and peaceful times in invoking good luck without being so blatant by shouting it out. In a highly developed and unique Chinese invention, it symbolically represents a communication of social messages by the 'language of food.'

Having discussed the background of the Moon Cakes, it is now necessary to know how it is made. The following are some selected recipes of Cantonese-style and Swatow-style Moon Cakes.

Fried Soft Moon Cakes

Ingredients: Dough
  1/4 cup wheat starch flour (Têng-mien-fên)
  2 cups glutinous rice flour (No-mi-fên)

3 Tbs. vegetable shortening
1/4 cup boiling water
1/2-3/4 cups water
1/4 cup sugar

Ingredients: Filling

6 oz. canned bean paste (tou-sha) or canned lotus paste (lien-jung)
2 salted duck's egg yolks (optional or if preferred)

Method:

1) Sift the wheat starch flour in a mixing bowl and add boiling water and mix well.
2) Sift glutinous rice flour onto pastry board or table and make a hollow in the center. Place sugar, vegetable shortening and wheat starch dough in the center. Adding water, gradually work together and knead into a soft dough.
3) Cut off half of the kneaded dough and steam it in a steamer over high heat for approximately 8-10 minutes. Take it out and knead it with the other half of the raw dough, making sure that it is completely combined. Roll into a long sausage shape and cut into 32 equal pieces.
4) Shape the bean paste into 32 marble sized balls. If egg yolks are used, they must be steamed first and then cut into pieces and wrapped into the centers of the bean paste.
5) Take a piece of the dough and form it into a ball. With a rolling pin, roll out into a small round. Place the filling into the center and bring up the edges, sealing it firmly and press it out flat.
6) Heat a flat-bottom frying pan and brush on a little oil. Place the cakes on it and fry each side over low medium heat until golden brown (approximately 5 minutes on each side).

Savory Fried Cakes with Chives

Ingredients:

2 cups flour	1/2 tsp. M.S.G.
1/2 tsp. salt	1/2 cup water
1/4 tsp. sugar	3 Tbs. chives (or scallions)
1/2 cup water	1/2 cup sesame seed
4 Tbs. raw pork fat	2 Tbs. vegetable shortening

Method:

1) Sift flour onto pastry board or table and make a hollow in the center. Place salt, sugar and M.S.G. and mix well together. Add vegetable shortening and water. Mix well and knead into a soft dough.
2) Wash raw pork fat with warm water and cut into small dices. Wash chives (or scallions) and finely chop into small pieces. Mix both chopped chives (or scallions) with the diced raw pork fat together.
3) Roll out the dough into a long sausage shape. Cut into 8 or 10 equal pieces. Take each piece and roll them into a thin square sheet.
4) Spread some of the mixture of pork fat and chives evenly on the surface of the rolled out dough sheet. Roll up tightly like a jelly roll into a long thin cylinder.
5) Take the long thin cylinder and coil in a spiral circle on the pastry board. Flatten slightly with a rolling pin and brush a little water on both surfaces to coat it with white sesame seeds.

6) Heat a flat-surfaced frying pan and oil slightly. Place the round cakes in and fry on low-medium heat for approximately 5 minutes on each side or until golden brown.

Steamed Soft Moon Cakes — I

Ingredients: Dough

    3 cups wheat starch flour (Têng-mien-fên)
    1 cup glutinous rice flour (No-mi-fên)
    2 cups water
    1/2 cup vegetable shortening
    1/2 cup sugar

Ingredients: Filling

    10 oz. canned lotus paste (lien-jung) or bean paste (tou-sha)
    4 salted duck's egg yolks (optional, if desired)

Method:

1) Sift both wheat starch and glutinous rice flour together into a large mixing bowl.
2) Dissolve the sugar in boiling water and add to the flour mixture. Blend and stir together before adding vegetable shortening. Knead to a soft pliable dough.
3) Divide the lotus paste into 24 equal parts and roll into small balls. If egg yolks are used, they must be steamed first then divided into 24 pieces. Place a small piece into the middle of the ball of lotus paste.
4) Roll out the dough into a long sausage shape and cut into 24 equal parts. Shape each into a small ball and flatten in the palm. Fill each with a small ball of filling, drawing up the edges and seal it firmly.
5) Press each ball into an oiled shallow wooden cake mold and pat firmly. Turn the wooden mold upside down and tap on table's edge to release the molded cake.
6) Arrange cakes in a greased steamer and steam for about 10-15 minutes. Outer dough of cakes becomes transparent when cooled.

Steamed Soft Moon Cakes — II

Ingredients: Dough

    2 cups wheat starch flour (Têng-mien-fên)
    1 cup cornstarch (Ling-fên)
    2-1/2 cups water
    6 Tbs. sugar
    2 Tbs. oil

Ingredients: Filling

    10 oz. canned lotus paste (lien-jung) or bean paste (tou-sha)

Method:

1) Sift the wheat starch flour and cornstarch together into a large mixing bowl.
2) Dissolve sugar in boiling water and add to flour. Mix together then knead well into a soft dough. Roll out into a long sausage shape and cut into pieces. The size of the pieces should be 2/3 of the size of the mold to be used.
3) Roll each piece of dough into a ball, then flatten out in the palm. Place an amount of filling half the size of the ball of dough into the center and bring up the edges and seal firmly.

4) Press into an oiled shallow wooden cake mold and pat firmly. Turn mold upside down and tap on edge of table to release molded cake.

5) Arrange cakes in an oiled steamer and steam for 10-15 minutes.

Steamed Soft Moon Cakes — III

Ingredients: Dough
- 8 cups glutinous rice flour
- 1 Tbs. banana extract
- 2 cups sugar

Ingredients: Filling
- 12 oz canned lotus paste (lien-jung) or bean paste (tou-sha)

Method:

1) Dissolve the sugar in a small amount of boiling water, then allow it to cool before adding banana extract.

2) Retain and set aside a small amount of glutinous rice flour for dusting the cakes later. Combine the larger portion of glutinous rice flour with the cooled liquid mixture and knead into a soft but firm dough. Roll out dough into a long sausage shape and cut into pieces. The size of the pieces should be about two-thirds the size of the cake mold used.

3) Roll each piece of dough into a ball and flatten in the palm. Place a small portion of the filling, about half the size of each ball of dough into each flattened piece of dough and wrap around. Bring up the edges and seal firmly.

4) Press into an oiled wooden cake mold and pat firmly. Turn mold upside down and tap on edge of table to release molded cake.

5) Arrange the cakes in a steamer lined with a piece of damp cloth and steam for 15-20 minutes.

6) Stir fry the retained glutinous rice flour in a pan until cooked. Set aside. When the cakes are done, roll or dust each cake with it.

Old Wife's Melon Cake (Lao-p'o-ping)

Ingredients: Outer pastry dough
- 1 cup high gluten flour (high protein)
- 1 cup flour
- 4 Tbs. sugar
- 1/2 cup vegetable shortening
- 1/2 cup water

Ingredients: Inner pastry dough
- 1 cup flour
- 1 tsp. wheat starch (Têng-mien-fên)
- 1/4 cup vegetable shortening

Ingredients: Filling
- 1 lb. candied winter melon
- 1/2 cup toasted sesame seeds
- 1/3 cup sugar
- 1/2 cup water
- 3/4 cup cooked glutinous flour
- oil

Method:
1) Toast the sesame seeds in a pan over low heat and set aside. Stir fry glutinous flour in dry frying pan until cooked then set aside.
2) Mince candied winter melon and combine with sesame seeds and sugar. Add water gradually and stir together. Sift in cooked glutinous rice flour and add a few drops of oil and mix well. All this process could also be done in the food processor.
3) Sift 4 oz. of flour with one 1 tsp. wheat starch and add in 2 oz. of vegetable shortening and knead well to form the inner pastry dough. Roll out the dough into a long sausage shape and cut into 32 equal pieces. Roll each into a ball and flatten with the palm.
4) To make the outer pastry dough, sift the high gluten and plain flour onto a pastry board or table and make a hollow in the center. Add the sugar and vegetable shortening in the center and gradually add water to dissolve the sugar. Slowly work it into the flour and knead into a soft dough. Roll out the dough into a long sausage shape and cut into 32 equal pieces. Roll each into a ball and flatten with the palm.
5) Wrap one piece of inner pastry dough within a piece of outer pastry dough and roll into a long thin strip. Roll up strip, flatten a bit, then overlap both sides towards the center and knead pastry dough in a round shape.
6) Roll it out into a round pancake and place some filling into the center. Fold the edges together and seal firmly.
7) Place on a piece of small paper square with sealed end facing down and press with palm. Shape the cake into a round ball and flatten. Use a fork to form air holes on top of the cakes, brush on beaten egg wash and bake in heated oven at 200 degrees F. for 20 to 30 minutes or until golden brown.

Thousand-year-old egg cakes (P'i-tan-su)

Ingredients: Dough
  2 cups flour
  3 Tbs. vegetable shortening
  6 Tbs. water
Ingredients: Filling
  8 oz. canned lotus paste (lien-jung)
  3 Tbs. sugar preserved ginger
  2 thousand-year-old eggs (P'i-tan)
Method:
1) Sift half of the flour onto pastry board or table, making a hollow in the center. Add water and one third of the vegetable shortening. Mix and knead together into a soft dough. Roll into a long sausage shape and cut into 16 equal pieces.
2) Combine the remaining half of the flour and vegetable shortening. Knead them together into a lardy dough. Roll into a long sausage shape and cut into 16 equal pieces.
3) Take a piece each of the two doughs and press them together flat. With a rolling pin, roll it out into a long flat rectangular piece of dough. Dividing into thirds, bring the two ends into the center. Roll it out again and repeat this process two more times. Then roll it into a flat oval or round cup.

4) Cut each thousand year old egg into 8 pieces. Place into the dough cup, a slice of preserved ginger besides each piece of egg along with some lotus paste. Close the cup and seal tightly. Shape into either a round or oval shape and flatten slightly in the palm. Place it with folded edge down onto a small paper square. Brush top with egg wash and bake in medium heated oven for 20-30 minutes or until golden brown.

Date filled Moon Cakes

Ingredients: Dough
    2 cups flour
    6 Tbs. vegetable shortening
    2 eggs (beaten)
    2 tsp. baking powder
    6 Tbs. sugar
Ingredients: Filling
    small can of date filling
    5 whole dates.
Method:
1) Sift flour and baking powder together onto a pastry board or table and make a hollow in the center.
2) Beat the eggs well and place it into the hollow along with sugar and vegetable shortening. Mix by pressing the mixture together to form a soft dough and knead. Roll out the dough into a long sausage shape and cut into 20 equal pieces.
3) Knead each small piece and shape into a small round cup. Place date filling into the center and close up the edges, sealing it tightly. Place on small piece of paper square with open end facing down.
4) Cut each whole date into 4 pieces and place a piece on top of each cake as garnish. Brush the surface with egg wash and place in a medium heated oven and bake for 24-30 minutes or until golden brown.

Sweet Roast Pork Crescents — I (Ch'a-shao-su)

Ingredients: Dough
    2 cups flour
    7 Tbs. cooked oil
    2 eggs
    2 Tbs. water
Ingredients: Filling
    6 oz. sweet roast pork (ch'a-shao)
    1/4 tsp. chopped shallots
    1 tsp. vegetable oil
    1 tsp. sesame seed oil
    2 Tbs. oyster sauce
    3 Tbs. sugar
    dash of MSG
    1 Tbs. light soy sauce
Method:

1) Sift flour. Divide the flour into two equal portions. Add 1 Tbs. oil to one half of the flour along with 1 well-beaten egg and 2 Tbs. water. Mix and knead well into a dough. Roll it out and shape into a small loaf. Wrap it in wax paper and place in refrigerator and allow to rest and harden. Mark it as Dough No. 1.

2) Mix the remaining flour and oil together and knead well to form a lardy dough. Roll it out and shape into a small loaf. Wrap it with wax paper and place in refrigerator to rest and harden. Mark it as Dough No. 2.

3) Cut sweet roast pork into small pieces. Saute in oil the chopped shallots and add the roast pork. Add wine and the remaining ingredients. Sir and mix constantly. When mixture is cooked, stir in a solution of 4 Tbs. of cornstarch dissolved in 1/2 cup of water and slowly thicken. Take the mixture out and place it in a bowl and set aside to cool.

4) Take out Dough No. 1 and soften it by beating with the rolling pin. Then roll it out to a long thin rectangular shape. Take out Dough No. 2 and likewise soften it by beating with rolling pin. Roll it out into a long loaf the same length of Dough No. 1 but 1/3 the width. Place it in the center of Dough No. 1 and wrap by taking up the two outer ends and folding towards the center. With a rolling pin, roll the dough loaf until flat. Then divide in thirds, bringing in the two sides towards the center and again roll out. Repeat this process 3 or 4 times. After this is completed. Roll out the dough into a long sausage shape and cut it into 12 equal pieces. Shape each piece into a small round pancake.

5) Spoon some filling and place it in the center of the pancake and fold the two edges together to form a semi-circle shape and seal firmly. Brush egg wash on the surface and arrange on a slightly greased cookie sheet and bake in medium heat for 20-30 minutes or until golden brown.

Sweet Roast Pork Crescents — II (Ch'a-shao-su)

Ingredients: Dough
   2-1/2 cups flour
   1/2 cup butter
   1/2 cup vegetable shortening
   1/8 cup water

Ingredients: Filling
   6 oz. sweet roast pork (Ch'a-shao)
   6 Tbs. onion (diced)
   2 Chinese mushrooms (diced)
   2 Tbs. bamboo shoots (diced)
   1 Tbs. yellow chives (Chiu-huang)

Seasoning
   1/2 tsp. each of salt, sugar, oyster sauce, and wine.
   dash of white pepper

Method:
   1) Sift flour onto pastry board or table and make a hollow in the center. Place in butter, vegetable shortening and sugar. Mix well and work it into the flour adding water slowly. Knead it into a soft dough. Shape it into a loaf. Wrap with wax paper and place in refrigerator to rest and harden.

2) Soak, steam and dice mushrooms. Steam or boil bamboo shoots and then dice. Dice sweet roast pork and onions. Chop yellow chives.

3) Heat a pan with a little oil. Saute onion until limp and translucent. Add roast pork, mushrooms and bamboo shoots. Add all seasonings except oyster sauce. Mix well and stir. Add a mixture of 1/2 tsp cornstarch dissolved with a little water to thicken. Add oyster sauce and place in a bowl. Add chopped yellow chives and place aside or in the refrigerator to cool.

4) Take out the dough from refrigerator and soften with rolling pin. Knead it and roll it out into a long sausage shape and cut into 24 equal pieces.

5) Knead each piece and form into a ball. Flatten it in the palm and spoon in some filling. Bring the edges together and seal firmly, forming a semi-circle shape. Brush surface with egg wash and place on slightly greased cookie sheet.

6) Bake in pre-heated oven at 200 degree F. for 20 minutes or until golden brown.

Cantonese-style Moon Cakes

To make the popular Cantonese-style molded Moon Cake, a most important ingredient, an aged syrup, must first be prepared long ahead of time.

Aged Sugar Syrup

Ingredients:
    20 cups sugar
    10 cups water
    Juice of of 1/2 a lemon (strained)
Method:
    Dissolve 20 cups of sugar in 6 cups of water over high heat. When it comes to a boil and the sugar is completely dissolved, add the lemon juice. Add the remaining 4 cups of water in several stages. Stir constantly and lower to medium heat and allow the mixture to cook for approximately 30 minutes. Stir constantly. When the mixture has formed bubbles and when it coats the spoon and have small threads, the mixture is done. Remove from heat and allow to cool. Store in a sealed container for 15 to 20 days before using.

Basic Dough

Ingredients:
    20 cups of flour
    9 cups of syrup
    2-1/2 cups of vegetable shortening
Method:
    Sift flour and save 5 cups of flour and place aside. The remaining flour should be sifted onto pastry board or table and make a hollow in the center. Add syrup, sprinkled with a little water and mix and knead. Add vegetable shortening and work it into the dough and knead. When it is completely mixed, add the remaining flour and knead the dough again, working it into the dough completely. Cover with a towel and allow the dough to rest 20-30 minutes.

    When ready to use, knead the dough slightly and roll out into a long sausage shape. Cut pieces, 2/3 the size of the cake mold to be used. Roll each piece into a ball and flatten with the palm. Then slightly roll out with rolling pin to get a uniform thickness. Place some dough about the size of ball of dough but slightly smaller. (Remember that Cantonese-style Moon Cakes have a thin pastry crust with a great deal of filling.) Wrap the dough over the filling and press firmly in greased wooden cake mold with open end facing up. Turn cake mold upside down and tap on edge of table to release molded cake. Brush surface with egg wash. Place on slightly oiled cookie sheet and bake in moderately hot oven.

Various types of fillings may be used to make the Cantonese-style moon cakes. However, there is a special variety of moon cakes which have colored dough that were utilized by the upper class as an imitation of the Tzu-lai hung and Tzu-lai pai moon cakes of Peking. Instead of having only two colors, white and red like those of Peking, the Cantonese have added a third color, yellow. These are given auspicious names such as: Hung-ling lien-jung su, Pai-ling wu-jên su and Huang-ling tou-sha su.

Hung-ling lien-jung su (The red variety)

Ingredients:
    2 cups flour
    4 tsp. aged sugar syrup
    Red food coloring
Second dough:
    4 cups flour
    1 cup vegetable oil
    Red food coloring
Filling:
    4 cups lotus paste (canned)
Method:
    1) Sift flour onto pastry board or table, making a hollow in the center. Add sugar syrup and red food coloring. Knead into a non-sticky dough.
    2) In a bowl, mix the flour, vegetable oil, and red food coloring together to form the second pastry dough. Add the oil slowly. Knead the dough until it attains the softness of a lardy dough and with the same consistency as the first pastry dough.
    3) Cut the outer dough into two portions. Roll out each portion of the dough into two flat pieces with the middle a little thicker than the sides. Likewise roll out the inner pastry dough in the same way, but in one piece only. Wrap a layer of the second dough sandwiched between two outer layers of the first dough. Roll out with a rolling pin into a long rectangular shape. Divide into thirds and fold towards the center. Again roll out the dough and repeat the process three times.
    4) Roll out into a long sausage shape and cut into 8 equal pieces. Form a ball and roll out into a flat circular piece of dough.
    5) Place some filling in the center. Draw up the edges and roll out into a ball. Lightly flatten out each ball. The sealed end should face downwards.
    6) Place cakes on a cookie sheet and bake for 10 minutes in a moderate oven.

Pai-ling wu-jên su (The white variety)

Ingredients:
    2 cups flour

4 tsp. aged sugar syrup

a small amount of oil (from the oil used for the second dough)

Second pastry dough

    4 cups flour

    2 cups oil

Filling:

    2 cups toasted rice-flour (ch'ao-mi-fên)

    2 cups sugar

    1-1/2 cups vegetable shortening

    3 Tbs. walnuts

    2 Tbs. peanuts

    2 Tbs. toasted sesame seeds

    2 Tbs. almonds

    1 Tbs. melon seeds or pine nuts

Method:

1) Chop peanuts, walnuts and almonds. Mix and combine with sesame seeds. Toast mixture in a dry frying pan.

2) Sift fried rice flour (ch'ao-mi-fîen) into a large mixing bowl. Add sugar and vegetable shortening. Mix and blend together. Add toasted nuts and mix thoroughly. Divide and roll out into 8 balls. Set aside.

To make the dough, use the same procedure as that of the red variety, without adding any food coloring.

Huang-ling tou-sha su (The yellow variety)

Ingredients:

    2 cups flour

    4 tsp. aged sugar syrup

    Yellow food coloring

Second pastry dough

    4 cups flour

    1 cup oil

    Yellow food coloring

Filling:

    4 cups bean paste (canned tou-sha)

    3 Tbs. walnuts

    1 Tbs. melon seeds or pine nuts

Method:

1) Chop walnuts and combine with melon seeds or pine nuts. Toast them in a dry frying pan. Add to bean paste and mix thoroughly. Divide and roll out into 8 balls. Set aside.

To make the dough, use the same procedure as that of the red variety, except using yellow food coloring.

Chapter 3:
Food Offerings Used During the Moon Festival

Besides Moon Cakes, there are also a number of other food items used for making offerings to the Moon during the celebration of the Mid-Autumn or Moon Festival. These foods are chosen not only for their nutritional qualities but also as symbolic reminders of various events and values that one should honor and hold to be a good citizen and human being. The stories surrounding these food items encourage people to promote peace and harmony among themselves in society and in nature. The following are some stories of selected food items of the autumn season used in this celebration.

Taro

In the southeastern provinces of China which border the Pacific Ocean, besides the Moon Cakes, another important item used in the Mid-Autumn Festival celebration is the Taro root.

This custom began during the Ming dynasty (1368-1643) when China was being pillaged and plundered by Japanese pirates called Wo-k'ou. Using Taiwan, the Ryukyu Islands as well as some small islands off the China coast, these pirates raided the South China coasts and inflicted great suffering with the loss of life and property to the people living in these coastal and inland areas.

Ch'i Chi-kuang and the Wo-k'ou

As the Wo-k'ou raids along the Chekiang coast intensified, selected military officers were brought into the province to strengthen the military organization with tactical commands. One of these military officers was Ch'i Chi-kuang (1528-1588), who was from a hereditary military family.

From the bitter experience of inroads by the Japanese pirates, Ch'i Chi-kuang formed a plan to train volunteers to defeat the invaders. He decided that it was difficult to turn urbanites into good soldiers and suggested training farm boys only. One of his innovations in the training program was the tactical formation known as the *Yüan-yang-chên,* or Mandarin duck formation, composed of basic units of twelve men each, consisting of one leader, two shield men, two with bamboo lances, and four with long lances, two fork men, and a cook. They were to advance in that order, or in two five man columns

dividing the weapons equally, but with the strict ruling that all acted to protect the leader from being wounded. If the leader lost his life, during a battle that ended in defeat, any survivor of his unit was to be executed. Thus each man was drilled in the spirit of win or die.

At the same time, the weapons were designed especially to fight the Japanese pirates whose long bows were deadly and whose sharp swords could sever any Chinese hand weapon. In Ch'i Chi-kuang's tactics, the shield was to take care of the arrows, and the bamboo lance, with its bushy branches intact, could slow down the onslaught and entangle the swordsman making it possible for the other lancers to dispatch him. In his experience, the Japanese swordsmen were formidable combatants and he needed these five to one odds. He organized four basic units to a platoon, four platoons to a company, three companies to a battalion of approximately six hundred men.

In 1561, when the T'ai-chou coast was invaded by a large fresh contingent of Japanese pirates, Ch'i Chi-kuang led his newly trained volunteers to fight them, and of nine engagements within a single month he won every one. The enemy was annihilated, with only a few casualties among his own men. This complete victory won Ch'i Chi-kuang promotion to regional commissioner. The people of the coastal areas noticed a new phenomenon in China, the marching of a disciplined army, well-fed, well-led, and well-trained in coordinated fighting.

In June, 1562, Ch'i Chi-kuang led a relief expedition to Fukien against the Japanese pirates who had drifted south out of Chekiang. After several victories, he returned to Chekiang. A few months later, the Wo-k'ou, reinforced by newly arrived Japanese, captured a large area in Fukien, including the guard city of P'ing-hai and the prefectural city of Hsing-hua.

Ch'i Chi-kuang rushed back, but the troops there were forced to seek refuge in a mountain stronghold. Soon the Japanese pirates laid siege to that area. As the siege wore on, the food supplies were exhausted and hunger became a problem. Ch'i Chi-kuang ordered some of his men to secretly comb the woods, but there was no wild game to be found. Gathering only wild vegetables and roots they found a strange tuberous root in abundance. When boiled, not only was it tasty and

agreeable, but it satisfied their hunger. After Ch'i Chi-kuang had eaten it, along with his troops, he said, "We had been caught in a crisis with hunger being imminent. However, finding this strange tuber, we have averted this danger. Not knowing what its name is, I suggest that we should call it *Yü-nan* or 'caught in crisis'.

Having been fed and re-organized, the troops were now filled with vigor and enthusiasm. Ch'i Chi-kuang ordered a surprise night attack on the enemy. The Japanese pirates were feeling rather complaisant as they thought that the Chinese troops were all experiencing hunger and could not do battle. Thus the pirates were all caught sleeping soundly in the cool Autumn night. With his trained and disciplined men, Ch'i Chi-kuang was successful in dealing the Japanese pirates several heavy blows, and recovered both cities with resounding victories.

The term for the tuber which helped avert hunger and gave the strength necessary to defeat the enemy was gradually changed from *Yü-nan*, 'caught in crisis' to *Yü-nai* or popularly called in later time, *Yü-t'ou* or Taro root.

Since it was found in the bright moonlit night of the Mid-Autumn festival, it was used in the celebration as a reminder of this crisis and the sweetness of victory over the Japanese pirates. Therefore, Taro used in the Mid-Autumn festival celebration is boiled whole in plain water and then eaten with some sugar, or fried and candied.

It is interesting to note that besides the term *Chung-ch'iu chieh* or 'Mid-Autumn Festival', the people of Kiangsu and Chekiang also call this festival *Hsieh p'ing-an* or 'Thanksgiving'.

The Taro and the Manchus

In another popular story widely circulated both in Fukien and Kwangtung, it is told that when the Ming dynasty fell in 1643 to the invading Manchus, the Chinese were made to suffer greatly under this foreign rule. At the outset, the Manchus were afraid that the Chinese majority would rebel against them. Therefore, in all strategic and important locales, the Chinese were moved out and Manchus temporarily took up residence.

In addition, every five households were required to provide quarters and boarding for a Manchu soldier. The quartered Manchu was above the law and did whatever he pleased including violating the women folk. The Chinese households were forbidden to shut or lock their doors even at night so that the Manchus could have complete freedom everywhere.

The Chinese were greatly angered by this situation but were helpless against the conquering Manchu's arrogance and savage behavior. Wanting to rebel against such injustice, patriots held secret meetings. It was determined that in order to be successful, they must have a concerted effort and a carefully synchronized uprising, all at the same time. However, fearing that their activities would be discovered, they devised a scheme.

Giving an appearance of someone's wedding, they would order a large supply of *Pao-tzu* or buns, as was the custom, to be distributed to various relatives and friends, thus escaping suspicion. Inside of the Pao-tzu or buns would be placed a small piece of paper with the date and hour of the unified uprising. This was to be at the hour of the Rat (11 p.m.-1 a.m.) on the 15th of the 8th lunar month.

At the designated time, there was a unified rebellion and many Manchu soldiers were killed. Their decapitated heads were placed in a bag so that the dead corpses could not be recognized as being Manchus. There was a retaliation and many Chinese were executed for their unsuccessful attempt in trying to overthrow the Manchus. Fearing further out-breaks or problems, the quartering of Manchu soldiers in private homes was discontinued and the order of disallowing doors to be shut or locked was rescinded.

It is in memory of this event that a large taro is used as sacrificial food during the Moon Festival as it resembles a severed head. Sometimes sweet potatoes or yams are substituted.

This story is somewhat gruesome and seems to be a take-off of the story of the Moon Cake. However, it is interesting to note that Pao-tzu or buns usually have a piece of paper on the bottom as a reminder of this story. However, such an event could have happened as quartering occupying soldiers is not uncommon in history. This was also done in the United States when colonists had to provide quarters to British soldiers which was one of the reasons given for the American Revolution.

The Chinese eat the taro not just for symbolic reasons but because it is both delicious and nutritious while promoting good health by strengthening the stomach and large intestines.

Taro, called Yü (Cantonese: Oo) or T'u-chih is known botanically as *Colocasia esculenta*. It is a member of the *Arum* family *(Araceae)*. It is a large-leaved tropical plant that has been grown as a staple food crop in the Orient for thousands of years. Several species of *Colocasia* are cultivated in China, and it was known long before the Han dynasty (220 B.C.-206 A.D.). All parts of the plant are edible when cooked, although it is grown mostly for its fleshy underground corms and tubers which are rich in starch and protein. It is usually eaten as a potato-like vegetable or used to make flour. Hawaiian poi is made with cooked taro that is pounded into a pasty mass and sometimes allowed to ferment. Taros are richer than potatoes in carbohydrates and most vitamins and minerals.

The corms and tubers, as well as the other plant parts, contain needlelike crystals of poisonous calcium oxalate that give the plant a bitter taste, but that can be destroyed by cooking. There is a variety of taro called *Dasheen*, probably from the French 'de la Chine' meaning 'from China', which is less bitter. The Chinese call this variety, Pin-lang.

Although only the taro corms and tubers are eaten by most people, the Chinese also eat the leaves and leafstalks as green vegetables which are rich in vitamin C. The blanched shoots obtained by growing the corms in the dark have a delicate flavor somewhat like that of mushrooms and considered a great delicacy by the Chinese. The flower of the taro is similar to that of the Jack-in-the-pulpit. The fleshy central spike or spadex, is enclosed by a pale yellow rolled bract, or spathe, which may be 6 to 15 inches long. Both the flower and the fleshy central spike are considered choice parts by Chinese gourmets and called Yü-chieh (Cantonese: Oo-haap).

According to Li Shih-chên in his *Pên-ts'ao kang-mu*, the seeds, as well as the leaves and stalks are used in medicine. The former are considered to be somewhat poisonous, and are recommended in indigestion, flatulence, and in disorders of partuient women. A decoction is prescribed as a wash in pediculosis. The leaves and stalks are recommended in similar cases and as an application in insect bites and other poisons. Following are some Taro recipes:

For the Mid-Autumn Festival, small taro corms are boiled in water until fully cooked, then cooled and eaten dipped in sugar. More involved recipes follow:

Taro Pudding with Dates

Ingredients:
2 lbs. taro	2 tsp. toasted sesame seeds
8 Chinese red dates	2/3 cup sugar syrup
1 Tbs. vegetable shortening	

Method:
1) Peel the taro and cut into thin slices and steam for 20-30 minutes or until soft. Mash with potato masher until smooth.
2) In a large bowl, combine mashed taro, sugar syrup and vegetable shortening and mix well.
3) Remove pits from red dates and decorate the top of the mixture, sprinkling some sesame seeds over it.
4) Cover the bowl tightly with cellophane wrap and place in steamer and steam for approximately 1 hour. Allow to cool and serve.

Taro Pudding with Gingko Nuts

Ingredients:
1 medium sized Taro	1/2 cup vegetable shortening
1/4 cup fresh Gingko nuts	1/2 cup water
1/2 cup Chinese rock sugar candy	

Method:
1) Shell Gingko nuts and steam until cooked then set aside.
2) Dissolve rock sugar candy in 1/2 cup of water over heat. Then set aside.
3) Peel taro and cut in slices and steam for 15 minutes or until soft. Then mash with potato masher until smooth.

4) In a pan, melt the vegetable shortening, add the mashed taro, and sugar syrup. Place over low heat, stir constantly. When thoroughly mixed, add the Gingko nuts and continue to cook and stir. When all is nicely combined, remove from heat and serve.

Spicy Fried Taro

Ingredients:

1 lb. taro

3 cloves garlic

Ginger

1/4 cup chicken broth

Vegetable oil for deep frying

4 Tbs. light soy sauce

Chili pepper powder

Scallions

MSG

Method:

1) Peel the taro and cut into thin slices. Place in a pan of boiling water and lightly blanch them to rid them of any powdery starch. Drain and place aside.

2) Heat oil in pan and deep fry taro slices. Remove when golden brown and drain.

3) Pour oil out, leaving 1 Tbs. oil remaining. Add ginger, garlic and chili pepper powder. When garlic is browned, add light soy sauce and taro slices. Stir-fry and add chicken broth. Add MSG and scallions. Remove and serve hot.

Stewed Taro

Ingredients:

1 lb. taro

1/2 tsp. salt

1-1/2 Tbs. wine

2 slices ginger

2 cloves garlic

3 Tbs. peanut oil

3 Tbs. light soy sauce

2 scallions (cut in 2 inch sections)

3/4 cup chicken broth

Method:

1) Peel taro and cut into slices.

2) Heat oil in pan and add salt, garlic, ginger. Stir-fry.

3) Add taro, light soy sauce, wine. Stir constantly. When taro changes color, add chicken broth. When it comes to a boil, cover and lower heat and simmer.

4) When taro is cooked, add scallions, salt and MSG. Stir-fry. Remove and serve hot.

Cooked Taro Shoots

Ingredients:

Taro shoots (Oo-haap)

1 Tbs. cornstarch

1/2 tsp. sesame seed oil

1/2 cup vegetable oil

MSG

1/2 tsp. sugar

2 tsp. soy sauce

1 tsp. wine

1 cup chicken broth

Method:

1) Wash taro shoots and cut into pieces and set aside.

2) Heat vegetable oil in pan and add taro shoots. Stir-fry, then remove and drain.

3) Pour out the oil from the pan, leaving only about 1 tsp. behind. Then put the taro shoots back into the pan and add sugar, soy sauce, wine, chicken broth and MSG. Cover and stew over low heat for 3-5 minutes. Make a mixture of

cornstarch and water. Add this mixture plus sesame seed oil and stir quickly.
Remove and serve hot.

Pomelo

One of the important food items for the Moon Festival celebration is the Pomelo.
The Chinese call it 'Yu' but more specifically 'Sha-t'ien-yu' after the place where
production is the best. How did this tradition come to be and how did the Pomelo get
its name? There is an interesting legend from the
Ch'ing dynasty during the reign of Emperor Ch'ien-
lung (1736-1796).

In the province of Kwangsi, there is a village
called Sha-t'ien which is located 20 *li* north of the
district capital of Jung-hsien.   There lived a
person named Hsia Chi-kang, who was intelligent,
upright, faithful and sincere. At age 40, while he
was serving as an official in Chekiang, he became
very friendly with a young provincial graduate
with the highest honors (chieh-yüan) named Ch'in
I, who was from the nearby Yang-k'o village.

In time, his friend, Ch'in I received orders
from the capital to serve as prefectural magistrate
of Ningpo. By coincidence, it was about the same
time that Hsia Chi-kang's term of office terminated.
Before his departure for his native home, Hsia
Chi-kang asked his friend if he could have a seedling of a tree whose fruits he greatly
enjoyed. His friend complied by presenting two healthy young plants for him to take
back home.   Returning to Sha-t'ien village in Kwangsi province, Hsia Chi-kang
immediately employed two full-time gardeners to care for his gardens and orchards.
He entrusted the two young seedlings to these professional gardeners to plant and
care for them.

After three years cultivation, the fruit trees bore their first fruits. They were
quite large with a beautiful yellow color. The elated Hsia Chi-kang quickly picked the
largest fruit that he could find and cut it open. He invited all to have a taste of this
exotic fruit which he had brought back from Chekiang province. Anxiously and with
great curiosity, everyone took a piece of the fruit. Placing it in their mouths, they
started to pucker and make disgusted faces as they were greeted with an extremely
sour, bitter and astringent taste.

Hsia Chi-kang was perplexed and greatly puzzled as these trees were grown
from young plants that he personally brought back from Yang-k'o village in Chekiang
province. There could be no mistake of it being something else. Yet how could there
be such a drastic change from the delicious fruits that he had so enjoyed before? He
remembered the fruit as being sweet and juicy and now this fruit grown in his orchard
was sour, bitter and astringent in taste. There must be some explanation for this

drastic change as the fruits looked the same. He tried to find an explanation so he could, if necessary, make changes in their cultivation. After much thought and agonizing, he came to the conclusion that due to the change in environment, climate and soil conditions, the fruit trees in adapting themselves to these new conditions altered so drastically that the changed fruits were the result.

Convinced that this must be the answer, he quickly had his gardeners carefully dig up the trees that were growing on the hillside and transplant them nearer to his house so that they may receive greater and careful tending. He personally saw to it that the soil was clean and fertile and that they were watered daily with fresh and cool spring water.

In the spring of the fourth year, Hsia Chi-kang's cow had given birth to a young calf, but it died shortly after birth. Hsia Chi-kang ordered his gardeners to bury the dead calf near the two fruit trees. That same year, during the fall at the time when the hoar frost had descended, Hsia Chi-kang again went to look at his two fruit trees. They were full of large and beautiful yellow-colored fruits. Hsia Chi-kang arbitrarily picked one of them, but from his earlier experience, before he had cut it opened, he began to pucker and make faces in anticipation of the sour and bitter taste. After cutting it open, he hesitated. Sticking his tongue out to taste with the tip of his tongue, he closed his eyes. To his amazement and great surprise, his tongue met with a juicy and honey sweet taste. Opening his eyes wide in disbelief, he tasted it again and again, each time with greater delight and enjoyment. Excitedly, he called out to his gardeners and servants. "All of you come here quickly! This fruit is sweet and delicious!" Everyone took a piece and after tasting it, smiled and started to talk and praise the pleasing flavor of this exotic fruit. Before long, the news had spread throughout Sha-t'ien village and everyone wanted to have a taste and were gleefully welcomed.

Hsia Chi-kang was so proud that he selected the largest and best looking ones to be presented to the Prefectural Magistrate of Jung-chou who had jurisdiction over the Sha-t'ien village. After tasting the fruit, the Magistrate was so pleased that he encouraged the mass growing of this fruit. He said to Hsia Chi-kang, "We must place all our efforts and labors in growing and cultivating this exotic fruit. It is a wonderful delight that it may serve as a 'kung-p'in' or tributary gift to the Throne."

Hsia Chi-kang was greatly encouraged by these words. Returning home, he talked with his gardeners about plans to expand the orchards planting more trees. Carefully they selected large and plump seeds from the largest choice fruits and planted them. Three years later, during the autumn months, a few of the new trees started bearing fruit. However, these fruits were only slightly larger than goose eggs, with thin segments containing little flesh. Moreover, its taste was so bitter and astringent that it could not be eaten. Hearing the disastrous results of this crop, the people from the nearby villages teasingly remarked, "The seeds from the exotic fruit of Sha-t'ien if planted will have such a harsh and bitter taste that it will turn your insides out!"

These jokes and cruel remarks became a dilemma for Hsia Chi-kang and caused him untold anxiety. He was determined to find the cause and correct it. He studied the propagation of various fruit trees and found that in the case of the Lychee and Longan (Dragon-eyes), they are propagated by grafting or air-layering branches. Hsia Chi-kang after much investigation and study, decided to follow suit in the same technique with his original two trees. Continuing this method of propagation over the period of three years, he began to have quite a number of trees bearing fruit on the third year. He was most anxious to taste the fruits on these new trees. This time, the golden-colored fruits were honey sweet and delicious in taste. Satisfied and pleased, Hsia Chi-kang now knew exactly how to cultivate and propagate this exotic fruit.

When Emperor Ch'ien-lung took one of his Southern Tours (Nan-hsün) and visited the Huai River Delta, Hsia Chi-kang took some of the choicest fruits as tribute to the visiting monarch. After Emperor Ch'ien-lung had tasted the fruits, he was most pleased and said, "Excellent! This is an excellent delight! Summon before me the bearer of these most desirable tributary presents!" When Hsia Chi-kang received an audience with the Emperor, he was asked what this delightful fruit was called. Hsia Chi-kang dutifully answered, "Your Majesty, your loyal subject had brought two young plants home from Yang-k'o village in Chekiang province when I had retired from government service and planted them in Sha-t'ien. Not knowing its proper name, the people in Sha-t'ien have named it after the place of origin as 'Yang-k'o-tzu' or 'the fruit from Yang-k'o'."

"Yang-k'o-tzu, is an awkward name," said the Emperor, "we must think of a better name befitting of such a pleasurable and delightful fruit."

One of the attending high officials, an elderly minister, spoke up saying, "Your Majesty, this humble official had formerly resided in Sha-t'ien village and am familiar with how far it is from here. Yet from such far distances, the grower of these wonderful fruits has personally come to present them to your Majesty. Therefore, if I may be permitted to make a suggestion, I think that the phrase, 'Sha-t'ien-yu' or 'presented from Sha-t'ien [to His Imperial Majesty] would be most appropriate. However, since this is a fruit, the character 'Yu' (from) should be classified with an appropriate radical denoting it being botanical. By adding 'Mu' or the wood radical, it does not alter the pronunciation but more exactly describes it as a fruit and also gives its origin. Perhaps, Your Majesty might consider calling this favorable fruit 'Sha-t'ien-yu'."

Hearing this suggestion and the background of philology and logic in choosing this term, Emperor Ch'ien-lung was most pleased and exclaimed, "That is a most appropriate and wonderful suggestion. Henceforth, this fruit shall be called 'Sha-t'ien-yu'!"

More than two hundred years have passed since this name had been bestowed on this fruit by the Ch'ing dynasty Emperor. The fruit has continued to improve in bearing larger and sweeter fruits and more bountiful harvests on the trees. The term 'Sha-t'ien-yu' has come to be used for an excellent variety of pomelo. These fruits are large, plump and yellow-colored. The skin is thin and the fruit large with small seeds. It is fleshy and not pulpy and contains a lot of juice. It is sweet and refreshing to eat, moreover, it is healthy and nutritious.

The more common variety of Pomelo is called 'Lu-yu' (Cantonese: Luk-yau). The term 'Lu' could either mean 'roundish' or 'common.' Therefore, the Cantonese, mainly from the Chung-shan area have started calling it 'Boo-luk' (Mandarin: Pu-lu), meaning a pomelo that is 'pu' or a healthy tonic to strengthen one's health. Since it is considered good for one's health, the Cantonese use it in almost all their festivals. Moreover, since this tree was approved and its name bestowed by the Emperor, it is considered sacred and so the leaves of the Pomelo are used as an Imperial Edict to ward off all malevolence. As such, it is similar to coins with the name of the Emperor's reign. It is believed that the Emperor, being the Son of Heaven and a Dragon, has jurisdiction over all things on earth, including spirits and demons. Also, according to the legend, all bitterness and things bad could be averted and be gotten rid of by understanding, intelligence, diligence and hard work. The result is sweetness and delight! To the practical Chinese, this is certainly a wonderful symbol to be used as an offering.

Superstition has it that, if there is a hollow in the center, there is a space in the middle

where the segments come together, it means good luck. However, the 'Sha-t'ien-yu' are always found in such a condition. This makes it more of a good marketing device for fruit vendors to call all their pomelo 'Sha-t'ien-yu.'

The Pomelo which is a globular fruit is rich in vitamins B and C and high in potassium. It has a thick, pale yellow peel and a juicy, acid, pale yellow, greenish white or pinkish flesh that is divided into segments. Besides eating the fleshy segments both fresh and also cooked, the Chinese use the thick peel, extensively in cooking and candies They are eaten for indigestion and also to improve the appetite, relieve congestion in the chest, and alleviate mucous discharge and coughs.

For the Mid-Autumn Festival celebration, pomelos are eaten as a fresh fruit. However, some people separate and peel the segments, sprinkle them with brown sugar and some cinnamon and lightly broil them. These are eaten warm.

As for the pomelo peels, there are several methods of preparing the thick peels which to the Chinese gourmet, are a special treat. The following are some recipes for pomelo peels.

Oyster-sauced Pomelo Peels — I

Remove the outer rind or skin of the pomelo peels and set out to dry in the sun. After it has been dried, boil it in water for 30 minutes (add a little Chien-shui or Potassium carbonate solution). Rinse thoroughly with cold water. Squeeze out all the water and allow to completely dry out. Then boil in water again for 20 minutes. Rinse and soak in cold water. Squeeze dry. Place in a covered ceramic steamer. Place some bamboo matting in the bottom. Place the pomelo peels on it and a piece of toasted Ta-ti fish then a bamboo matting to separate and another layer of pomelo peels and toasted Ta-ti fish. Finishing with a layer of peels on the top. Add some vegetable shortening, MSG and some chicken stock and slowly steam for 1 hour. Before eating, add some oyster sauce.

Oyster-sauced Pomelo Peels — II

Ingredients:

3 pomelo (unripened green ones)	1/2 cup vegetable shortening
2 Tbs. oyster sauce	7 cups chicken stock
1-1/2 Tbs. wine	3 Tbs. water chestnut starch
1 tsp. MSG	1 tsp. salt
2-1/2 Tbs. vegetable oil	1 Tbs. baking soda
1/2 lb. dried Ta-ti fish	

Method:

1) Take about 1 Tbs. baking soda dissolved in 1 cup of cold water. Using a potato peeler, remove the outer rind of the pomelo. Then dip and rub baking soda mixture over it and allow to soak in baking soda solution. When there is a bright greenish color on the pomelo, remove and cut the pomelo peel open into 4 large pieces. The pulp may be discarded or broiled with some cinnamon and sugar.

Scrape out the very soft parts of the pomelo peel then place in a pot of boiling water and boil for 30 minutes. Remove and rinse thoroughly. Allow to soak in a pan of water for 1 day. Change the water 3 or 4 times. Each time rinse and squeeze out the water before allowing to soak in clear water.

2) On the second day, boil the pomelo peels again in a pot of boiling water for 20 minutes. Again soak them in a pan of water for another day, repeating the earlier process until there is no bitter taste in the pomelo peels.

3) Wash and wipe dry the dried Ta-ti fish and coat it with vegetable oil. Fry over low heat on both sides until toasted.

4) Into a large covered pottery steamer, place a piece of bamboo matting on the bottom and place a layer of pomelo peels followed by pieces of the toasted fish. Repeat this with the top layer being that of pomelo peels.

5) Add vegetable shortening, salt, wine, MSG, and chicken stock over the pomelo peels. Cover pottery steamer and place in a large steamer elevated on a trivet and over high heat, steam for 30 minutes. Then lower heat and steam for 1-1/2 hours.

6) Remove pottery steamer and allow to cool a short time. Carefully remove the pomelo peels, discarding the dried fish and place on a platter. Reserve any liquid. Adding oyster sauce to it and a mixture of water chestnut starch and water. In a saucepan, cook for about 1/2-1 minute then pour over pomelo peels.

Note: The dried Ta-ti fish after toasting, could be placed in a food processor and chopped fine. Then it could be sprinkled or spread onto the pomelo peels.

Candied Pomelo Peels

Ingredients:

2 cups pomelo peels cut in thin strips

1-1/2 cups cold water

Syrup: 1 cup Sugar + 1/2 cup water

Method:

1) Bring slowly to the boiling point, 1-1/2 cups of cold water and pomelo peels. Simmer for 10 minutes or longer if you do not like a bitter taste. Drain. Repeat this process 3 to 5 times, draining well each time.

2) Make a syrup by dissolving 1 cup sugar in 1/2 cup water over heat.

3) Add peels and boil until all syrup is absorbed and the peels are transparent. Roll in powdered sugar and spread to dry.

Note: Both orange and grapefruit peels may be used with this recipe.

Stewed Spare Ribs with Pomelo Peels

Ingredients:

Peel of 1 large pomelo	1-1/2-2 lbs. spare ribs
2 Tbs. light soy sauce	1 tps. sugar
1/2 MSG	Ginger
Cornstarch	

Method:

1) Remove the hard outer rind of the pomelo. Boil in water for 30 minutes. Rinse and soak in cold water. Squeeze dry. Repeat in boiling, rinsing and soaking in cold water 2 or 4 times until the bitter taste is eliminated.

2) Cut spare ribs into 2-inch lengths. Parboil 15 minutes and rinse in cold water. Pat dry then coat with a mixture of cornstarch, sugar and light soy sauce and set aside.

3) Heat the oil and add ginger. Then add the spare ribs and brown. Then add pomelo peel and water. Cover pot, bring water to boil. Reduce to simmer, and cook spare ribs until tender. Uncover. Gradually add cornstarch and water mixture. Stir continuously until gravy thickens. Serve over or with steamed rice.

Shrimp Paste with Pork Tongue and Pomelo Peel

Ingredients

1 pound pork tongue   1/2 pomelo peel
3 Tbs. Shrimp Paste   1/2 tsp. minced fresh ginger root
1/2 tsp. MSG   1/2 tsp. sugar
Vegetable oil

Method:

1) Parboil the pork tongue sufficiently and with a knife, scrape and remove the outer skin. Wash, pat dry and cut in pieces, 1/4-inch thick.

2) Remove the hard outer rind of the pomelo peel. Soak in cold water for 1 day. Then squeeze dry. Cut into strips.

3) Heat pan with oil and place pomelo peels in pan and cook until all the water has been drawn out of the peels. Then remove in a plate and set aside.

4) Heat 3 Tbs. of oil in a pan and add the pork tongue and stir-fry. When it is done, remove and set aside.

5) Heat 2 Tbs. of oil in a pan and place the pomelo peels and when it is half done, add the shrimp paste. Stir-fry a little and add mixture of light cornstarch and water. Add pork tongue and a little salt. Cover and continue cooking. When it is done, add some chopped scallions and a dash of sesame seed oil. Remove and serve.

Note: Stewed pork tongues which can be purchased from many Chinese barbecue shops may be used. Steps 1 and even 5 could then be eliminated.

Steamed Pork Patty with Pomelo Peels

Ingredients:

1-1/2 lbs. ground or finely chopped pork containing some fat
1 tsp sliced ginger   1 tsp soy sauce
1/2 tsp. sugar   1 tsp. wine
sprinkle of ground pepper   Sprinkle of MSG
1 Tbs. cornstarch   Slices of Processed pomelo peels
1/2 cup water chestnuts diced   Chopped scallions (optional)

Method:

1) Mix all ingredients except the processed pomelo peels, thoroughly until all are completely blended. Transfer to a platter and press into meat patty about 1/2 inch thick.

2) Processed pomelo peels could be bought from Chinese grocery stores. Cut in thin slices and arrange on top of the meat patty. Sprinkle with a little light soy sauce, wine and sugar.

3) Place patty elevated on a trivet in a large steamer with tight fitting lid. Cover and steam cook at high heat 25-30 minutes or until pork is done. Serve immediately with hot steamed rice.

Steamed Pork with Pomelo Peels

Ingredients:

1 lbs. lean pork (julienne)	1 tsp. ginger (sliced)
1/2 tsp. sugar	1 tsp. wine
1 tsp. light soy sauce	1 tsp. cornstarch
1 Tbs. oyster sauce	Processed pomelo peels (sliced)

Method:
1) Marinate pork in sugar, wine, soy sauce, ginger, cornstarch and add pomelo peel slices. Set aside for 5-10 minutes.
2) Place marinated pork in shallow dish, elevated on a trivet in a large steamer with tight fitting lid. Cover and steam cook at high heat 25-30 minutes or until pork is done. Serve hot.

The Case of the Snail

During the Ch'ing dynasty (1644-1911), there was a person named Liu Tsu-wang who was a native of the Liu-tu district, Min-ch'ing prefecture in the province of Fukien. He had served as a tutor in the Classics in Peking. However, after thirteen years of service, he was appointed a Chih-hsien or district magistrate of Wên-ch'ang-hsien in the province of Kwangtung. Upon his arrival at his post to assume his duties, he was confronted with a most unique legal battle dubbed, 'The Case of the Snail.'

This case took place during the reign of Emperor Ch'ien-lung, (1736-1796) involving the fact that the fields of Wên-ch'ang contained an abundance of snails. However, at that time, the natives of that area had not learned to eat them. They considered the abundance of snails as pests and dangerous to their growing crops. Having tried and found no effective method of preventing these snails from multiplying, the farmers resorted to deceptive and underhanded means of getting rid of the snails on their fields by transferring them onto their neighbor's fields. In the still of the night when there was no one around, clandestinely and stealthily, they would gather up and cast the snails onto their neighbors' fields thereby passing their problems to their unlucky and unsuspecting neighbor.

The snails gathered together and scattered about, led to gross confusion, animosity, deception, feuds, quarrels resulting in charges of assault and battery that filled the court dockets. The frequency and cumbersome nature of these law suits hampered any just trials and acted like a heavy yoke placed on several previous magistrates who struggled in their unsuccessful attempt to curb these re-occurring legal battles.

Unfortunately, shortly after Liu Tsu-wang took office as the Magistrate of this district, he inherited these unsolved law cases. In familiarizing himself with these legal cases and clearing the court docket, his first order of business was having the prisoners in this pending case brought before him.

When the two prisoners were led out, he saw that they each bore a heavy wooden cangue around their necks and on their shoulders. Although they were rugged, they were so thin that their bones were visible and their bodies were covered with filth. Without question, these two prisoners had been incarcerated for a long duration. The prisoners while on their knees were questioned about the charges filed against them. Without hesitation, they answered in a straight forth and truthful manner and fully admitted their guilt. After their confession, they asked for permission to speak out. Their request so granted, they related that inasmuch as they were guilty of all charges brought against them, they were only doing what had been the usual practice of transferring snails from their own fields onto their neighbors'. Admittedly, they said that this was a common and widespread practice.

After listening to these two prisoners, Liu Tsu-wang curiously inquired, "If this is an accepted and common practice, then why is this construed as a crime? Moreover, why were the two of you the only ones apprehended and imprisoned with pending criminal charges?"

"Your Lordship," the prisoners replied, "First of all, we belong to a minority race. Secondly, we haven't any money to buy gifts to present to the magistrates or officials. Thirdly, we know of no one with influence to speak on our behalf . . ."

Hearing this, Liu Tsu-wang slapped the table in a gesture of anger and roared, "Insolence!"

The two prisoners fell backwards and were greatly intimidated and frightened. They began to kowtow repeatedly, crying out and begging for mercy. They felt that they had offended and angered the magistrate and fearing a severe beating, they shook and shuddered as they bit their teeth tightly in anticipation of an order of punishment. Instead, they were astonished and greatly surprised when the District Magistrate ordered that their heavy wooden cangues be unlocked and removed. Moreover, he gave orders that they should be given a hearty meal and receive decent treatment while awaiting a formal trial.

The next day, the District Magistrate issued and posted a public proclamation.

> *To all, take notice! In Wên-ch'ang-hsien, there being an abundance of snails in the fields, it has been the cause of frequent squabbles and wranglings. This has incited unrest, animosity and even suspicion amongst the populace. With time, these angers have given to quarreling feuds which resulted in assault and battery and the disruption of the peace and tranquility of this area. This cannot be tolerated and allowed to continue. It is an infringement upon law and order and good orderly government. Therefore, it is hereby set forth that on the 15th day of the 8th month at the hour of ch'ên (7-9 a.m.), a public trial will be held in the district yamen or courthouse. All persons, regardless of race, sex or age are requested to be present at this public trial. Take heed of this notice!*

After reading the proclamation, many of the people felt that the newly appointed magistrate exhibited some fury and daring so that the public trial should not be missed as it should prove to be spectacular and interesting. Therefore, everyone eagerly awaited the appointed date of the 15th of the 8th month. On that day, people came from every hamlet, borough and village within the district of Wên-ch'ang-hsien. They crowded themselves outside of the small courthouse so compactly that they formed a tight and thick barrier that could even have dammed up a flooding river.

The magistrate, Liu Tsu-wang, had promptly ordered that a long table should be set up in the middle of the courtroom. On top of this table were placed ten large platters filled with large and plump morsels of snails, each the size of a large adult thumb. These snails had been delicately and carefully prepared by several noted chefs who had arrived with the magistrate at his new post. When all was ready, the Magistrate took up his position on the bench and ordered that the two prisoners be brought out before him.

The Magistrate quickly announced, "Coincidentally, today happens to be the Mid-Autumn Festival for which families gather together in celebration. Celebrating this important festival, I have ordered that a savory delicacy be specially cooked and prepared by my chefs. I hereby extend an invitation to all of you to first sample this gourmet delight before we should begin the business of this legal trial."

After saying this, he quickly ordered that he be served first. After taking the first sampling, he extended the invitation to the nobles and minor officials and office holders inside the courthouse. Although all were baffled by this strange gesture and behavior, nevertheless, they did not hesitate and complied with following the Magistrate's example of sampling the food. To their great surprise, it was tasty, flavorful and a delight to the palate.

Afterward, Liu Tsu-wang said to the people standing outside the courtroom, "All of you outside. File in an orderly manner and also partake some of this festive delicacy." The people responded to the Magistrate's words as an order and quickly did as they were told. Before long the entire contents of the ten large platters were quickly consumed so that nothing, not even a small morsel of sauce, remained.

When everyone had been given a taste, the Magistrate politely asked, "Did you find the food tasty and to your liking?"

Everyone nodded and gave an affirmative answer. Then Liu Tsu-wang asked, "Would any of you have any idea as to what you have tasted or what is the main ingredient of this savory dish?"

All were silent and a great hush and stillness reigned. There was not even a slight movement of any kind. After a while, there was a person who sheepishly, haltingly and hesitatingly spoke out, "Could it be that this excellent dish of food which we were granted the honor of sampling, possibly be that of snail meat?"

Liu Tsu-wang smiled and laughed aloud. Then he responded, "Absolutely perceptive and correct. Without any doubt it is a dish of snails. The tail end of the shell had been cut off and washed clean before it is boiled in water. After which the meat had been taken out from the shell. Combined with ginger, sugar, wine, scallions and other ingredients, it is then prepared as a delightful and savory dish. Ah. . . , it is delicious and very tasty. Moreover, it is also nutritious and highly beneficial to health. In fact, it strengthens and brightens one's eyes. In my native Min-ch'ing-hsien in Fukien province, people are delighted with this great delicacy which at times is quite expensive and difficult if not impossible to obtain. However, locally none of you seem to recognize that your fields abound with an abundance of these snails. In utter ignorance, you deceptively gather and scatter this wealth onto the fields of others. Yet those receiving this precious commodity exhibit greater ignorance. Instead of being grateful for this most valuable and costly gift, charges are brought against their neighbors for depositing wealth onto their fields. Do you not agree with me that this is a most strange and unique behavior? Moreover, feuds and fighting surround these quarrels, not to mention hard feelings, hatred, and animosity. Look here at these two culprits who have been imprisoned. They had snails deposited on their lands and in turn, gathered and passed it onto the lands of others. Fights began and they were arrested for assault and battery and a heavy wood cangue placed on each of them. They were disgraced and made to suffer the pains and hardships of imprisonment for several years. Yet, there was no curbing or curtailing of the problem, it continued. Therefore, why is there only two of them ever arrested and incarcerated? Why no one else?"

Everyone listened intently and with great interest as the Magistrate continued, "Concerning these two prisoners, they were unlucky and unfortunate that not only are they poor but of a minority race. Therefore, they were looked down upon, considered unworthy and even despised. This is an example which the Classics term, "Jo-jou ch'iang-shih" or the weak serves as a prey to the strong — a weak country being annexed by a stronger one. If you were to change places with them, how would any of you feel? Do you call this justice or even reasonable treatment?"

Everyone was caught speechless and they lowered their heads in shame. Hearing no response, the Magistrate then gave his verdict. "I find these two prisoners before me not guilty and absolve them of all charges placed against them. Today is the 15th of the 8th month and the Mid-Autumn Festival. In celebration, all families should be united and joined together. Likewise, I am freeing these two persons so that they may rejoin their respective families. This is the only just, reasonable and dutiful order that should be discharged. Case dismissed!"

After this trial, people went about saying, "This new magistrate could be described as "Ming-ching kao-hsüan" or like a clear mirror which hangs on high as he conducts a just trial with clear intelligence. He is certainly a most worthy official."

News of this unique trial quickly spread like fire in the open plains. Henceforth, farmers no longer looked at the snail as a pest or even hideous. Instead of ridding their fields of snails, they fostered and encouraged their propagation. This became a most valuable crop and the area of Wên-ch'ang-hsien in Kwangtung became famous for their large, plump and succulent snails which were eagerly sought by not only gourmets but everybody.

The snail is a mollusk, whose soft body is protected with a spirally-coiled shell. Snails usually hide out in a dark and damp place during the day and emerge at night to search for food.

There are more than 22,000 kinds of snails found all over the world, with the largest concentration in wet temperate and tropical zones. Among them, only the apple snail *(Helix pomatia),* garden snail *(Helix aspersa),* and agate or giant African snail *(Achatina fulica)* are edible.

To the Chinese, the term 'T'ien-lo' or 'Shih-lo' means a savory gourmet's delight. The Cantonese chefs excel and are the most famous for their recipes in preparing this fine dish. This term, 'T'ien-lo' is used to designate edible snails as opposed to Kuo-niu the common snail. Just as we have used the word 'Pork' instead of 'Pig', perhaps if we are to, likewise, use the French term 'escargot' or 'Escargot de la chinoise,' it may prove to be more acceptable and appetizing to Westerners instead of the common word 'Snails.'

This dish eaten as part of the Mid-Autumn Festival food is a reminder of equal justice and equal rights for all and that racism and prejudice is wrongful thinking. It also reminds us that the wealth of the land should be fully utilized. Rich in protein, snails have high economic value as a food and tonic. The snail, although a lowly creature is not only tasty and delicious, but also nutritious and nourishing to our health. This dish is even more delicious when served with a good wine. After all if it were living in the sea, we would not blink as it would be the meat of the conch for which we place great delight in this expensive dish. Why not consider the snail or escargot in the same way? The following are some recipes for preparing 'Escargot de la chinoise."

Cooking Escargot

Escargot may be purchased live in the shell or canned without shell. The live escargot must be purchased several days before cooking and must be cleaned. In cleaning them, place in a pan of water and change the water several times daily for two or three days. The dead ones should be removed and discarded at each changing of the water. This constant changing of fresh water should suffice in obtaining clean and healthy snails. There is an earlier popular practice of placing a rusty cleaver into the pan of water. It was believed that the snails would eat some of the rust and expel all the dirt in their system. However, such a practice based on old wive's tales, could be dispensed with as daily changing of the water suffices. A Chinese cleaver is only necessary when preparing to cook the escargot. The pointed end of each must be tapped against the flat blade or something hard in order to both facilitate the cooking and eating of the escargot as the meat is dug out with toothpicks.

Escargot with Black Bean Sauce

Ingredients:

1-1/2 to 2 lbs. cleaned live escargot
2 large cloves garlic (minced)
2 Tbs fermented Black Beans (tou-shih)
1/2 tsp. minced fresh ginger
2 tsp. soy sauce   1 sprig Tzu-su (Shiso or Beefsteak)
2 Tbs. vegetable oil   1/2 tsp. salt
1 tsp. wine

Method:

1) Heat oil in pan and add garlic, ginger, salt, soy sauce, and fermented black beans. Stir-fry over high heat.
2) Add live escargot and Tzu-su and continue to stir-fry over high heat. Add wine. Remove and serve hot.

Escargot with Shrimp Paste

Ingredients:

1-1/2 to 2 lbs. cleaned live escargot
3 Tbs. Shrimp Paste   1/2 tsp. minced ginger
1/2 tsp. MSG   1/4 tsp. sugar
1 sprig Tzu-su (Shiso or Beefsteak)
2 Tbs. vegetable oil   2 tsp. garlic (minced)
1 tsp. wine

Method:

1) Heat oil in pan and add ginger, garlic, shrimp paste, and sugar. Stir-fry over high heat.
2) Add live escargot, Tzu-su, wine and MSG. Continue to stir-fry over high heat. Remove and serve hot.

Stir-fried Escargot

Ingredients:

1-1/2 lbs. escargot   1/2 red pepper (seeded and sliced in
    strips)
3 scallions (chopped)   1 clove garlic
1 tsp. sugar   1 Tbs. sesame seed oil
1 Tbs. wine   3 Tbs. soy sauce paste (Chiang-yu-kao)
1 Tbs. vinegar   1 sprig Tzu-su (beefsteak or shiso)
1/2 tsp. MSG   vegetable oil

Method:

1) Heat oil in pan, stir-fry red pepper, scallions, garlic, tzu-su. Add Escargot and continue to stir-fry over high heat.
2) Add wine, sesame seed oil, soy sauce, sugar, vinegar and MSG. Mix and stir-fry. Remove and serve hot.

Escargot meat with Black Bean Sauce

Ingredients:

Canned or frozen escargot meat   2 Tbs. fermented black beans
3 cloves garlic   3 scallions (chopped)
1 red pepper (seeded and slivered)
1 Tbs. sesame seed oil
1 Tbs. wine   1/2 tsp. sugar
1 Tbs. soy sauce paste (Chiang-yu-kao)
1/4 tsp. MSG
3 Tbs. vegetable oil   Tzu-su (beefsteak or shiso)

Method:

1) Rub some coarse salt into escargot with fingers. Rinse with water and drain.
2) Marinate escargot with sesame seed oil, sugar, wine, soy sauce paste, MSG. Set aside for ten minutes.
3) Heat oil in pan. Add fermented beans, garlic, scallions and stir-fry.
4) Add marinated escargot, red pepper and stir-fry. Remove and serve hot.

Tzu-su

One of the main ingredients in cooking escargot is Tzu-su. Tzu-su *(Perilla ocimoides)* of the mint family, is the purple variety commonly known as the beefsteak plant or by its Japanese name Shiso. The leaves are used mainly as a garnish and in pickles, but the young leaves are also eaten as a vegetable. They are also used to prepare a fragrant beverage. The stalk and leaves are used for driving away colds, as a stomachic and tonic, in cholera, and to benefit the alimentary canal. They are considered to be diaphoretic and pectoral and antidotal to fish and flesh poison. Tzu-su are thought to be highly nutritious. They are also prescribed in rheumatism, seminal losses, asthma, and obstinate coughs.

During the autumn season, the leaves are plump and thick. The northern Chinese and especially the Manchus, pick these leaves to make a pastry called Po-po which is eaten with sugar or light syrup. This is eaten with great relish.

Tzu-su wrapped Po-po

Ingredients:

2 cups glutinous rice flour   1 cup water
1/4 cup vegetable shortening   large Tzu-su leaves
6 oz. can of bean paste

Method:

1) Wash Tzu-su leaves and set aside to drain.
2) Sift the glutinous rice flour onto the table or pastry board. Make a depression in the center and pour water in little at a time and knead into soft dough. Add lard and knead until thoroughly blended.
3) Roll dough into a long sausage shape and cut into pieces (size of walnuts)
4) Shape each piece of dough into a small nest and fill with a spoonful of bean paste. Bring all edges together and roll into a ball. Then lightly flatten out like a cookie.
5) Take a piece of Tzu-su leaf and wrap over each cake.

6) Arrange in a platter and place in steamer and steam for 3-4 minutes. Remove and serve with a dish of granulated sugar or light syrup.

The Water Caltrop

The rustic pavilion called 'Ts'ai-ling-tu' is one of the 72 scenic spots within the Imperial summer palace called Pi-shu-shan-chuang in Jehol. It is but a resting spot or ferry stop for the Emperor and the royal family when they are boating on the lake. However, there is something very strange and unique about this spot. The pavilion was named 'Ts'ai-ling' or gathering water caltrops for these are found in abundance in the nearby waters. These water caltrops are unique. Most water caltrops have a deep dark green or dark brown color. However, those found in this area are black. Why is this so? What strange tale explains these black water caltrop?

It is said that after the Ch'ing dynasty Emperor Ch'ien-lung (1736-1796), had completed his ten great military campaigns, solidified his rule and strengthened the border areas, he was exceedingly happy to boast that his military accomplishments were unequaled by any ruler since antiquity. However, he did not want to be known only as a martial Emperor so he looked towards some literary and aesthetic accomplishments.

Following the example of his grandfather, Emperor K'ang-hsi, he ordered the compilation of the *Ssu-ku ch'üan-shu* or the 'Four-treasure Library' which is a huge and vast collection of rare books. Aesthetically, he decided to expand and improve on the Pi-shu-shan-chuang or the Imperial Summer Palace which had originally been built by Emperor K'ang-hsi. However, it had only 36 scenic spots. Emperor Ch'ien-lung decided that he would not only improve these 36 scenic sights but add another 36, making a total of 72 scenic spots. In his determination for such a massive construction, there was a nationwide recruitment of skilled artisans, craftsmen along with general laborers and other workmen.

Of the great numbers recruited, there was a young artisan in his early twenties named Ah-nan. He was a native of T'ai-hu and was highly skilled as a decorator, both as a draftsman and painter. He was also talented as a sculptor, with a specialty in carving pillars and beams. There was little in the decorative arts that was beyond this versatile young artisan's skills and talent.

Ah-nan had been newly wed to a beautiful young girl named Ling-hua or Water Caltrop blossom. After three days of marriage, he was summoned and had to answer to the government's recruitment orders. It was a sad and tearful departure for a pair of newlyweds married only three days. As a parting gift, Ah-nan brought out a matching pair of carved stone seals. These seals were carved with the same inscription, one in intaglio and the other in relief script. The inscription read: "Never to be apart whether in life or in death."

Ah-nan gave the stone seal bearing the intaglio script to Ling-hua while keeping the one with the relief carving. While holding her hands, he comforted his new bride and assured her that he would return after the work period was fulfilled. He also asked that she would look at the seal that he had carved as a reminder of him and his love for her. Before Ah-nan's departure, they each took a solemn vow to uphold and abide by the inscription on the seals.

Time passed like an arrow in flight, and before long it was three years since Ah-nan's departure. Seeing that her husband still had not returned, young Ling-hua decided to make the long journey to Jehol in search of her husband. With great difficulties and hardships, she made this journey of more than a thousand *li* on foot. Having arrived in Jehol, she found out that all workmen both entered and exited through the South Gate. She proceeded there and waited nearby to find her husband.

The sun was just beginning to set behind the mountains when the groups of workmen started to leave through the South Gate. Anxiously looking at everyone exiting, she became elated when she caught sight of her husband and shouted out, "Ah-nan!" Both rushed forwards into each other's arms, crying as they were both happy and sad while exchanging words at the same time. They were so excited and intensely involved with themselves that they did not hear the beating gongs to clear the way as some important official was approaching. It was too late for them to run and hide so they merely stood quietly on the side of the road with their heads bowed in respect.

Exactly who was this official that was approaching? It was none other than the notorious minister Ho-shên. This official was an opportunist and had gained the confidence of the Ch'ien-lung Emperor. When he saw the beautiful Ling-hua, he thought to himself, "Could there be such a person so beautiful on earth that had escaped my notice? Yet she is but a mere peasant girl." His evil and cunning mind began to scheme as he felt that he would gain greater favor with the Emperor should he present such a beautiful maiden to him. In a loud voice, he shouted out, "It is forbidden for anyone to be within a hundred feet of any palace enclosure. This carriage is an imperial gift so that it falls within the same category. Therefore, I charge both of you for trespassing within forbidden confines. Guards! Arrest these two!"

When both were seized and brought before Ho-shên, he ordered, "Take this man and give him forty lashes. As for this maiden, take her back with us. She will be a slave girl!" Both Ah-nan and Ling-hua knelt down and pleaded for mercy and leniency. However, Ho-shên turned a deaf ear to them. Without saying a word, Ho-shên arrogantly waved his hand as a signal for his guards to carry out his orders.

As soon as Ho-shên arrived at his quarters, this shrewd and conniving person immediately sent a message to His Imperial Majesty that he had found an extraordinarily beautiful young maiden whom he would present as a gift. The Emperor was extremely delighted and as it was the time of the Mid-Autumn Festival, he passed an Imperial Edict. He would be celebrating and viewing the moon at an area called 'Yüeh-sê chiang-shêng' (A beautiful moon over the sound of water), near the edge of the lake and there he desired to have this beautiful young maiden presented before him.

When Ling-hua got word of this, she thought to herself, "My abduction by Ho-shên would certainly not have been known by His Imperial Majesty. Since I am being summoned by an Imperial Edict, I will use this opportunity to relate my hardships and sufferings of journeying over a thousand *li* to seek out my husband. His Imperial Majesty governs the entire empire and is a wise ruler. I am certain that he will understand and allow both my husband and I to be reunited and live together again." With that thought stirring in her mind, she was filled with anxiety and anticipation as she changed into magnificent court dress and tidied her appearance for the Imperial audience.

Escorted by various palace maids, she was led to the place called 'Yüeh-sê chiang-shêng.' Emperor Ch'ien-lung was leisurely enjoying the beautiful bright moon and upon seeing Ling-hua, he was dazzled by her magnificence and beauty. He even thought that the heavenly Ch'ang-O, the Moon Goddess, had descended to earth. He had seen none so beautiful or charming. Neither the Queen, Concubines nor the numerous Ladies-in-waiting could compare with the stunning beauty of Ling-hua. He was exceedingly pleased and happy. Besides her physical beauty and charm, he wanted to know about her intelligence. Without hesitation, he inquired if she was capable of composing poetry.

Ling-hua was excited and had intended to tell the Emperor about her abduction. However, when she heard him inquire if she knew poetry, she stopped for a moment. She felt that if she was over-anxious and brought accusations against one of the Emperor's officials, it may reflect poor taste. Moreover, this may be a violation of court custom for which she would be faulted.

In answering the Emperor's question, she nodded. The joyful Emperor said, "Excellent! We shall settle on the magnificence of the bright moon as the subject for which you must compose a 4-line poem of 5 characters each."

Ling-hua smiled and thought that she would use the poem as a means to plead her case. Quickly she took up the brush and wrote:

Stone-chimes ringing while viewing the moon over the hills
The moon's brightness gloriously beams in the four directions
Sincerely, I wish to borrow the sparkling Milky Way
To help me wash away my grieving anxiety

After finishing writing out her poem, it was presented to the Emperor who after reading it aloud, applauded and called it a unique poem. He had thought to himself,

"Not only is this young maiden beautiful she is also intelligent." However, the Emperor had misread and misinterpreted the last two lines of her poem. He thought that it meant that like the lovers in the Milky Way, she wished to be with the Emperor forever. In great delight and joy, the Emperor asked her to kneel so that he would bestow honors on her.

When Ling-hua heard the word 'bestow', without hesitation, she said, "A peasant like me does not wish to have any honors bestowed. She wishes only that Your Majesty would release and allow her permission to return home to rejoin her husband."

The gleeful Emperor Ch'ien-lung was taken aback and in shock when he heard that this beautiful maiden was married and had a husband. Disappointed and dejected, he sadly said, "Retire and leave me!" The palace maids quickly escorted Ling-hua away back to her quarters in the Summer Palace.

Emperor Ch'ien-lung summoned Ho-shên and said, "Why have you selected a married woman with a husband?"

Ho-shên replied, "Your humble and obedient servant had been completely ignorant that she had a husband."

"Well, what should be done now?" asked Emperor Ch'ien-lung.

The crafty Ho-shên rolled his eyes and gave a little smile and said, "I don't think that this is much of a problem. I'm certain that her husband is no more than a common craftsman. He must also be poor so should we offer him a large sum of money, I'm sure that he will write a bill of divorcement and that will be that."

Thinking that this would be the solution, the anxious Emperor Ch'ien-lung said, "I will allot you three thousand taels of silver for this mission."

After this discussion, Ho-shên took his leave and went to the treasury and obtained three notes, each for the amount of one thousand taels of silver. Before setting out to see Ah-nan, he pocketed one of the treasury bills for himself.

Visiting Ah-nan, Ho-shên placed the two treasury bills for two thousand taels of silver on the table before Ah-nan and demanded that a divorce note be written. When confronted, Ah-nan said, "As husband and wife, we have vowed, 'Never to be apart whether in life or in death.' Therefore, no amounts of money, gold or silver could entice me to write out a bill of divorcement."

Ho-shên sneered at Ah-nan as he thought to himself, "I really don't need him at all as I could very well forge a document myself. In this way I would benefit with an additional two thousand taels of silver." Snubbing Ah-nan, Ho-shên dusted off his garments and left in a huff.

Ah-nan was greatly filled with remorse and melancholy but could not find any solution to remedy his problem. Taking a stroll, he stopped at a little wine shop called 'Erh-hsien-chü' to wash away and forget some of his sorrows. Here he met one of the overseers on the construction project. Previously, this officer had held a position as a minor official in the capital. However, he was unafraid to speak out and had offended his superiors and was thereby banished from Peking to serve as an overseer in the outpost of Jehol.

When this officer had heard Ah-nan's unfortunate story, he was furious and wanted to help him seek justice. He said, "I have a niece named Ch'iu-ch'ü who is one of the personal waiting maids of the Empress. Should she be informed of your problem, she would surely relate it to the Empress. The Empress is an intelligent, righteous and just person. I am sure that she will have mercy on you and speak to the Emperor on your behalf."

As things happened, Ch'iu-ch'ü when informed of the situation, did relate it to the Empress who was greatly stunned that such a situation had occurred. She had thought of confronting the Emperor, but upon consideration did not wish to make such a shameful situation public. She decided on a better and less public plan to assist Ling-hua's escape out of the Summer Palace so she might flee with her husband to distant parts.

Quickly, she ordered her personal waiting maid, Ch'iu-ch'ü, to escort Ling-hua out the Pi-fêng Gate late at night. She also sent word secretly to Ah-nan to meet his wife there. Unfortunately, this secret plan was overheard by the many spies of Ho-shên who without hesitation reported it to him.

Late at night, the maid Ch'iu-ch'ü led Ling-hua out through the Pi-fêng Gate without incident where she met her waiting husband Ah-nan. They stood outside the Gate for a short time when suddenly some commotion was heard. There were pursuers with lighted lanterns rushing towards them. Ling-hua saw that their situation was hopeless and there was no escape. Thinking of both her father-in-law and mother-in-law at home, she said to Ah-nan, "You . . . You must run away and make your escape. I hope that we will meet and be together again in the next life!"

Ah-nan responded, "A man who could not protect his own wife should deserve only death!" He rallied all his courage and charged his pursuers only to be cut down. He met his death by Ho-shên's sword. Again, Ling-hua was abducted and taken away.

The next morning, the Emperor Ch'ien-lung summoned the Empress and accused her of meddling and the crime of freeing Ling-hua. The Empress countered with the argument that an Emperor had no right to engage in abduction or kidnapping. This developed into a bitter quarrel. Seeing that the Emperor would not admit to any wrong-doings or set Ling-hua free, she took out a pair of scissors and cut off the top of her headdress and swore that she would take the vows of a Buddhist nun. This action infuriated and angered the Emperor so greatly that he ordered the Empress to be held as a lone prisoner in the Inner Palace away from everybody.

With the Empress cast aside, Emperor Ch'ien-lung ordered that Ling-hua should be brought to him aboard his boat on the lake.

Accordingly, Ling-hua was brought before Emperor Ch'ien-lung who took great pleasure in just viewing this magnificently beautiful maiden. However, the almond-shaped eyes of Ling-hua were filled with hatred for this immoral monarch. With a twist and turn, she freed herself and plunged herself into the lake thus drowning herself.

The surprised Emperor Ch'ien-lung hastily ordered that the lake be dragged. However, even after half-a-day's time of dragging the lake, there was no success. Ling-hua's body could not be recovered, instead only some black-colored water caltrop were netted.

Emperor Ch'ien-lung was startled, he thought to himself, "Water caltrops are usually dark green in color, but why are these black? It must reflect Ling-hua's grief at injustice. The water caltrop was her namesake so Heaven, taking pity on her had changed the color to symbolize the wrongs committed against her." Emperor Ch'ien-lung was greatly frightened and feared retribution and punishment from Heaven. Therefore, he ordered that a rustic pavilion be built at the water's edge and named

"Ts'ai-ling-tu" or Water caltrop ferry point in honor of this virtuous and beautiful maiden, Ling-hua. This pavilion still exists and the water caltrops have remained black in color.

At the Mid-Autumn Festival, people eat boiled water caltrop to remind themselves of Ling-hua, a dutiful and faithful wife. Not only was she beautiful and intelligent but she exemplified all the best qualities of womanhood in China. Children break open the hard shell of the water caltrop and place them on their fingers fashioned like claws and act out the evil Ho-shên trying to get you. Some ingenious toy makers hollow out the insides of the water caltrop and place a small piece of stick inside and fashion it into a type of Yo-yo and peddle these in marketplaces. These Yo-yos symbolized the ups and downs of the fortunes of Ho-shên. However, more conservative Chinese who are superstitious about anything evil, look at the water caltrop as resembling a bat. The bat called *Pien-fu* or *Fu-shu* is a homonym for prosperity and good luck. Therefore, when a dish of boiled water caltrops is placed on the table they shout out, "Man-fu! Man-fu!" or Full of Prosperity, Full of Good Luck. Some families boil the water caltrop with a red food color and call it 'Hung-ling' or 'To have many wishes come true!' The term 'Ling' is also a homonym for intelligence, so children are encouraged to eat plenty of them. What great meanings have become associated with such an ordinary water caltrop.

Botanically, the Water Caltrop is called *Trapa bispinosa* and grows plentifully in the ponds, lakes and rivers of China. The common variety is the two-horned, but there are those with three and four horns. 'Ling' refers to the two or four horned varieties although people commonly use the term 'Ling' for all varieties.

It had been used from very ancient times as a food item and is included among the things to be offered in religious ritual. The author of the *Pên-ts'ao kang-mu*, Li Shih-chên gives a very good description of the plant, its fruit, and the manner of cultivation. It is said that if eaten raw, it will injure the digestive tract, producing worms and intestinal disorders. Boiled, it is eaten in great quantities with great relish. It is regarded as nutritious and constructive and being a water product, it is thought to relieve thirst, reduce fever, and to be useful in sunstroke. The flowers and shells of the fruits are used for dyeing the whiskers and hair, and as an astringent in fluxes. Water Caltrop are only sold during the time of the Mid-Autumn Festival, however, Ling-fên or the starch made from the fruit is available at all times. The following are some recipes.

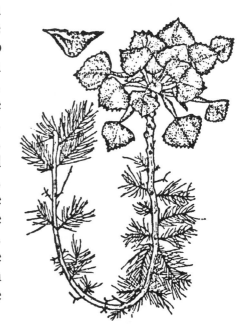

For the Mid-Autumn Festival celebration, Water Caltrops are washed and cleaned then boiled in water and then eaten like boiled peanuts.

Water Caltrops with Spare Ribs

Ingredients:

12 oz. Water Caltrop	1 lb. meaty spare ribs
2 cloves garlic	1 slice ginger
1/2 tsp. salt	Vegetable oil
1/2 tsp sugar	MSG

Method:

1) Wash Water Caltrop and soak in a pan of water then drain. Make an incision in the Water Caltrop or else, cut them in half.

2) Cut the spare ribs in 2 inch pieces.

3) Heat pan with oil and add ginger, garlic. Brown spare ribs. Add 1 cup of water and seasonings. Add the Water Caltrops and stew until spare ribs are fully cooked.

Chapter 4:
Other Food Offerings

There are a number of food items that are traditionally used as offerings to the Moon. These are mostly items selected from the bounty of the Autumn harvest.

Pear

Many, many years ago, just on the outskirts of a small hamlet located somewhere near the gulf of the sea, there was an elderly mother and her son living in a small humble hut. The young son was called Hsiao-mu-wa or Little Wooden Doll as he was a cute and lovable child. His mother loved this name so much that even though he was already 13 years old, she continued to call him by this pet name. Little Wooden Doll was intelligent, obedient and very helpful to his elderly mother who was over 60 years of age. His mother was a virtuous woman who was kind-hearted and charitable, hard-working and diligent. Both mother and son derived a living by fishing the nearby waters. Although they always had enough to eat and warm clothing to wear, they were still poor.

Located behind their house was a sizable parcel of salt flats that always sparkled with flakes of salt. This area was always swept by cool winds and was almost completely barren save for some red thorny bramble and some stunted russet pear trees.

One day in the autumn when Little Wooden Doll was returning from fishing and crossing the salt flats, he discovered that there were some small fruits on the russet pear trees. He was delighted and carefully picked several of the fruits and rushed home with them. As he burst into the hut, his mother was busily reeling thread. "Mother!" he excitedly called out, "Look at what I have brought you!" His mother turned and gazed upon the fruits and happily asked, "Did you find them washed up on the shores of the gulf? I have never seen such fruits here before. Tell me, where exactly did you find them?"

Smiling proudly, Little Wooden Doll remarked, "They were picked off those small trees behind our house on the salt flats. His mother insisted that he take her there so that she could see for herself. When they reached the trees, his mother upon seeing the fruit bearing trees, turned to her son and said, "Child, you must cut and clear away all the thorny bramble that is growing near these trees. Then carefully dig out these trees without injuring them and transplant them nearer to the rear of our house so that they may receive better care." Hearing his mother's approval of these trees and her desire to have them planted near the house gave Little Wooden Doll much happiness.

After that, Little Wooden Doll seldom went out to fish. He devoted much of his time daily to clearing the thorny bramble and digging the hard-packed salt flats in order to move the stunted trees. He was both diligent and careful in digging out and transplanting the trees. He then spent considerable time in their care; loosening the soil, fertilizing, watering and seeing to it that they were free of insects and disease. With such devoted care and cultivation, the trees grew larger, taller and more bountiful in fruit. However, upon tasting these fruits, Little Wooden Doll found them sour and astringent. He was perplexed. "How could this be so?" he thought, "I've given the trees excellent care." As he did not have any answer, he rushed in and asked his mother.

His mother calmly said to him, "I'm afraid that this condition is because in all the areas surrounding us are salt flats, the soil is mixed with salt and so the plants growing in this poor and sour soil are greatly affected in their growth and the production of their fruits."

Thinking about his mother's explanation, the clever and intelligent young son thought to himself, "If I were to remove these layers upon layers of poor soil and replace it with good fertile soil, then I would be able to alleviate and correct this problem." Resolved in his mind that this was the best plan, the youngster at once started digging up the soil all around. Placing the removed soil in baskets, he laboriously carried them on a pole down to the sea to dump them. He continued this laboring into the night.

Seeing her son, so determined and working so diligently and hard, the elderly mother laid aside her reeling of thread and went outside to assist him. Working together side by side, they dug, removed and carried away the infertile soil. However, although their intentions were correct, the work was both too difficult and the project too large for an elderly woman and a young boy to do alone. Before long, the old woman became ill with overwork and could not continue, leaving only Little Wooden Doll working alone. How much could just a young lad accomplish? Yet, he was determined and worked hard alone. After a while, his cute round young boyish face started to wear thin and his complexion darkened into a deep reddish black. His eyes became puffy and swollen yet all these discomforts did not deter him from continuing to dig and remove the poor soil.

One evening as Little Wooden Doll was laboring hard into the night and was feeling the pain of overwork, he stopped and sat down on a nearby rock pile to rest a moment. All of a sudden, he became startled as he heard a painful high pitched squeaking sound coming from the group of trees. Turning around to discover the source, he saw a small white rabbit hiding under the trees. Overhead and above the trees, a circling giant owl was just descending and catching the rabbit. However, the owl did not have a tight hold on the rabbit and so there was a struggle. The owl was flapping its wings violently with great fury while the rabbit was tugging and struggling, trying to pull away. The struggling rabbit was squeaking loudly in a painfully high shrill. Seeing that the rabbit was losing the battle, Little Wooden Doll picked up several sizable stones and threw them at the owl with all his might. One of the stones hit the owl squarely and in pain it screeched loudly and released the rabbit as it flew away.

Little Wooden Doll rushed over and took the scared rabbit in his arms and tried to calm the frightened animal as he examined it for any injuries. Luckily, the rabbit was only frightened and not hurt. Cradling the rabbit in his arms and stroking it calmly, the youngster took the animal home with him.

His elderly mother saw what Little Wooden Doll had brought back and knew he wanted to have it for a pet. She exclaimed, "I have seen grey and brown colored rabbits in these parts, but never a white one. Especially one whose fur is a shining snow-white. I guess that you may keep and care for him."

Placing the rabbit in his mother's charge, the happy youngster fashioned a caged-pen which he lined with grasses to keep the rabbit. When he had finished with it, he placed the rabbit into the caged-pen and sat before it admiring the cute little white rabbit for a long time before he went to bed.

At midnight, his mother was awakened from a sound sleep. The entire house was aglow and lit with a shining light as bright as sunlight. Startled and somewhat frightened, she quickly tried to wake up her son. Little Wooden Doll sat up rubbing his eyes and upon opening them, he too became startled and baffled of this brilliant glow. Surprised, he asked, "What is this glow and where is its source?" Both mother and son, holding onto each other looked about in all directions. To their surprise, they saw that the light was emanating from the little snow-white rabbit. As they came closer to the caged-pen, the white rabbit stood up and called out, "Kind-hearted mother and son!"

Hearing a rabbit calling out, they both fell backwards and were frightened. Little Wooden Doll, holding onto his mother said, "Mother, could it be that we have caged a rabbit monster? If it isn't a rabbit spirit, how could it call out to us? I'm frightened!"

Again, the white rabbit called out, "Good and kind-hearted mother and son. I am the Jade Rabbit from the moon and belong to the Moon Goddess, Ch'ang-O. Tonight my mistress had been invited out to a banquet for immortals, allowing me the chance to escape from the moon and descend to earth. I had met with misfortune when an angry old owl tried to seize me. I would have been killed, had it not been for Little Wooden Doll's coming to my rescue. However, I must return to the moon before the fifth watch (3-5 a.m.). If I should fail to do so, then my Mistress upon discovering my absence would punish me severely. I would have to suffer hard labor for a hundred years in the area of the Bitter Waters. Please save me by releasing me and allowing me to return to the moon!" The rabbit then started to sniffle and cry. His crying sounded so sad and painful and was so moving that it touched the sympathetic emotions of both mother and son.

The mother said, "Little Wood Doll, release the white rabbit to return to his Mistress. We could not allow him to be punished because of our keeping him here!"

Obediently, Little Wooden Doll did as instructed and opened the caged-pen to release the white rabbit. Before leaving, the white rabbit, sensing the virtuous qualities of the youngster, quickly said, "Little Wooden Doll, I know that you are a good and kind person. You are a diligent, charitable and self-sacrificing youngster and a dutiful and filial son. I will never forget your saving me and now your willingness to set me free. Whenever you should have any difficulties or hardships, I will come to your aid and assist you!" As he was talking, he pulled out some hairs and gave them to Little Wooden Doll saying, "These hairs which I am entrusting to you could summon all the animals at night should you need their help and assistance. They will do whatever you ask."

Hearing these instructions, Little Wooden Doll thankfully took the rabbit hairs and said, "Jade Rabbit, look yonder at these salt flats. They are barren of any tall trees, except for a few stunted russet pear trees. However, their fruits are so small and sour. Could there by any remedy by which they could become bigger and their fruits sweeter?"

The Jade Rabbit after some thought responded, "On the moon, there is a tall pear tree. If you are able to go there and take home some cuttings to be grafted onto those stunted trees, then the trees would become tall and bear large and sweeter fruits. The fruits of the Heavenly Pear tree are large and delicious. They have thin skins and are very juicy to eat. Their taste is heavenly sweet with a lingering fragrance."

Looking out the window, the Jade Rabbit saw that the moon was already in the west and he had little time to rush back. In haste, he jumped out and started to fly towards the moon. He shouted back in a loud voice, "After you have removed all the sour soil that is mixed with salt, then take some of the hairs and blow on them and they will change into a white cloud to transport you up to the moon. When you arrive, you should not have any fear. First go across Ruby Mountain, climbing it you will pass the area of the Bitter Waters and beyond that Poisonous Snake Creek and Cassia Grove. Do not be greedy and take anything that you may see from these areas. Following the Cassia Grove along a small winding path, turn right and you will come to the Garden of All Flowers. Thereupon you will have arrived at the Moon Palace. Go straight into the palace and you will come to the Golden Phoenix Hall. There is a large fan-shaped gate which looks like a peacock spreading its feathers. Through that gate there is the tall Heavenly Pear tree. Climb up and cut off some healthy cuttings and return quickly with them to earth. Should I be present at the palace, I will certainly assist you." Having said that, the Jade Rabbit kept soaring upwards and changed into a puff of white cloud disappearing completely before Little Wooden Doll's eyes.

After the Jade Rabbit's departure, Little Wooden Doll was determined to remove all the poor sour soil mixed with salt near his house and the nearby salt flats. He worked hard in its removal and as before labored late into the night. One day, he began to think of the Jade Rabbit's instructions and the bunch of rabbit hairs given to him. He brought out the hairs and holding them up before his face, he timidly and softly said, "Jade Rabbit's hairs, quickly help me! I need assistance! Let all the animals large and small come forward to hear my directions." Repeating these words thrice, he paused and thought for a moment. Becoming somewhat skeptical he pondered, "Could there be magic in these hairs?" Almost immediately, there were large numbers of wild animals surrounding him. There were rabbits, foxes, wild cats and dogs and a multitude of animals emerging from all directions and everywhere. All the animals converged towards Little Wooden Doll to be directed by him. Little Wooden Doll, holding the bunch of hairs said, "Jade Rabbit hairs, quickly command all the animals to assist me in clearing away all this poor, sour soil and deposit it into the sea. Command them also to find and bring back good fertile soil to nourish these russet pear trees." Having told them what he wanted done, they immediately commenced working at their tasks. They scratched and dug into the ground, hauled away the salted soil and brought back fresh, fertile soil. All knew exactly what to do and like well-oiled machinery, all worked at their assigned tasks. They covered the area like a moving carpet of fur, all busily working.

Little Wooden Doll was astonished and amazed as he sat on the side fascinated and mystified by all that was happening. The constant motion of the animals was rather hypnotic and Little Wooden Doll was watching them so intently that he was quickly put to sleep. When he awoke, it was already daylight. Looking about, he could not believe his eyes. All the animals had disappeared and so had the poor, sour, salty soil. It was completely removed and dark, fresh, fertile soil was in its place. The area looked fantastic and the russet pear trees looked so nice growing in the rich soil. Little Wooden Doll was so excited and happy that he had to rush home to tell everything to his elderly mother.

Time just seemed to flash by like the dazzle of the sun and before long, it was the 6th lunar month. The russet pear trees burst out with an exuberant and vigorous growth of green leaves. Little Wooden Doll said to his mother, "Today is the 15th day of the 6th lunar month and there will be a full moon. I think that it is time for me to go to the moon and gather some cuttings off the Heavenly Pear tree to be grafted." After receiving his mother's approval, Little Wooden Doll brought out some of the Jade Rabbit's hairs. Softly and in a low voice, he said, "Jade Rabbit's hairs, quickly transform into a white cloud and transport me up to the moon." As quickly as he said this, there was a cloud before him. Little Wooden Doll mounted the white cloud, and soared upwards to the moon.

Little Wooden Doll was floating upwards and flying at such high speed that he could not even open his eyes. The winds brushing across his face forced him to keep his eyes closed. Moreover, there was a whistling wind blowing in his ears which caused him to experience a ringing in his ears. However, these discomforts were not long in duration as very soon, he landed safely on the moon.

Little Wooden Doll was extremely happy and delighted to see so many new and exciting sites. However, he was mindful of the instructions given him by the Jade Rabbit and his purpose in coming to the moon. Quickly, he proceeded to Ruby Mountain, then traversed the Bitter Waters. He then courageously negotiated Poisonous Snake Creek and tracked through Cassia Grove which seemed to be surrounded by a variegated cloud of mist. Through this mist, he saw the Moon Palace which was mentioned by the Jade Rabbit. Entering the palace, he made his way through until he found the gate shaped like an opened peacock's tail. Beyond that, he found the tall Heavenly Pear tree. Without losing any time, he climbed up and carefully selected some healthy and strong branches with fruits and took cuttings from them.

When he had gathered enough of the cuttings, Little Wooden Doll placed the cuttings inside of his tunic, climbed down and began making preparations for his homeward trip. At that moment, Little Wooden Doll saw the Jade Rabbit rushing out towards him from the Moon Palace. The Jade Rabbit told Little Wooden Doll that he had made a detail report to his Mistress, Ch'ang-O, informing her of all that had happened and of his assistance and instructions of gathering cuttings from the Heavenly Pear tree on the moon. He said that Ch'ang-O was pleased and agreed that what had been done met with her approval. Moreover, she had sent him with instructions to give further assistance to Little Wooden Doll to help get the cuttings safely back to earth. This had to be done in the quickest time possible or else the cuttings would dry out and become useless. In a flash, Jade Rabbit turned around and transformed himself into a large white cloud. Little Wooden Doll mounted the cloud for his return home to earth.

In record time, they had arrived at the doorsteps of Little Wooden Doll's house. The Jade Rabbit said, "Quickly dismount!" Little Wooden Doll was very surprised to have arrived home so quickly and said, "Jade Rabbit, How can I thank you!"

Jade Rabbit responded, "When you left, it was in the middle of the 6th lunar month. Presently, it is already the beginning of the second spring season. Hasten to your mother as she is worried about you. Should there be any need for my assistance, call out my name thrice at midnight and I will come to your assistance. Should there be great and grave dangers or matters of vast importance, then call out my Mistress' name, Ch'ang-O, thrice and together we will come to give you aid!" Having said that, the Jade Rabbit again transformed himself into a cloud and floated upwards to Heaven.

When his elderly mother saw Little Wooden Doll, she became overwhelmed with joy and gladness. She was so happy that it brought tears to her eyes. "My child," she said, "You have been gone for nearly a year and a half! I had gotten so worried that I thought you may never return." While talking to him, she hugged him dearly and cried for joy.

Little Wooden Doll cried also and said, "Mother, I had been up in the moon and I have brought back cuttings from the large Heavenly Pear tree. Henceforth, we will have deliciously sweet pears to eat."

Without wasting any more time, he rushed out to where the russet pear trees were growing and quickly proceeded to graft the Heavenly Pear cuttings onto them. He performed this operation carefully and with great enthusiasm. He then wrapped and sealed them. He carefully cultivated and watered the trees daily.

After the passing of some time, the grafted trees grew even taller than a tall adult. The healthy branches provided not only fruit but also allowed the taking of more cuttings to be grafted onto the other russet pear trees found in the area. Little Wooden Doll considered the propagation of these Heavenly Pear trees as a crusade and worked tirelessly throughout the year. Even the inclement weather conditions of wind or rain did not interfere with his work. He planted so many trees that in five years time, the whole area surrounding his house was a large and vast orchard of this grafted Heavenly Pear. The bountiful harvests taken each year were tremendous and because of the large and beautiful fruits which were fragrantly sweet, juicy and delicious, their fame spread through the entire country. People came from near and afar to either buy fruits or plants from Little Wooden Doll. He and his mother became wealthy and enjoyed a happy life together. In honor of and in thanksgiving to the Jade Rabbit and Ch'ang-O, they always picked the largest and choicest pears to be made sacrificial offerings to them on the 15th of the 8th lunar month, the Moon Festival. Thus, the pears have been one of the most essential items for this festive celebration.

The pear has been known in China from very ancient times and is probably indigenous. It was introduced into India and Japan from China, and may have been carried to other parts of the world. The eating of the fruit in the cool weather is thought to produce weakness and those suffering from wounds, nursing women, and the anemic should not eat it. The pear is considered to be antifebrile, peptic, quieting to the nerves, and lubricating to the lungs.

In the Mid-Autumn Festival celebration, pears are sliced and eaten as fresh fruits, however, pears can also be cooked, candied or pickled. The following are some recipes:

Chicken with Pears
Ingredients:
4 firm and ripe pears   1-1/3 cup chicken broth
2 whole chicken breasts   1 cup peas
4 Tbs. soy sauce   2 Tbs. vegetable oil
6 scallions (chopped)   4 Tbs. cornstarch
2/3 cup water chestnuts (sliced)
Method:
1) Peel, core and dice pears into 1/2 inch pieces.
2) Bone chicken breasts and cut into 1-1/2 - 2 inch pieces.
3) In a pan, heat oil and stir-fry chicken for 2 minutes.
4) Add chicken broth, water chestnuts, peas and scallions. Bring liquid to the boil and cook for 2 minutes.
5) Add the pears and a mixture of soy sauce and corn starch. Stir constantly, mixing until sauce is thickened and smooth. Remove and serve.

Note: Dried pears may be used, however, the amount of chicken broth should be doubled as the dried pears would soak up much of the liquid.

Gingered Pears

Ingredients:

6 firm ripe pears   2 cups water
2 cups sugar   3 pieces of cinnamon stick
4 Tbs Chinese candied ginger   1 lemon (juice and zest)
1 piece (1-1/4 inch) fresh ginger (chopped)

Method:

1) Peel, core and quarter pears.
2) Combine water, sugar, cinnamon, ginger, lemon juice and zest in sauce pan and bring to a boil. Uncovered, cook for 8 to 10 minutes until the mixture becomes a sugary syrup.
3) Add the pears and simmer uncovered for 15 to 20 minutes or until tender but still holding their shape. Turn off heat and allow pears to cool in the syrup.
4) Remove pears and place in a dish with syrup poured over them. Chill before serving and garnish with candied ginger.

Stuffed Pears

Ingredients:

4 firm ripe pears   1/4 cup raisins
2 Tbs. chopped nuts   2 Tbs. sugar
1 Tbs. lemon juice   1/2 cup of light syrup
Cinnamon   Granulated sugar

Method:

1) Peel, core and cut pears into halves
2) Combine raisins, chopped nuts, sugar and lemon juice and spoon mixture into the hollow of the pears.
3) Sprinkle some granulated sugar and cinnamon on top of the pears and place under the broiler until golden brown. Serve immediately.

It is interesting that in a Ch'ing dynasty medical prescription book, *Wên-t'ang chi-yen-fang* by Ho Ching, there is found the following remedy for asthmatic breathing or difficulties of breathing accompanied by the collection of phlegm and coughing. "Take the autumn pear and core it and place it into one mace (1/10 of a Chinese ounce) of Bird's nest. Place all in hot water and add one mace of rock candy. Steam until done." These instructions are better expressed by the following recipe:

Bird's Nest and Pears

Ingredients:

1 large white juicy pear (Hsüeh-li or round Asian pear)
Bird's nest   Rock sugar candy

Method:

1) Cut the pear in half and remove the core and seeds.
2) Place the bird's nest and rock sugar candy in the hollow and secure with tooth picks or bamboo skewers. The rock sugar candy may be broken up into small pieces as to facilitate being placed into the pear.

3) Place the stuffed pear into a covered pottery steamer pot with a support of a bamboo mat so that the pear does not sit directly on the bottom of the pottery container.

4) Place the covered pottery steamer pot into a pan of water and steam until cooked. Serve hot.

Soft Fruit Candy

Ingredients:

2 cups sugar

3 envelopes unflavored gelatin

2 or 3 tsp lemon juice

1 tsp. Rose water

1 cup apple sauce

1/4 cup water

1 cup chopped nuts

Method:

1) Soak the gelatin in 1/4 cup cold water and 1/2 cup apple sauce for 10 minutes and mix well.

2) Boil the remaining applesauce and sugar. When it comes to a boil, add the gelatin mixture and boil for 20 minutes. Stir constantly.

3) Add Rose water and nuts and pour into buttered cake pan. When cooled, cut in oblong pieces and roll in powdered sugar.

Peanuts

The peanut grown in ancient times were very similar to those grown today, with the exception that they did not have an inner red skin lining and they grew above ground like bush beans. However, how did the peanut evolve or change to being an underground fruit? An interesting traditional story attempts to explain the change.

In ancient times, there was a small hamlet called Li-chia-chuang, which consisted of some 30 households. Every household in this hamlet had a surname of Li except one which was Lo. The Lo household consisted of an elderly couple in their late fifties and a young son who was barely twelve years of age. The father was weak and always suffered with illness so he was unable to perform much work. This left most of the responsibilities of the family's work to be taken up by his wife. The family was poor and had little. They labored hard from sunrise to sunset in their half *mou* (1 *mou*=733-1/2 sq. yds.) of poor farm land.

The young boy was quite intelligent, however, his family being poor, they could not afford for him to go to school. Being young, he helped by scouting the hillsides for sticks and pieces of wood along with dry grass and wild vegetables to be used by the family. Whenever he had a little time, he would remain outside of the classroom, listening to the teacher giving lessons to rich children. He would listen attentively and with a stick scratch on the ground to practice writing. When the old teacher discovered that this young boy was anxious to learn but impeded by being impecunious, the kind-hearted teacher admitted him for instruction without charging tuition. The teacher was so pleased to have found a bright and intelligent youngster willing to learn that he even supplied the books which his student could not afford. The young boy showed great promise and enjoyed studying which greatly pleased the old teacher.

One day, the young boy went up to his teacher and said, "Teacher, I'm afraid that from now on, I will not be able to continue to attend classes. My family needs me and I must go to the hillsides and watch over our crop of peanuts." Although sad to see the youngster go, his teacher knew well that this work was necessary. Knowing of the young boy's fondness for learning, the teacher gave him several books and instructed him that he should not neglect his studies and should read these books whenever possible. The young boy thanked his teacher before taking his leave.

The Lo family's land, although not very large in acreage, was a long narrow strip of land on the hillside. In these parts, there was an abundance of crows. Anyone planting a peanut crop would have problems with them as the crows would flock together and descend on the fields and eat up everything in sight. In order to protect the crop until harvest, there must be someone always in the fields to scare off the crows. In the Lo household, the father was ill and could not perform this duty and his wife had to remain home to look after him, leaving only the young boy to do this work. Therefore, it was essential that he leave school to attend to their field of peanuts or suffer the consequence of having nothing to harvest.

Earlier, the young boy and his mother had gathered together some tree branches and straw and dry grass and had constructed a small thatched protective shelter near their fields as a shield against the sun and rain. Every morning, at dawn, the young boy would come here and take up a vigil to scare away the crows thus protecting the peanut crop. He would take with him some dry provisions and a jug of cool water as he had to remain there until just after sunset when all the birds took to roost.

After three days of strenuous work, the youngster became depressed and melancholic. The field that he had to stand guard over was narrow and long. When he ran to the north end to chase away the crows, another flock of crows would descend upon the south end. This caused him to run back and forth all day with hardly any time to sit and rest. When would he be able to find time for any studying or reading of books? At the end of the day when he returned home, his body and legs would ache. With pain, he could not concentrate on his reading. He felt that should such a situation continue, he would be completely robbed of a good education.

At noon one day the heat was exceedingly hot as the sun was shining brightly like a blast furnace. It became so hot that even the crows would not venture out into the open fields but took shelter in the branches of the nearby woods. This gave the young boy some rest so he sat in his small thatched shelter, wiping perspiration and reading his book. Suddenly he heard a weak moan and cry for help. Quickly he laid down his book and ran outside to investigate. Not far away there was a skinny old man, who had fallen and injured himself. His hair, eyebrows and beard were dirty white and his face was covered with leaves, grass and dirt from his fall. He just looked awful and could only manage to crawl while moaning and crying for mercy. He unsuccessfully tried to get himself up several times but he was too weak and exhausted and quickly collapsed, further hurting himself.

Seeing this pitiful old man suffering, the young boy quickly rushed over to the old man to assist him and carefully helped him to his shelter. When the old man was out of the burning sun's rays and settled in the thatched shelter, the young boy inquired, "Elderly Sir, are you all right? Where were you going?"

The old man heaved and sighed, "I . . . I was going to visit my daughter. Not realizing how far the distance, I . . . I was passing nearby when both hunger and thirst gripped me and I . . . I lost my footing and fell down and injured myself."

The youngster took out the dry provisions that he had for his lunch and offered it to the old man along with his jug of water. Without hesitation, the old man greedily ate up all the food and drank all the water.

After consuming everything, the old man felt rested enough so he said, "I think that I am able to continue my journey now. However, go to the southern end of the woods and find and cut me a branch that is neither too short or long, strong but not so thick or weighty and comfortable in the hand that I may use as a walking stick."

Obediently, the young boy, without hesitation took his woodcutter's knife and went into the woods. Conscientiously, he searched for just the right kind of material as described by the old man. After some time, he found just the right tree branch. Not only did he cut it down, however, diligently he shaved off the rough bark to fashion it into a handsome walking stick.

The heat was so intense and since he had not had anything to eat or drink, the youngster felt a bit weak. Without complaint, he walked and found a mountain spring from which he drank several mouthfuls of water. He pulled up some wild vegetables growing nearby and ate them. Although they were somewhat bitter and astringent in taste, nevertheless, his hunger was satisfied and he regained his strength to allow him to return to his thatched shelter to the waiting old man.

Seeing the old man, the youngster proudly and courteously with both hands made his presentation saying, "Elderly Sir, May I present you with this walking stick. I hope that it meets with your approval and satisfaction."

Taking and examining the walking stick, the old man smiled and said, "You are certainly a good youngster!"

Having said that, suddenly there was a gust of cool wind and the old man disappeared completely out of sight. This startled and frightened the youngster and he fell backwards onto the ground. There on the floor of the shelter, he found a piece of writing left by the old man. Resting on top of the piece of paper was a large, bright, sparkling red jewel. The surprised young boy picked up the red jewel and held it in his hand while excitedly he read what was written on the piece of paper.

Good and kind youngster:

I am the local mountain spirit. Before the sun should set behind the mountains, you must take this jewel and bury it in the middle of your field of peanuts from which great benefits would be gotten. However, you must carefully follow these precise instructions:

1) The jewel must be buried in a pit three feet in depth

2) You may not use any tool of any description or type for digging except your bare hands.

As it was already late afternoon, the youngster took the red jewel and quickly ran into the middle of the field. With astonishment, he noticed that all the peanuts plants bowed down before the red jewel. Without hesitation, he commenced his digging with his bare hands. Before long, he was able to easily dig down about a foot in depth. Beyond that point, he found the digging somewhat more difficult. However, he did not hesitate and diligently continued his digging. His hands became bruised and all ten fingers suffered opened cuts and were bleeding. With each handful of soil being dug, his fingers felt great pains like having needles piercing into them. With continued digging, not only did his hands and fingers hurt, but the pain reached his chest. Nevertheless, with great determination and resolve, the youngster bit down tightly on his teeth and continued his digging until the required depth was reached. There he buried the sparkling red jewel. By the time that he placed the last handful of dirt to fill the hole, the sun was just setting behind the mountains.

Tired and exhausted, he returned home and washed his bloodied hands. Inasmuch as he was in great pain and tired, he did not alter his regular routine and sat down reading his book. However, he could not turn the pages. Resourcefully, he place his left index finger in his mouth and slowly bit down on it until it could feel no pain then he turned the pages and continued his studying.

The next morning, when the youngster went up the hillside to the peanut field to assume his watch, he was amazed to find a strange phenomenon. All the peanuts had buried themselves into the ground and were completely out of sight and away from reach of the menacing flocks of crows flying overhead. Squawking and seeing no peanuts to feast on, the crows flew away. Henceforth, there was no need for the youngster to stand vigil over the fields so he could devote himself to reading and studying his books under the shade of the thatched shelter.

When it was harvest time, everybody else's peanut crop had been devastated by the crows and they had nothing to harvest. There was only the harvest of the Lo family's fields to meet the demands of people celebrating the Mid-Autumn Festival. These peanuts were not only bountiful but each had thin red inner skins which became very desirable and greatly sought after. Selling these peanuts brought enough money to the Lo household that they could now afford a more comfortable life.

In time, the young boy's diligent study allowed him to pass the government's civil service examination and he became a prominent and successful government official bringing fame and fortune to his elderly parents.

It is believed that the thin red inner skins on the peanuts were from the blood that was shed by the youngster in digging a pit to bury the red jewel. In honor of him, people began to call the peanut, 'Lo-hua-shêng', later abbreviated as 'Hua-shêng.' This youngster was Lo Pin-wang, one of the Four Savants of the T'ang dynasty.

Although this is an interesting story expounding the virtues of filial piety, diligence, hard work, sacrifice, generosity, humanity, determination and above all education and learning, the peanut was not named after Lo Pin-wang. The term 'Lo-hua-shêng' as it is recorded in ancient literature is derived from empirical observation of the development of the peanut. After the peanut blossom has been pollinated, it bends downwards and buries itself into the soil and a peanut is developed. Therefore the term is most descriptive, literally meaning 'the growth of the descending flower.'

The Chinese also observed that when the flower descends into the ground and the peanut is developed, it also sprouts a root as an anchor. Therefore the Chinese have an adage, "Lo-ti shêng-kên,' meaning to establish yourself by gaining a firm hold of whatever you are doing. This is a good motto for anyone starting out on a new career or any endeavor. All these qualities and symbolism that the Chinese have incorporated in the lowly peanut makes it so important not only as a nutritious food item but a reminder of what it is to be a good human being.

The peanut *(Arachis hypogaea)* is not indigenous to China, having been introduced from abroad some time prior to the 18th century. It is said to have been introduced from the country of Fu-sang by a priest during the first year of the reign of Emperor K'ang-hsi of the Ch'ing dynasty (1662). It was introduced into Fukien, and the peanuts from this province are still regarded as the best, although they are extensively grown all over China. There are two principal varieties grown in China. One, known as the native peanut, has a small, round pod with very sweet and tasty beans. The other variety, sometimes called the foreign peanut, which probably is of later introduction than the other, is larger and resembles those in the United States, although not so large, nor is the plant so prolific.

Peanuts are regarded by the Chinese with much favor as an article of diet, and very large quantities are boiled, roasted, stewed, fried, and candied. They are considered to be nutritive, peptic, demulcent and pectoral. They are often shelled, crushed and mixed with meat-broth as a remedy for those affected with chronic coughs. Oil made from the peanut is used by the Chinese for cooking and is considered laxative and pectoral. Peanut oil is also used to rub and massage the forehead and temples of a sick person with fever or fainting spells. For a child, peanut oil is rubbed briskly between the palms and when hot, the palms are immediately placed on the forehead and held there for a moment. The procedure is repeated. Both the child's palms and the soles of the feet are also rubbed in order to bring the fever down. The following are some recipes using peanuts.

Peanuts and Pork Trotter Soup

Ingredients:

4 pork trotters (pig's feet)   1 Tbs. wine
6 Chinese red dates   2 Tbs. salt
1 cup raw peanuts (without skins)   1 small piece ginger
6 pieces dried bean curd (Fu-chu)   1 tsp. MSG
3 qts. boiling water   6 dried oysters (optional)

Method:

1) Pour boiling water over pig's feet and let soak for 20-30 minutes. Chop into large pieces. Set aside.

2) In a sauce pan, place dried oysters in hot water and bring to a boil. Remove from heat and allow to soak 10-15 minutes. Clean thoroughly and set aside.

3) Soak dried bean curd in warm water for 20-30 minutes.

4) In a deep pot, heat a little oil. Add ginger, salt, wine, drained oysters, and pig feet. Fry until pig feet are golden brown, then add 3 quarts of boiling water. When it comes to a boil, cover, lower heat and simmer. Add red dates, soaked bean curds and raw peanuts. Allow to simmer for 3-1/2-4 hours. Before serving, add MSG and adjust seasonings to taste.

Peanuts and Pork Tails Soup

Ingredients:

4 pork tails   1 Tbs. wine
1 cup raw peanuts (without skins)   2 Tbs. salt
6 Chinese red dates (scored)   1 thick slice ginger
1 small piece dried orange peel   MSG
3 qts. boiling water

Method:

1) Pour boiling water over pork tails and allow to soak 30 minutes. Chop into large pieces. Set aside. Soak orange peel in warm water.

2) Heat a little oil in a pot, fry ginger and salt for 1 minute. Add wine and chopped pork tails. Fry pork tails until golden brown then add 3 quarts boiling water. Lower heat. Cover pot with lid and allow soup to simmer. Add orange peel and red dates. Allow soup to simmer 3-3-1/2 hours. Before serving, add MSG and adjust seasoning to taste.

In the Mid-Autumn Festival celebration, peanuts are usually boiled in salted water and eaten as boiled peanuts in their shells. Along with these boiled peanuts, boiled soybeans which are prepared in the same manner are also served.

Soybeans

The soybean *(Glycine max)* is an annual herb of the family *Leguminosae* and is now cultivated throughout the world. It was first cultivated in North China in ancient times and later introduced into Japan, Korea and throughout Asia and elsewhere. Soybeans are rich in protein, Vitamin B complex and fat. Along with the peanut, they have traditionally been an important source of nutrients. Many products are made from it such as tofu, soy sauce, bean paste, bean sprouts, fermented beans, etc. A full stalk of the soy bean plant with leaves and beans is always planted in the middle of the incense burner to represent the Heavenly Cassia tree in making offerings to the Moon at the Mid-Autumn Festival celebration. For this celebration, the soybeans are boiled in salted water like peanuts. However, there are many other ways to prepare and use both the soybeans and peanuts. The following are some recipes:

Boiled Soybeans

Ingredients:
    Fresh Soybeans in pods
    15 Szechwan peppercorns
    Salt
Method:
    1) Wash the soybeans and drain. Then using a pair of scissors, cut off the two ends of the pods.
    2) Place soybeans in a large pot of water and add salt and peppercorns and over high heat, boil for about 20 minutes. Remove and drain. Discard the pepper corns and serve.

Red Bean Pudding

Ingredients:
    1 lb. red beans   1 lb. rock sugar
    8 cups water   1/2 cup lard
    1-3/4 cups rice flour mixed with 3 cups of water
Method:
    1) Wash red beans and drain.
    2) In a sauce pan, cook the beans in 8 cups of water over medium heat. When it boils, lower heat and simmer for 1 hour or until beans are tender.
    3) Add rock sugar and lard, stir and blend well
    4) Slowly add mixture of rice flour batter. Stir constantly and blend well.

5) Pour mixture into oiled round cake pan and place in steamer and steam for 1 hour until completely done. Remove and allow to cool. Cut into pieces and serve.

Persimmon

During the Ch'in dynasty, 221-107 B.C., there was a regional magistrate named Hsüeh Tê. He was a pilferer and a corrupt and immoral official who had no virtue. He took pleasure in seeing the people suffer in pain and anguish. The people hated him terribly and referred to him as 'Ch'üeh-tê,' a pronunciation closely sounding like his name but meaning 'having a deficiency of virtue or moral conduct.'

One day word came to Hsüeh Tê that living on the P'an mountains were two persons, a father and son. The father was called Chang Lao-kuei and his son, Chang Hsiao-kuei. They were bee-keepers and from their apiary they derived lots of honey. Quite often, they would share their honey with the poor or needy. This, of course, was contrary to Hsüeh Tê's concept and he was greatly infuriated as he was not made a recipient. He felt slighted. In anger, he mounted his horse and led three squads of armed men into the P'an mountains.

When the townspeople became aware of Hsüeh Tê's motives, they quickly sent word to Chang Lao-kuei of this impending action against them. As soon as they were informed, both father and son immediately gathered up all the honey from the bee hives and placed it into a large earthenware jar. They had intended to place the jar in concealment, however, searching here and there, they found no suitable place to hide the large jar of honey. Finally, the young son said, "Father, there being no other alternative hiding place, let's seal up the jar tightly and bury it near the roots of the large persimmon tree. I'm sure that that corrupt official, Ch'üeh-tê, would never find it there!" With time working against them, there was not time for further discussion. They hastily struggled to dig a pit near the persimmon tree to bury the large jar of honey.

No sooner had they completed their work then Hsüeh Tê appeared with his men. He was haughty and arrogantly displayed his might and power. In contempt, he pointed to Chang Lao-kuei and sneeringly said, "What uncalled for daring! What audacity! How dare that you should raise bees and gather honey without my permission. Moreover, to sneak behind me and distribute the honey to the poor! What daring! Not only do you not respect the law, you also disregard my authority. Never once had you even presented me with a little of your honey. Do you mean that you prefer the poor over me? Poor people are made to suffer and only taste the bitterness in life. It is someone like myself who should enjoy life and taste all that is sweet! Yet, you accord me no respect or reverence. Bring out your honey immediately and give it all to me or your flesh will suffer the sting of my whip. I'll teach you obedience!"

Both father and son stood mute. Seeing this, Hsüeh Tê waved his hand and like a swarm of attacking bees, his soldiers rushed forward and entered Chang Lao-kuei's small hut. Overturning and destroying everything without regard to rights or property, they searched everywhere. They had completely demolished the hut but found no honey and so reported back to a disappointed Hsüeh Tê.

However, this report did not discourage Hsüeh Tê. With beady eyes he sneered and slowly glanced in all directions. Then with a disgusting snorting sound, he said, "Hmmph! You are a bunch of good-for-nothings. Imagine that all of you should allow yourselves to be tricked by these two simpletons. However, they can't fool me in any manner. Look yonder at that large persimmon tree. Isn't there a heap of freshly dug dirt beside it? It is so recently dug that the soil is still moist. Certainly this is where they had hid the honey. Quickly dig it up and bring it to me!"

Doing as ordered, the soldiers discovered the large jar of honey. When Hsüeh Tê saw it, he laughed and said, "How could simple-minded persons like you two hide anything from my sharp vision? Bring the jar of honey along. When I return home, I will savor the sweetness of the honey which is intended for me alone!"

As the soldiers were preparing to fashion some poles to carry the large heavy jar of honey, the young son, Chang Hsiao-kuei with great anger and fury, rushed forward. Seizing one of the spades that were used for digging, he struck and hammered the large jar until it was completely smashed and the total contents lost. Then in a loud voice, he shouted out, "This honey is more fitting to be given to this persimmon tree than to accord one drop to a filthy and corrupt dog official such as you!"

"What!" exclaimed a surprised and excited Hsüeh Tê. He saw the honey flow and ooze into the ground and could do nothing. His burning anger completely blinded him as if he had gone mad. He maliciously shouted out, "Seize that bastard! Tie him against that big tree there and gather wood to burn him alive. I'm going to allow that tree to taste his blood and flesh. Burn him up alive! That bastard, he deserves nothing better!"

Seeing his son burning and suffering, the father, Chang Lao-kuei, tried to rush forward to embrace his son, but was seized and restrained by the soldiers. In anguish and sadness, he shouted out to Hsüeh Tê, "You're an animal! A heartless beast! Why can't you even allow me to die with my son?" Sobbing and crying out, he could do nothing but witness his son being burned to death.

Hsüeh Tê, without even blinking or showing any sympathy or emotion, remarked,

"Heh . . . heh! Die? You want to die? I'm afraid that that would be letting you off too easily. Take him away!" Then turning once more to Chang Lao-kuei, he said with intended malice, "I'm going to ship you to labor in building the Great Wall. There you may die if you are lucky by either hard labor, by freezing in the cold or starvation. Whatever the case, you will be reduced to a homeless and wayward hungry ghost when you die!" The poor old man was led away to suffer the hardships of building the Great Wall.

After Chang Hsiao-kuei's death, the large persimmon tree seemed to have grown larger and bore an even greater abundance of blood-red fruits. The persimmons were so sweet that they seemed like to taste like honey. The youngsters who were especially became fond of eating these persimmons called them 'Mi-kuan-êrh' or 'small cannisters of honey.' Likewise, the aged also found delight in these persimmons and called them 'Lao-t'ou-lo' or 'old people's delight'

The people of the area, whenever they ate the persimmons, were reminded of the sacrifice of young Chang Hsiao-kuei and his father. Knowing that the father was still alive and laboring in building the Great Wall, they wanted to send some persimmons to him. They made cakes and filled them with persimmon paste and had someone take them up north to him.

When the old Chang Lao-kuei saw these cakes, tears flowed yet he was proud of his son and considered him a hero. He shared the cakes with the poor, hungry and sick people recruited to build the Great Wall.

The people of the area where the original persimmon tree was growing also began air-layering branches to be grafted onto other persimmon trees growing elsewhere. It was their way of sharing with all people the sweetness of these special persimmons. Moreover, it was a reminder to all people to stand up against tyranny and to be generous to others. Later, besides making cakes filled with persimmon paste, the people also dried and flattened them and used them as gifts to be presented to friends and relatives. They also found that the persimmons were nutritious and strength building.

The persimmon, *Diospyros kaki*, is a large, thin-skinned juicy fruit of an orange or yellowish color and having a sweet taste when fully ripe. It is common in China and Japan. The taste of the unripened fruit is exceedingly astringent. The Chinese ripen the fruits artificially by inserting one or more splints of bamboo into them by the side of the stem, which hastens the process of softening. These, however, lack the fine flavor of the naturally ripened fruit.

The persimmon appears in several forms in Chinese medicine. There is an artificially ripened fruit called Huang-shih which is produced by placing the unripe fruit in a vessel containing leaves and allowing a process of fermentation to go on until the fruit is ripe. It is said to become as sweet as honey under this process and is used as a antifebrile, antivinous, and demulcent remedy. Another form is called Pai-shih or Shih-shuang. This is prepared by removing the skin of the fruit and exposure to sunlight by day and dew by night until they are dried and a whitish powder appears. The white powder on these dried persimmons is called Shih-ping. The medical properties are thought to be much enhanced by this process of drying. It is considered to be restorative, expectorant and anti-hemmorrhagic and is recommended in virulent sores and ulcers. There is also a persimmon confection, Shih-kao, which is prepared by beating together glutinous rice flour and dried persimmons then steaming the mixture until it is fully cooked. It is recommended to be eaten by children in cases of autumnal dysentery as well as in other forms of flux.

In the Mid-Autumn Festival celebration, persimmons are eaten as a fresh fruit. However, there are several recipes for cooking and serving them.

Persimmons and Taro Dust

Ingredients:

2 tsp. Shih-shuang-fên	2 lbs. Taro
1 cup sugar	6 small red dates
2 tsp. candied winter melons	1 cup vegetable shortening
4 tsp. scallions (white part only)	5 Tbs. vegetable oil
5 Tbs. water	

Method:

1) Peel taro and cut into slices. Steam for 30 minutes and mash with potato masher while hot.
2) Dice candied winter melons. Remove the pits of the red dates and cut dates into small pieces. Finely chop the scallions (white part only).
3) Heat pan with oil and stir-fry scallions until golden brown. Remove and set aside.
4) Over heat, dissolve the sugar in water and add 3/4 cup vegetable shortening. Blend well into a smooth syrup. Remove and set aside.
5) To the mashed taro, slowly add the syrup. Mix well until completely blended and smooth. Place in a pan of water and steam until cooked. Remove from heat and allow to cool.
6) Heat pan with the remaining 1/4 cup vegetable shortening. When it is hot, add the taro mixture and stir. When the taro mixture starts to bubble, remove into a serving bowl. Place the diced red dates, and onions on top of the taro and onto one side. On the opposite side, place the diced candied winter melons sprinkled with the Shih-shuang-fên. Serve immediately.

Coconut

Sometime in the remote past, there lived a young man whose surname was Yeh. As it was the custom then, people called him Yeh-tzu or the young man of the Yeh family.

When Yeh-tzu was very young, his father became violently ill. His complexion changed color to a waxy-yellow. A variety of medical doctors were called upon but seeing their patient's depressing appearance, they did nothing but shake their heads and leave. In desperation, the family prayed at various temples and even engaged Shamans and Taoist priests to perform exorcist rites. However, all measures were unsuccessful. The situation seemed so hopeless that friends and neighbors counselled Yeh-tzu to make preparations for his father's departure from earth. Hearing this made Yeh-tzu sad and he grieved, crying day and night.

One day, a 'Fang-shih' or Necromancer passed by the Yeh household and heard Yeh-tzu crying. He sensed the bitterness and pain of the young boy and was greatly moved. He inquired of the youngster about the cause of all his sadness and was told of the father's incurable illness. The Necromancer had some herbs at hand and he took some and waved them across the father's nostrils. Like magic, the patient's complexion started to change back to normal and before long, he was able to get up as he was completely cured of his ailment. The astonished Yeh-tzu gleefully jumped up and down with tears in his eyes as he was overly happy to see his father well again and in good health and spirits.

Yeh-tzu rushed over to hug his father and openly cried in happiness. All of a sudden, Yeh-tzu realized that he had not even thanked the Necromancer. However, turning around, he could not find him as he had already disappeared.

However, man does not live forever, so after a number of years, Yeh-tzu's father, without even being sick, suddenly died. The saddened Yeh-tzu accorded his father the necessary funeral rites and proper burial. After the period of mourning, on his way home from the grave-site, Yeh-tzu chanced upon meeting the same Necromancer who had saved his father years before. Rushing forward, Yeh-tzu knelt down and repeatedly bowed before him begging to be accepted as a disciple. "I want to devote my life in learning the healing arts," said Yeh-tzu, "so that I may assist people in curing sickness and promoting good health."

The Necromancer was won over by young Yeh-tzu and consented to accept him as a disciple. After a number of years of diligent and devoted study and practice, Yeh-tzu also became a noted and able Necromancer.

During this time, the ruling monarch was engrossed in the fascination of achieving and gaining immortality. He had ordered a number of Necromancers to search everywhere for the elixir of immortality. There was a Necromancer who after going abroad in his search, returned and sent a Memorial to the Emperor. It read in part:

> *The elixir of immortality could be found on a fairy island called P'êng-lai. On this fairy island, there are golden palaces and jade halls. As we observed from a distance, the fairy island appeared to be floating above the water. In another moment, the fairy island seem to have reversed its position and was below the water. Approaching nearer, the fairy island seemed to be hastened by the wind in escaping us. We were stunned and could do nothing but watch it*

move away. This elixir of immortality is most difficult to obtain. It is an impossible task.

Having read this Memorial, the Emperor was utterly furious as he raged, "My power and authority are vast, extending to the four seas. My vast number of subjects have been enriched as they hold me up high in honor as the Son of Heaven. What is there that forbids me from obtaining anything I desire. Nothing is impossible! I am the conqueror of the entire world!"

So saying, the Emperor ordered Yeh-tzu and a number of accompanying Necromancers to form an expedition to find the fairy island of P'êng-lai and search for the elixir of immortality.

After putting out to sea, the expedition experienced innumerable hardships and perils. Nevertheless, in spite of all these disasters, they were successful in reaching and even landing on the fairy island. Immediately they formed search parties and combed the island in their hunt for the elixir of immortality. After some time, they were successful in finding a type of strange herb. Yeh-tzu looked and examined it and recognized it to be the same herb that had previously cured and saved his father. "Certainly, this must be the divine herb which we seek," he said to himself as he smiled and was fully satisfied. Quickly he instructed everyone to gather all they could find of this herb. After a time, they had enough to fill their boat as they made their way homeward.

On their return trip, they met with a typhoon. The skies darkened and the gusting winds and heavy downpour of rains were so strong, violent and noisy that all sense for direction was lost. Steering the boat was senseless, so they just allowed the boat to ride the waves, tossing and turning every which way. How long this continued or where the boat was heading was totally unknown and uncontrolled.

Suddenly and abruptly, there was a loud crashing sound as the boat ran aground on the rocky shoals near some island. Gradually, the winds died down and the rains stopped. All became silent and calm. They waited until daylight to assess to what extent their ship had been damaged. They found that the ship was resting in shallow waters on a sand bank. The barrels of fresh water were either washed away or suffered great damage and were mixed with saltwater, leaving no fresh water for drinking. Even in such a dilemma, Yeh-tzu, being loyal to his charge, was greatly concerned over the cargo of herbs. He ordered that they be quickly moved and taken ashore.

It was still early morning when they came ashore and the sun was barely up in the skies. However, as the day progressed, the blasting heat of the sun became so intense that the sands on shore became hot and created great discomfort to everyone. Some started to shed their clothing and raise it above them as shields against the burning sun. Some dug down three or more feet in search of water to refresh themselves but only found salt water. Everyone tried to find some means of escaping from the heat. However, none met with success.

Yeh-tzu looked all about. All around, as far as the eye could see, there was nothing but sand without any trees at all to give shade. The only relief that this expedition party had was at night when the sun went down. After several days of this suffering heat and no water to drink, a number of them collapsed and fainted. Likewise Yeh-tzu also became exhausted by the heat and fainted. Upon awakening and regaining conscientiousness, he took some of the divine herbs and administered it to those most seriously affected by the heat and those seriously suffering from sunburn. However, the herbs remained ineffective. In disgust, Yeh-tzu remarked, "Now that everyone is suffering, some nearing death, we find that this herb is ineffective. It is useless as it cannot avert thirst or heat. It cannot save or cure the people who are dying from heat exhaustion and lack of water. What good is this divine herb anyhow?" He was so discouraged and furious that like a maniac, he seized supplies of the divine herb and flung it into the sea. Afterwards, these divine herbs transformed themselves and became edible seaweed.

Yeh-tzu had become somewhat delirious as he stumbled and fell on the sandy shores. Suddenly there was a light gust of cool wind which struck his face. He heard a voice calling, "Yeh-tzu!" He was frightened and baffled as he looked about him in all directions. To his amazement, he looked up and saw his teacher, the old Necromancer standing before him.

Yeh-tzu had intended to give a frank and honest report of his throwing away the divine herb into the sea. However, he wanted to spare his teacher the anguish of knowing about his foolish act. Yet, in excitement, he tearfully said, "This divine herb is incapable of saving people dying of thirst. Look at these people, what they need is relief from thirst and heat. Divine herb? What use is it to these people suffering? Please, Master, what can we do? Where can we find something to relieve their thirst and heat exhaustion. How can we save them from dying? There must be some thirst quenching plant! There must be!" Having said this, Yeh-tzu looked upwards and closed his eyes and fell down dead.

The old Master was greatly moved by his disciple's words. After burying Yeh-tzu, he took up the search for a thirst-quenching plant.

Not long after, from Yeh-tzu's grave site, there sprouted a young shoot. Stretching upwards towards the sun, it grew rapidly. Several days later, it became a tall tree bearing some large round fruits. The fonds on the top of the tree spread widely in all directions in a form of an opened umbrella giving cool shade to passersby. When the fruit was picked and broken open, there was a sweet milk, fragrant, delicious and refreshing. It was most ideal as a thirst quencher. Moreover the flesh of the fruit could satisfy hunger.

Later, the people realized that this tree must be Yeh-tzu in transformation. He became the thirst-quenching plant which he wanted to find to save those suffering from thirst. Unselfishly, he became this divine plant giving shade and providing refreshment and nourishment. In honor of his ultimate sacrifice and concern for his fellow human beings, the people called this plant 'Yeh-tzu' or Coconut.

Interestingly, the coconut is also called 'Yüeh-wang-t'ou' or King Yüeh's head. There is a rather gruesome story found in the *Pên-ts'ao kang-mu*. It is said that the ruler Lin-i harbored resentment against the King of Yüeh. On one occasion, he invited the King of Yüeh to be his guest at a party whereby he made him drunk. He beheaded his guest and hung the head of King Yüeh on a tree. This tree was then transformed into the Coconut tree. The coconut took on the appearance of a woeful face with two round eyes and a small round mouth and became known as Yüeh-wang-t'ou or King Yüeh's severed head. So it seems that the slang, "My Coconut," referring to one's head has its origin in an ancient Chinese legend.

The coconut is found mostly on the island of Hainan and the adjacent China mainland of the Kwangtung province and as far north as the 21st degree latitude. To the Chinese, it is considered to be very beneficial, promoting a healthy plumpness of figure and face. Fresh coconut milk is considered to be cooling and if fermented as heating. The intoxicating properties of the latter are recognized, and it is said to increase thirst instead of relieving it as fresh coconut milk does. Coconut milk is said to be nutrient and serviceable in hematemesis and dropsy.

In the Mid-Autumn Festival celebration, coconut is made into desserts and confections and even cooked with other foods, but not served as fresh fruit. The following are some recipes:

Coconut Pudding (Yeh-tzu kao)

Ingredients:
- 1 cup wheat starch (Têng-mien-fên)
- 1-1/2 cups glutinous rice flour
- 2 cups sugar
- 2 cups coconut milk
- 1/3 cup milk
- 2 Tbs. vegetable shortening

Method:
1) Over heat, blend sugar, milk and vegetable shortening into a smooth sugar syrup. Set aside.
2) Combine glutinous rice flour and wheat starch with coconut milk and mix well.

3) Slowly add sugar syrup to flour and mix well into a smooth mixture.

4) Pour into an oiled baking dish or pan and steam for approximately 2 hours.

5) Remove when well done and set aside to cool. Slice and serve.

Note: This coconut pudding could be eaten cold and plain. However, it could also be coated with a batter of 1 beaten egg and 2 Tbs. of flour and fried in a pan and served hot.

Coconut Pudding with Pine Nuts

Ingredients:

2 Tbs. pine nuts	2 Tbs. water chestnut flour
6 Tbs cornstarch	1/2 cup coconut milk
1 small can evaporated milk	1-1/4 cup sugar
2-1/2 cups water	

Method:

1) Over heat, dissolve sugar in water and set aside.

2) Combine cornstarch and water chestnut flour and slowly add the hot syrup. Place into a pan and over heat stir constantly into a smooth mixture and bring to a boil.

3) Add pine nuts, evaporated milk and coconut milk and bring to a second boil. Remove from heat and pour mixture into a shallow pan and allow to cool and refrigerate. Cut into rectangular pieces and serve cold.

Chapter 5:
More Festival Delicacies

Symbolic food items used in the celebration of the Mid-Autumn Festival, include some foods that have greater medicinal values to strengthen and fortify the body for the anticipated cold season.

Melons

A long time ago in the province of Hopeh, there was a family named An who for a number of generations had become famous as melon growers. The present generation of the An family growing melons was An P'ing and his father. An P'ing was a young lad of 18 who was intelligent and perceptive. An P'ing diligently learned all about melons and melon cultivation and care from his father and together they became very successful in the management of their melon patch.

Sometime later, An P'ing's father somehow had offended a member of a wealthy family in the area. Being just farmers, they were powerless against the rich and powerful so their only recourse was to pack up and remove themselves from the area. They went to the mountainous region of Kuan-tung and built a small thatched hut at the foothills.

An P'ing and his father scouted the area and found that on the hillside, there was a stretch of dark black soil. They had brought some melon seeds with them and felt that this spot was most appropriate for them to grow their melons.

They worked very hard clearing this hillside and planted their melons. After planting, there was the care of cultivating, carrying water up the hillside to water the melons, clearing of weeds and insects and other duties connected with growing melons. They worked from Spring to Summer, and Summer to Autumn, continuously and tirelessly. However, in spite of their busy and hard labor, the melons planted turned out poorly. The melons were so small, they were only slightly larger than a pea pod. They were neither sweet nor fragrant and also rather ugly and odd in appearance. There would be problems even giving them away free of charge not to mention having to sell them for a price.

Both father and son became so troubled and distressed about their melons that they could neither eat or sleep. They thought to themselves, "What are we going to do? It may be possible for us to provide for ourselves this year, but what about the coming year? Should we also have a repeat of poor melons, we may be reduced to starvation!" These thoughts lingered and haunted them continuously.

It was now the 15th day of the 8th lunar month, the Moon Festival time, and at night, there was a large and bright moon shining in the skies. Young An P'ing trying to forget some of these distressing problems, left his house and followed the mountain path up to the melon patch. There, in solitude and under the moon light and tranquil surroundings, he hoped to find peace of mind and possibly think of some solution.

Entering the melon patch, An P'ing found a grassy area and comfortably sat down. The full moon was slowly rising up in the skies and the silver glow of the moon light created a peaceful and beautiful setting. There was a light cool breeze and with the skies bright and clear, sounds of insects could be heard and their chirping was pleasant music to the ears.

An P'ing had brought with him a vertical flute and inspired by this beautiful scene, he began to play a tune. The clear, mellow, and deep tones that he blew on his flute were so moving and serene that even the insects stopped their chirping to listen. Even the wind ceased to blow and the tree branches stopped their swaying. All listened quietly as it was a lovely and inspiring tune.

As he was playing his flute, he became somewhat lost in the music. In his dreamy state, he suddenly noticed a brilliant greenish reflection on the stony ground which startled him. Looking up, he saw that on top of one of the large green rocks on the edge of the melon patch were two young maidens calmly sitting. One appeared to be 16 or 17 years of age and the other, 18 or 19 years old. They were dressed similarly with pale light green colored blouses and lively pastel green skirts. The older of the two, pointing to the hillside of melons said, "These melons have been altered due to the change of environment. All this hard work has been a disappointment and wasted effort! I deeply sympathize with the growers."

The younger maiden spoke up and said, "Older Sister. Do you have any good remedy for such a situation?"

The older sister responded, "I have with me some melon seeds for a variety of melon which is most appropriate and suitable for growing in this area and climate."

An P'ing had stopped playing and was holding the flute in his hands. He was so greatly astonished at what he saw that he stood motionless and silent staring at the two young maidens. However, when he overheard one of them mentioning some good melon seeds, he could not restrain himself and allowed himself to let out a soft, "Aaah . . . !"

Hearing that sound and sensing some movement, the startled young maidens immediately stood up. They saw An P'ing embarrassed and scratching his head and looking ashamed. They both giggled and vanished quickly as a shining green glow moving hurriedly behind the ridge of the hill.

After An P'ing regained his composure, he cautiously moved, step by step, towards the large rock where he had seen the two young maidens sitting. Reaching the large rock, he found a green silk pouch left behind by one of them. With the bright moonlight shining overhead, he opened the silk pouch and was delighted when he discovered that it contained large plump melon seeds.

It was getting rather late in the night and An P'ing felt too tired to walk all the way back to his house. Instead, he decided that he would sleep in the melon patch under the beautiful clear sky. Protecting the silk pouch of melon seeds like a bag of precious jewels, he held onto it tightly as he laid down on the ground to sleep. As he was very tired, it was not long before he was fast asleep. There was a gust of cool breeze accompanied by a shining green-colored glow as the older maiden appeared in the melon patch. An P'ing was awakened and quickly sat up. The young maiden walked up to him and in a soft and gentle voice said, "Take these 'Lu-i-hsiang' variety of melon seeds and utilizing all your skills and knowledge, plant and cultivate them. I guarantee that you will be happy with their bountiful harvest." When she spoke to An P'ing, he saw that she was a most beautiful young maiden having great finesse and charm. He found himself falling in love with her at first sight. He was so fascinated by her that without reserve, he allowed himself to say what his heart felt. "Would you be my life-time partner and assist me in planting melons?"

Hearing these words, the young maiden blushed and became greatly embarrassed. She placed her delicate hand near her mouth and silently gave a slight nod without saying a word. Then in a sweet and soft voice, she said, "Hurry home and inform your father and ask his approval first. I will be waiting under the twin pines beyond that ridge over the hill. Reaching there you should call out, "Lu-i ku-niang' (young maid dressed in green) and I will come out to greet you." Again after saying these words, she vanished as a shining green glow moved over the ridge beyond the hill. Somehow, An P'ing was placed back in his original position on the ground to resume his sleep.

When he awoke next morning, the sun was already up in the skies. He was puzzled. "Was I dreaming or did the events of last night really happened?" he thought to himself. He wondered and pondered for a while. But when he looked down at the green silk pouch in his hands, he realized that he had not been dreaming. Excited and happy, he hastily ran down the hillside towards his house. Arriving home, he informed his father in great detail of all that had happened. His father, upon hearing all this, shared in his son's excitement and happiness.

After gaining his father's approval, An P'ing and Lu-i ku-niang were married. Time passed and it was now spring with flower blossoms everywhere creating a beautiful sight to greet the new year. It was also time for spring planting and the newly wedded couple began a new melon patch with their treasured melon seeds. They were engaged in busy work throughout the spring and summer seasons. However, when harvest time came in the fall, they were rewarded with a bountiful crop of large delicious melons. Remarkably, these melons were all a large uniform size. They exuded a wonderful and sweet fragrance. Tasting these melons was like eating honey and the delicious flavor was a great refreshing delight.

One day, An P'ing carried two baskets full of these melons from their first harvest down the hillside to the market place. It caused a great sensation and excitement. Not only were these melons sweet and delicious, they were also beautiful. They had a wonderful form and color. Moreover, the wonderful sweet fragrance filled the air all around. Even if not eaten, they could serve as beautiful displays, filling the rooms with their sweet smell. They were so wonderful that no one could resist buying them. The melons sold without much effort by An P'ing. In fact, as soon as An P'ing brought his melons to the market place, immediately they were completely sold. Still there were customers calling for more, with a few wanting to accompany him to his melon patch to make their purchases. An P'ing was so happy and delighted that he gleefully consented to all their demands.

An P'ing was by nature altruistic and he was always willing to lend a helping hand to anyone. He had also a happy disposition and was always glad to share whatever he had. Therefore, with some customers wanting to go up the hillside with him, he could only give an affirmative answer.

An P'ing was personable and outgoing so that he had continuous conversations with the group of young men as they accompanied him up the hill. In this group of young men, there was one who was the chief accountant to the richest man in these parts. Unlike the rest of the young men, he had already made his purchase of some melons, so why was he joining in this group hiking up the mountain? This accountant had bought some melons, tasted and liked them. Being suspicious by nature, he thought to himself, "It is strange to have such delicious melons in these parts." Never before had he seen or tasted anything so wonderful. Even long after the eating of these melons, there was a lingering sweet fragrance. The person selling these melons seemed to exude this delightful scent. He was curious and was determined to investigate this.

From the market place to the melon patch was quite a distance and by the time the group reached their destination on the hillside, everyone was exhausted and out of breath — all except An P'ing. Looking at the whole lot of young men, An P'ing laughed and poked fun at them. Then after the joking and ribbing, he invited them all to have slices of melons to refresh themselves.

There was a time-honored custom that anyone eating melons in a melon patch may eat his fill. An P'ing was a generous person and his dutiful wife brought out large platters of these delicious melons for them to eat. Eating the melons, the guests could not stop praising them as they savored the sweet delicious flavor.

The accountant also joined in their praise but he was acting more as a spy. While pretending to be enjoying himself, he was developing a scheme. He was envious that such a young maiden whose beauty was like a heavenly goddess should be married to a poor farmer. At the same time, he suspected something unique and strange. Both An P'ing and his beautiful wife had a lingering sweet fragrance on their bodies. He thought to himself, "Could they be immortals? Could these be heavenly melons that we are eating? Under these unique and strange circumstances they must not be mortals but immortals! Should my wealthy employer acquire these lands and melon patches, there would be no telling how much his wealth would multiply. As for me, I'm sure that I would be substantially rewarded and my authority expanded."

After everyone ate their fill, they thanked An P'ing and his wife. Purchasing some melons they all made their way down the hillside to their respective homes. The cunning accountant hurriedly sought out his wealthy employer to make a full report and to influence him to take some action to acquire the properties.

To convince his employer, the accountant served some of the melons to him. It was no great surprise that the greedy employer found these melons to be delicious and delightful so that he continued eating them. Meanwhile, the accountant told his employer of his plans of gaining possession of these melon patches. His avaricious employer listened more intensely while eating. Savoring these delicious melons, he became impatient and wanted to take possession of these lands and melon patches. However, the scheming accountant cautioned him to first take proper procedures so that the lands would be legally his without interference from anyone.

In the meanwhile, An P'ing continued to harvest his melons and take them to market. Each day, he successfully sold everything and happily returned home. Those purchasing his melons, were always glad to see him and buy these delicious melons. In fact, there were usually small crowds gathering each day to await An P'ing's arrival with his supply of melons. An P'ing did not disappoint them and always brought more melons but it seemed to be never enough for his many customers. However, all those who bought his melons were always greatly satisfied with their purchases.

One day, as a crowd of customers was gathering around An P'ing who had just arrived, the young accountant with several attendants pushed the crowd aside and walked over to An P'ing. Pulling on An P'ing's sleeves, the accountant said, "Melon grower. From where did you acquire these melons?"

One of the angry customers who was pushed aside, replied, "That's a silly question, they were grown from the ground!"

The accountant snubbed and said, "That may be so, but where is this ground located?"

An P'ing being an honest person, pointed to the mountains, and straight forwardly answered, "It is on the hillside of the eastern slopes of those mountains there."

Sneering and with his eyes closed to a slit, the accountant arrogantly said, "Do you know whose lands they are?"

An P'ing excitedly replied, "It was my hard work in clearing those lands to cultivate and plant the melon patches up there." The accountant answered, "As far as a bird is able to fly for three consecutive days, all those areas belong to my wealthy employer! Do you know that you have been trespassing on his private lands and also illegally clearing and disturbing the natural surroundings. Do you know that such acts are criminal and an infringement of personal property rights that is punishable by law? My wealthy employer wants all his lands back! He demands it!"

An P'ing was flabbergasted and angry. "You are tyrants! Usurpers! I have labored hard on these public lands and now you intimidate me by saying that you own these lands." He shook his head in great disappointment.

Chuckling and feeling superior and greatly pleased with himself, the accountant haughtily said, "Whatever you may say, you have infringed on my wealthy employer's property rights. Attendants! Take all of these melons away as they are not his! We are the legal owners!"

There was great confusion and grumbling amongst the surrounding crowd. Several brave young men felt that there was great injustice and attempted to interfere by blocking the removal of the melons. An P'ing realized that there would only be more problems and trouble. So he quickly tried to stop the young men from interfering and painfully allowed the accountant and his men to have their way in seizing and taking away his melons. Having not even empty baskets, An P'ing, frustrated and angry, hurried home.

When An P'ing arrived at the melon patch, he told his wife everything that had happened in the market place. To his surprise, his wife only smiled but said nothing and was not even disturbed. An P'ing seeing that his wife was unmoved, suspected that she may have some plan in mind so he too calmed down and relaxed.

Shortly afterwards, the accountant and his wealthy employer along with some attendants made their way up the hillside to the melon patch. The greedy employer saw that there were some selected melon seeds being aired and dried on large flat bamboo mats for next year's planting. Immediately, he ordered his men to seize them. In spite of the men taking the melon seeds, An P'ing's wife made no move to stop them nor say anything.

This emboldened the wealthy employer who again ordered his men to strip all the melons which they quickly did as commanded. As the men were stripping the melons, An P'ing's patience was wearing thin and he had wanted to rush forward and stop them, but he was restrained by his wife. Not satisfied, the wealthy employer, seeing An P'ing's beautiful wife, instructed his men to kidnap her and take her home with them.

A strange thing happened. As the men rushed forward towards her, An P'ing saw her merely flicking her long sleeves at them. There was a bright green glow on the ground and the greedy employer, the accountant and attendants were all enveloped by the bright light. In a moment, they had completely vanished leaving behind only a pile of green-colored rocks.

Even to this day, the pile of green-colored rocks remains. The larger size stones are the size of a human skull and the small ones like melons. Although the pile of rocks remained, what happened to An P'ing and his family? Some say that there was a green-colored mist that came and transported An P'ing, his father and wife over the ridge beyond the hill where they continued their happy life together in peace and tranquility.

An P'ing and his family generously distributed their melon seeds and taught the people in the area melon cultivation and care. To their honor and to remember them, they called this variety of melons, 'Lu-i-hsiang' or 'green-colored fragrant melons.'

The melon, called 'Kua' in Chinese, is the general term for the fruits of cucurbitaceous plants. The Chinese, according to the *Pên-ts'ao kang-mu*, divide these into two categories, one called Kuo-kua (under the classification of fruits), includes musk melons, watermelons, cantaloupes, honey-dew melons, etc. The other category called Ts'ai-kua (under the classification of vegetables) encompasses cucumbers, squashes, pumpkins, gourds and the like. The melon is probably indigenous to China and there are varieties that are almost mealy when ripe while others are firm and more like a cucumber in texture. None are so juicy as the western kinds, but all have more or less an aromatic flavor and fragrance. Some are quite small and egg-shaped, while others are longer and more cucumber-like. The skin varies from a bright yellow, through greenish-yellows, to a pure green, being sometimes striped in darker shades.

The eating of melons is regarded by the Chinese as somewhat deleterious. Notwithstanding their slight fear of these melons, large quantities are ingested every season. Melons are considered to be resolvent, cooling, diuretic, antivinous, and peptic. But if eaten to excess, they are thought to cause pimples, to bring on ague, and to produce general weakness of the body. If eaten during the month of great heat, sunstroke may be prevented as they are regarded as cooling. The kernels of the seeds are considered as a stomachic, pepatic and constructive remedy.

Melon Seeds (Kua-tzu)

The Chinese are especially fond of melon seeds (Kua-tzu) of which the most favored is that of the watermelon, which is extensively grown in China. It was introduced from Mongolia in the 10th century, having been brought there at an earlier period by the Khitans from the country of the Uighurs farther west. This is the reason that it is called 'Hsi-kua' or 'melon from the west,' and not as some have supposed, because it was introduced from what is now called 'the west.' Several varieties are grown; some having white pulp, some yellow, and some red. The seeds of these varieties are of different colors — white, red, brown and black. The black-seeded variety with red pulp is usually the finest flavored.

Melon seeds are extensively eaten wherever tea is formally or informally served. They are prepared for this purpose by salting and parching. In eating, the shells are cracked with the teeth and the kernels extracted. To crack the seed, extract the kernel, and spit out the shells without using the hands, is an accomplishment that is considered to be evidence the good breeding of the gentleman. The melon grown to produce these seeds is of a special variety, evidently the result of a long period of selective breeding. It is not so large as the other varieties, containing little tasteless pulp but a mass of seeds. The kernels are said to be demulcent, pectoral, and peptic. Much of their good effects, however, may be attributed to their saltiness and the masticatory effort made in eating them. The rind of the seed watermelon is dried and incinerated, and after being finely powdered, is used in the treatment of sore mouths. This preparation could be purchased in Chinese herbal shops as Hsi-kua-shuang. It is extremely bitter in taste and is used also for tooth-aches and cold sores in the mouth. The rind of the sweet watermelon can be pickled or cooked.

Sauteed Watermelon Rind — I

Ingredients:

Watermelon rind	1 onion (finely chopped)
6 thick-sliced bacon (diced)	Salt and Pepper

Method:

1) Trim the green from the rind. Using a coarse shredder, prepare 6 cups of shredded rind.

2) In a skillet, render the bacon until crisp. Remove it to absorbent paper and set it aside. In the remaining fat, cook the onion until translucent.

3) Add the prepared watermelon rind. Stir and cook the rind, covered, for 10 minutes or until it is just tender. Season it to taste with salt and pepper and garnish it with the reserved bacon bits.

Sauteed Watermelon Rind — II

Ingredients:

2 cups Watermelon rind	1 lb. lean pork (julienne)
2 tsp. soy sauce	1/2 tsp. ginger
1 tsp. wine	1 tsp. sugar
2 Tbs. chicken stock	Vegetable oil

Cornstarch mixed with water, a few drops of sesame seed oil, a pinch of sugar and some oyster sauce.

Method:

1) Trim the green and the pink parts from the rind, leaving only the white parts. Slice into thin strips.

2) Saute the pork in soy sauce, sugar, ginger, and wine. Allow to rest for about 20 minutes.

3) Heat pan and brown the pork. When pork is half cooked, add the watermelon rind and chicken stock. Stir and cook until done. Add the cornstarch mixture and thicken the gravy. Remove and serve hot.

Cantaloupe Soup

Ingredients:

1 large ripe cantaloupe (diced)	6 cups of chicken stock
1/4 lb. lean pork or ham (julienne)	1/2 tsp. salt
1 tsp. sugar	2 tsp. soy sauce
6 Chinese mushrooms (soaked and julienne)	

Method:

1) In a pot, bring the chicken broth to a boil.

2) Add diced cantaloupe, pork or ham, salt and sugar. When the soup returns to a boil, reduce heat to a simmer. Uncovered, simmer for 5 minutes.

3) Stir in soy sauce and adjust the seasoning as needed and serve hot.

Ham and Winter Melon

Ingredients:

2 lbs. winter melon	1 tsp. salt
1/2 lb. ham	1-1/2 Tbs. wine
3 Chinese mushrooms	1 scallion
6 cups chicken stock	MSG

Method:

1) Remove the winter melon rind. Cut into 12-14 thick slices. Make an incision in the middle of each piece, but do not cut all the way through.

2) Cut ham into the same size and as many slices as winter melon. Place in a plate and steam both ham and scallion with 1 Tbs. wine and 2 Tbs. sugar. When cooked, remove and set aside.

3) Place a piece of ham inside of each piece of winter melon. Arrange in a deep dish. Add Chinese mushrooms, 1 tsp. salt, MSG, 1/2 tsp. wine and 6 cups of chicken broth. The juice from steaming the ham may also be added. Place in steamer and steam for 1 hour. Remove and serve hot.

Banana

In a small, peaceful hamlet, there lived two poor young men who were intimate friends. One was surnamed Wang and the other Li. They were the best of friends and were very close to each other, sharing and doing everything together. Everyday with the rising of the sun, they would go to work in the fields together and nearing evening, after they had their supper, the two men would always enjoy a game of chess.

In time, they each took a wife but their amicable relations and cooperative spirit continued. Pooling their savings, they jointly purchased a tract of land. Clearing the area, they planted a small number of banana trees. After a few years, with diligent work, they were successful in expanding and having an entire grove of banana trees.

About this same time, each of their wives gave birth to a child, one following the other. The Li family first had a son who they named Ch'ing-sung. The Wang household followed with a girl named Ts'ui-lien.

Time passed quickly and before long ten or more years had passed. Ch'ing-sung and Ts'ui-lien grew up together. Before they were 15 years old, Ch'ing-sung's father died. Before his father died, he gave his son a musical instrument, a P'i-p'a (Chinese guitar) and taught him to play a number of tunes. Ch'ing-sung loved his father dearly and would remember him often by playing this musical instrument. Each day when his work was completed, he would seat himself in the banana grove beside a small creek and play his P'i-p'a. He was so talented and became so proficient in his playing that not only the birds and animals, but also the fish in the creek would stop and listen. The leaves on the banana trees would sway to the lovely tune in a form of dancing. All appreciated his playing on the P'i-p'a. Whenever Ts'ui-lien heard him playing, she would put aside her embroidery and needlework and run out to the banana grove to sit and listen to the music. Although she was always happy and delighted, she often cried as she shared with Ch'ing-sung his tender feelings for his father. She was, to say the least, not only in love with the music, but also in love with the performer, Ch'ing-sung. This was no great surprise.

Both grew up together, worked and played together and always shared things with each other. With the passing of time, it was only natural that they should come to care for and love each other. However, when they reached the age of 18, things started to change. Having matured, whenever Ts'ui-lien saw Ch'ing-sung, she would cover her face slightly and turn with the feeling of embarrassment. Likewise, Ch'ing-sung's face would turn bright red and even his ears would have the color of cooked lobsters as he would turn slightly away while scratching his head. They were in love yet by custom and tradition they had to show embarrassment.

When Ts'ui-lien's father, Old Wang discovered them acting this way, he pretended that he had not noticed them. However, he had in his mind to separate the two for good. He saw that his daughter was maturing and getting prettier and more beautiful with each year. He was against her marrying Ch'ing-sung as he considered him merely a poor farmer. He thought little of him and wanted his daughter to marry into a rich household. There was a wealthy person living in this area called Master Jung. Although he was exceedingly wealthy with a large mansion and rich holdings, he was an old man who was nearly 70 years of age. Not only was he old, he was also physically and morally deformed. His only assets were that he had money, lots of money. Because Old Wang craved money, he would have sacrificed his daughter's future happiness to have her marry that old and ugly man.

One day, while Ts'ui-lien was doing some fine embroidery, she overheard her father and mother discussing her betrothal to Old Jung. She was shocked and completely shaken. She felt like a caged bird caught and restricted. She had to flee and get away quickly. However, as luck would have it, her mother caught her trying to escape and immediately had her returned and locked in her room with constant surveillance. She was now exactly like a caged bird without any freedom whatsoever.

Like Ts'ui-lien, Ch'ing-sung had matured into a rather handsome young person. He was strong and with bushy eyebrows and round eyes, he looked alert and bright. He was well coordinated and a diligent worker. To say the least, he was a fine handsome young man. As always, each day after work, he would seat himself in the banana grove and play music on his P'i-p'a.

One day, as he routinely came to the banana grove and started to play on his P'i-p'a, suddenly, a young maiden dressed in green approached him from behind. She sat herself before him and listened intently to the music. As Ch'ing-sung played, he would occasionally steal some quick glances at the strange young maiden. He noticed that she had a round face, a dainty and well shaped mouth and a slender figure. From all appearance and mannerisms, she differed little from Ts'ui-lien. In fact, she was so much like Ts'ui-lien that he thought that it must surely be her. In a soft low voice, he called out, "Ts'ui-lien, I have not seen you for quite some time."

The young maiden made a soft muffled laughing sound and smiled as she said, "Who is this Ts'ui-lien whose name you had just called out? I am called Chiao-ku (Banana maiden). Each day, I have been listening to you play on the P'i-p'a for many years. Do you not recognize me?"

Seeing that this girl was so clever, bright and friendly, Ch'ing-sung started to have a delightful and interesting conversation with her. Chiao-ku was able to direct their conversation to discussion about Ts'ui-lien. At that time, she seemed to have lowered her head and her fingers moved as though counting. Raising her head, her complexion seemed to have changed color as she said, "Ch'ing-sung! All is not well. I must inform you that Ts'ui-lien is in grave danger at this moment. Her father has consented to give her as a bride to Old Jung who in reality is the animal spirit of an old Banyan tree. At this very moment, she is being placed into the wedding sedan-chair to be taken to this monster's house."

When Ch'ing-sung heard this, he was frightened and taken aback. Without hesitation, he asked Chiao-ku if there were any suggestions to save Ts'ui-lien. He was so sincere in his pleadings that she could only comply. She said to him, "Alright! I will help you. There is a saying that when killing someone it should be quick. Likewise in saving someone's life, it should be direct and without wasting time. You must not lose a moment's time. Go quickly to save her by meeting the wedding sedan-chair en route to the groom's house. Get near the sedan-chair and cast this large banana leaf into it and Ts'ui-lien will be saved!"

Taking the banana leaf, Ch'ing-sung in all haste made his way quickly to where the wedding procession would be passing. Remembering well the instructions given him by Chiao-ku, he was resolved and determined to carry out the instructions. Disregarding any danger to himself, he rushed out to the middle of the road as the wedding procession approached. The wedding party ran forwards, surrounding him and began to hit and kick him for blocking the road. Ch'ing-sung endured the beating and pain with great determination as he pushed his way nearer to the wedding sedan-chair and cast the banana leaf in. By that time, he had fallen onto the ground and was unmercifully beaten by the members of the wedding party. When satisfied, they resumed the wedding procession by stepping over the fallen Ch'ing-sung as they continued onto Old Jung's mansion. Ch'ing-sung was left crawling on the ground, his face swollen and discolored. His entire body was covered with wounds and blood. Gradually and with great difficulty, he got himself up and painfully made his way slowly home.

When the wedding procession reached the main entrance of Old Jung's mansion, the groom and his party came out to invite the bride to emerge from the closed wedding sedan-chair. After calling out several times and having no response, they opened up the sedan-chair but found no bride in it. There was only a large banana leaf in its place. Seeing this, Old Jung was so flabbergasted and furious that he lost his balance and fell onto the ground. Everyone rushed forward to assist him in getting onto his feet. The angry raving old man shouted out, "The banana spirit has gone too far! Her meddling has infuriated me and I will see her dead before I am satisfied!"

Clasping his hands then counting with his fingers, this old monster was able to do fate calculation. He knew that Ch'ing-sung and Ts'ui-lien had already become husband and wife. This revelation angered him even more. But who was this old man who had such great powers? Well, he was a metamorphosis of an ancient Banyan tree which was over a thousand years old. His breathing of the ethereal essence over a long duration gave him the ability to transform himself into human form. However, he was wicked and cruel and practised his tyranny on earth. Demanding revenge, he transformed himself into a young peddler and carried two baskets filled with wares balanced on a pole. In a flash he made his way to Ch'ing-sung's house. In a clear and loud voice he shouted out, "I have fine threads and needles. Everything needed to do embroidery and fine needlework! Come out and look for yourselves! Come out and buy my wares!"

Hearing the sales calls of this peddler, Ts'ui-lien was delighted and very quickly she came out of her house to buy some thread and needles. As she was very fond of needlework and embroidery, she carefully examined all the needles by opening one pack after another in order to make her selection. After a while, she came to a package containing some poisoned needles. The young peddler, immediately took the package of needles and opening it and holding one of the needles said to Ts'ui-lien, "Mistress! This is the finest needle that you will every find. Just look!"

Ts'ui-lien was unsuspecting and unaware that this was a plot against her. As she turned around to look at this fine needle, the young peddler stabbed her in the lungs with the poison needle. Ch'ing-sung was sitting in the house but when he heard his wife's painful cry, "Aieee . . .!" he dropped everything and rushed out of the house to see what was the matter. He saw Ts'ui-lien's body stiffen and both arms and legs go limp as she bent over and collapsed onto the ground. She had fainted and was unconscious. Looking for the peddler, Ch'ing-sung saw no one. There was nothing in sight except some root hairs off a Banyan tree which were scattered all about the ground.

Ch'ing-sung rushed over to hold onto his wife and frantically called out her name repeatedly. But he got no response. Ts'ui-lien not only made no sound, there was also no movement of any kind. Ch'ing-sung leaned over to listen to her heart beat and was greatly startled to hear nothing. Feeling her pulse and placing his hand near her nostrils all resulted in no sign of life. Ch'ing-sung now cried out in a loud cry of pain as he realized that Ts'ui-lien had been killed and laid dead. He cried for a long time, but he realized that all his crying could not bring his wife back to life. He had to find some help. He carefully carried his dead wife's body to the banana grove.

As he entered the grove carrying Ts'ui-lien, he was met by Chiao-ku. When Chiao-ku saw that Ts'ui-lien was dead, she began to weep and together she and Ch'ing-sung, cried for some time. Finally, Chiao-ku took hold of herself and stopped her weeping and turned to Ch'ing-sung and said, "A dead person could not be brought back to life. Ch'ing-sung, your wife has been killed and all the crying will not bring her back. Instead it may be injurious to your health. I should be frank with you and tell you exactly how I feel. I am the spirit of the banana tree but I have never harmed anyone. Because I had listened daily to your music for many years, I developed a liking and a love for you. However, I had never suspected that you were so deeply in love with Ts'ui-lien. When I was made aware of your intense love, I tried to save her from danger and allow both of you to join together as husband and wife."

"Chiao-ku," interrupted Ch'ing-sung, "You are a good and kind-hearted person and I owe much to you. Since we are being frank with each other, allow me to tell you my deep feelings. I sincerely thank you for all you have done for me for which I will be eternally grateful. However, I am deeply in love with Ts'ui-lien and my heart belongs to her. Even though she had been so unmercifully killed and taken away from me by that mean old monster, I cannot alter my love for her. My love for her is eternal and I vow never to marry another."

When Chiao-ku had heard Ch'ing-sung's words, she let out a deep long sigh and lowered her head saying, "What ill-fortune surrounds me!" She slowly lifted her head and with down-cast eyes she lowered her head again. She was sad to hear Ch'ing-sung say that there would be no other woman in his life except Ts'ui-lien. In painful sadness, she bit down on her lips and stood up erect. Then as her face became filled with a strange glow, she faced Ch'ing-sung and said, "Alright! Giving aid to anyone must be complete and without reserve. I will help you both to finish what needs to be done!"

After saying these words, Chiao-ku knelt over Ts'ui-lien's lifeless body. She held onto her and touched her face gently. Then searching for the poison needle which had pierced Ts'ui-lien's lungs, she found and removed it. She bit her own finger until blood oozed out then placed her finger onto the spot from where she had extracted the poison needle. She held her hand there. As her blood flowed into Ts'ui-lien's body, there seemed to be some remarkable change in the dead lifeless body. The color of Ts'ui-lien's face started to return and she appeared young and fresh again. Quickly she started to breathe and her heart beat resumed. Ts'ui-lien even started to cough and sit up as she became alive again. She sighed and yawned like just having awakened from a deep sleep. As she opened her eyes, Ch'ing-sung became extremely excited and happy as he jumped up in joy to see Ts'ui-lien alive again!

However, as life had returned to Ts'ui-lien, life was being taken away from Chiao-ku. She started to gasp and with difficulty tried to speak. She had become so weakened from saving Ts'ui-lien that she could hardly open her eyes. However, she had a smile on her face. Both Ts'ui-lien and Ch'ing-sung held tightly onto her hands as she said to them, "I must bid both of you farewell. I will not be able to resume a human form again. I want you both to be happy and love each other dearly. Let your love be forever. Remember me . . . please do not forget me!" After saying these words she fell backwards. Her clothing had changed into banana leaves and her now lifeless body became the trunk of the banana tree.

Ch'ing-sung and Ts'ui-lien caressed the banana tree and burst out in great sorrow. Tears flowed as they cried out without stopping. Kneeling before the banana tree, they bowed in respect as they continued their wailing. They vowed that they would never forget the ultimate sacrifice that Chiao-ku had made on behalf of their happiness. "Oh why?" cried the young couple, "Why must such a good, kind-heart and unselfish soul have to die! Why do good people die and cruel and wicked ones live?"

Ch'ing-sung was so filled with anger that in a great rage he swore revenge. He quickly seized an axe and rushed to the entrance of the small hamlet where there was an old Banyan tree. Raising his axe overhead, he struck the tree with all his might. There was a great cry of pain, but Ch'ing-sung was single-minded and without stopping, chopped and chopped at the Banyan tree until it was completely cut down.

From the main trunk of the severed Banyan tree flowed a thick black sap somewhat resembling blood. The curious villagers witnessing this said that the Banyan tree had become a monster and they all rushed to assist Ch'ing-sung in setting fire to it and burning down the tree completely.

As flames engulfed the Banyan tree, painful cries were heard. Simultaneously in the Old Jung mansion, the wicked old man fell over and mysteriously was caught in flames, burning to a crisp leaving nothing of himself or the large mansion except a pile of ashes. Everything connected with the Banyan tree was wiped out and disappeared completely as though fire had cleansed the area of all evil, leaving the area peaceful again and without tyranny.

Afterwards, it was rumored that both Ch'ing-sung and Ts'ui-lien lived happily together and became prosperous. They both enjoyed the blessing of longevity and lived to be over 100 years of age before they passed away peacefully in their sleep together.

While they were alive, they had 3 sons and 4 daughters. All of their sons grew up as strong brave young men with all the virtues of their father Ch'ing-sung. The daughters were all intelligent and beautiful like their mother Ts'ui-lien. It is said that throughout her life, in memory and in respect of Chiao-ku, Ts'ui-lien was always attired in green. Together her entire family would gather in the banana grove playing musical instruments and dancing to entertain the banana trees. Whenever Ch'ing-sung played his P'i-p'a, the banana trees would respond by swaying their leaves as if dancing to his music.

The Chinese make little distinction between the plantain and the banana. Both are generically called 'Chiao.' However, the different varieties are given specific names under the general category of chiao. The banana is grown mostly in the southern provinces but it also grows in the Yangtze valleys although the fruit seldom ripens.

The banana is considered to be very cooling, and should not be eaten in excess. As a precaution, the Chinese always eat a bit of the lining of the banana peel. Eaten in the raw state, the banana relieves thirst, moistens the lungs, purifies the blood, heals wounds, and is antivinous. Steamed, it promotes the circulation of the blood and enriches the marrow. Bananas are a good source for potassium. The viscid sap of the plant called Chiao-yu, is procured by thrusting a bamboo tube into the stalk and collecting the sap in a bottle. It has the antifebrile properties of the other parts and the Chinese use it in epilepsy, vertigo, to prevent women's hair from falling and to increase its growth and to restore its color.

Usually the bananas are harvested when green as they bruise easily. From very early times, the Chinese had learned that if the bananas are placed in a dark room and smoked, the bananas would turn a bright yellow color which makes them more appealing for sale.

In the Mid-Autumn Festival celebration, bananas are either eaten as a fresh fruit or else caramelized and eaten as a dessert.

Caramel Bananas

Ingredients:

4 ripe bananas	1 Tbs. vegetable oil
2 eggs	6 Tbs. sugar
4 Tbs. cornstarch	2 Tbs. water
5 Tbs. flour	Oil for deep frying
6 Tbs. water	1 tsp. Sesame seeds (toasted)

Method:
1) Combine eggs, cornstarch, flour and 6 Tbs. of water into a smooth batter.
2) Cut bananas into 5 diagonal pieces. Dust with some flour prior to coating them with the batter.
3) In a pan, heat 1 Tbs. of oil. Add sugar and 2 Tbs. of water over low heat. Stir continuously until it turns into a thick syrup that coats the spoon.
4) In a separate pan, heat oil for deep frying. When oil is hot, fry the bananas until golden brown.
5) Transfer the fried bananas into the pan with the thickened syrup and mix thoroughly. Remove and place on a serving platter lightly oiled with sesame seed oil.
6) Before serving, sprinkle some toasted sesame seeds on the bananas. Plunge into a bowl of water with ice cubes. Remove and serve.

Gingko Nut

In the area of Chên-p'ing at the foothills of the Hsing-hua mountains, there is a monastery called P'u-t'i-ssu or Bodhi Monastery. In the temple courtyard grew three large Gingko trees. Two of the trees had only lush growth of leaves without ever bearing any fruit. The third tree was always covered with Gingko nuts in the autumn. Standing beside these trees was a bell tower with an ancient bell as tall as a person and slightly chipped and cracked due to age.

Legend has it that long ago, there lived in the Bodhi Monastery a kind-looking old monk who in spite of his outer appearance, was really mean, cruel and greedy. He had served as the abbot of this monastery which housed several hundred young monks. This old monk was extremely greedy and was always in league with the corrupt authorities. He claimed for himself all the lands within ten or more *li* in radius of the Bodhi Monastery. He became a tyrant and grossly mistreated the people in these areas and heavy-handedly extorted money from them. He stripped them of all their belongings and reduced them to complete poverty and life as slaves.

The three Gingko trees and the ancient bell standing near each other for such a long time had become friends. Since the bell tower was erected higher than the Gingko trees, from the lofty heights, the ancient bell became a witness to the painful sufferings of the people. To escape from seeing the misery during the daytime, each night, the ancient bell would take flight away from the temple's courtyard and went elsewhere to seek solitude. Each morning at the fifth watch (3-5 a.m.) the bell would return to the bell tower. Although this had continued for quite some time, nevertheless it was completely undetected and escaped the notice or suspicion of the wicked old monk.

One morning when the ancient bell had just returned, one of the Gingko trees in a soft and low voice asked, "Mr. Bell, every night you seem to take flight and go elsewhere. What is there outside the monastery that you find so attractive?"

The ancient bell answered, "Miss Gingko, I'm so glad that you spoke out as I had intended to speak to all of you on a matter of great importance. Tonight as I flew over the villages, I saw people suffering everywhere. There was not a single household in which I could not hear the crying of the people. I listened closely and found that the people have been stricken by some sickness of epidemic proportions. However, they have no money to either engage a medical doctor or buy the necessary medication. Therefore, many people had already died and many more are suffering and near death."

Shocked at what they heard, the Gingko trees in unison quickly interrupted saying, "Mr. Bell, what could be done about this? Quickly think of some solution to remedy this situation. You are old and wise, you must know what to do. We must do everything to save the people!"

The ancient bell lowered his head and sighed as he responded, "Saving the people is not a difficult problem. The problem is how much courage would the three of you have to do what is necessary?"

The third Gingko tree spoke up, "As long as the people are saved, we are willing to make whatever sacrifices are necessary. Even to have a violent wind uproot us. We are completely resolved and unafraid!"

Satisfied by these remarks, the ancient bell said, "On the overhanging cliffs of the mountains behind us, there are patches of herbs which we seek. They could provide miraculous cures of illness and are considered to be an elixir of immortality. If we should gather up some of these herbs and process them into medicines to distribute to the people, we will be successful in healing them and strengthen their bodies. However, we must do this without the old monk's knowing as he considers these divine herbs as his personal property. He prizes them greatly as valuable jewels and anyone caught stealing them may lose their life!"

The tree Gingko sisters together said, "Old Mr. Bell, we are unafraid of any consequences that may ensue. We are fully determined to save the people. Quickly, tell us exactly what we should do!"

Immediately the ancient bell transformed himself into a white bearded old man and the Gingko trees into three young maidens. Together they made their way to the overhanging cliffs to gather the divine herb.

As daylight came, the old monk discovered at once that both the bell and the three Gingko trees had disappeared. He ordered the monks to form search parties to hunt them down. By the time that the sun was shining overhead, the old monk with a number of accompanying monks had arrived at the foot of the mountains. Looking ahead in the distance, the old monk could see an old man along with three young maidens gathering his prized and valuable divine herbs. Without hesitation, he hastily climbed up the mountains shouting, "You culprits! You can't fool me with your disguises! You are the ancient bell and Gingko trees!"

The four realized that their transformations had been discovered by the old monk. Standing up erect they proudly admitted, "We are the ancient bell and Gingko trees. We have come here to gather some of the divine herb so that we may assist the people in curing them from their illness!"

The old monk roared out in great anger like a wild animal as he shouted, "All of you! Stop what you are doing and return with me to the Monastery! If you should even consider a no in your thoughts, I will immediately report your actions to the Supreme Heavenly Ruler and ask him to mete out your punishment!" Then bursting out in a sinister laugh, he continued, "If you have any fear of Heaven punishing you, then desist and return immediately!"

The older Gingko said, "Having been a monk for such a long time, praying daily and preaching charity and salvation, are you not concerned that the masses need to be saved from being afflicted with sickness?"

The third Gingko added another admonishment, "You are only masquerading as a charitable and kind monk. These qualities must have long disappeared from your body. What you say is nothing more than meaningless dog barking!"

The old monk was overcome by the flames of anger and hate. He could only see red before him. In great rage, he withdrew and rushed back to the Monastery. Lighting candles and incense, he filed a formal complaint to Heaven saying:

> *Memorializing and reporting with great respect to the Most August Jade Emperor in Heaven. This lowly monk is sad to report that unaccountable supernatural influences in the form of evil portents caused by a metamorphosis of an ancient bell and three Gingko trees have caused confusion and disruption in these areas. They dare to rebel and challenge the authority of Heaven. This lowly monk seeks justice and begs that Heaven should send someone to capture and punish them and clear away their bad influences. Let earth enjoy peace and tranquility and respect the Will of Heaven.*

Receiving such a complaint from the old monk, the Jade Emperor flew into a great rage. Immediately he commissioned a Heavenly General to descend to earth to quell this disturbance and return order to earth.

The Heavenly General, armed with a mighty iron whip, mounted a white cloud and descended to earth. Without any problem, he found the four still gathering the divine herb. In a loud voice, he roared, "I have an edict from the Jade Emperor ordering all four of you to stop your gathering of the divine herb and return to the monastery. Do as you are commanded!"

The disguised old man and three young maidens were engrossed in their gathering and ignored the Heaven General. This, of course, infuriated the Heavenly General. Being a military man and easily provoked, the Heavenly general, without showing any mercy, raised his iron whip to hit the old man. Quickly the old man handed the divine herbs to the eldest maiden, just before he was struck down. When the Heavenly General turned to the maidens, the eldest passed the divine herbs to the second and then to the third maiden. The attacking Heavenly General went from one maiden to another striking them without mercy. Fearing that the divine herb would be taken away from them, the third maiden quickly swallowed them in large handfuls before all four were subdued. Then they were taken back as prisoners to the Monastery and transformed back to their original forms as an ancient bell and three Gingko trees.

The noise and commotion that had taken place up in the mountains had brought the curious population up to the Monastery to investigate what had happened. By the time they arrived at the Monastery, all they could see was that the large ancient bell had some chips and large cracks and two of the Gingko trees had branches beaten down and the bark peeling with sap oozing out. It was a pitiful sight to see the trees in this condition and the people remarked, "They must be the two older sisters suffering pain and in great sadness for they are crying and bleeding!"

The third Gingko tree, because she had consumed the divine herb was left physically unharmed. But looking down at all the sick people and the punishments suffered by the ancient bell and her two sisters, she became extremely sad and filled with melancholy. "How could Heaven have been so cruel and unjust?" she thought. However, she was resolved to save the people so that all the pain and suffering of her sisters and the ancient bell should not be in vain. With great determination and with all her strength and concentration, she started to burst out with an abundance of Gingko nuts which fully covered the tree. Then shaking violently, she caused the Gingko nuts to fall onto the ground. The people were stunned and stood in great amazement as they could not explain what was happening.

Some were even frightened but a few of the brave souls picked up some of the Gingko nuts and bit into them. They found a sweet fragrance and delicious flavor in them. As soon as they ate them, they became filled with vigor and enthusiasm as they felt renewed strength in their bodies. Seeing this, more people tried them until everyone present ate some and became cured of their illness.

Soon the people realized that because the Gingko tree had consumed the divine herb, the miraculous curative qualities were transferred into the Gingko nuts. The Gingko nut became a life-saving drug, curing the sick and they were all greatly thankful.

Even to this day, people residing near the Bodhi Monastery visit this ancient Gingko tree during the autumn season to pick both the Gingko nuts and leaves. The Gingko became known as 'Pai-kuo hsien-i' or 'Gingko, the miraculous cure.' In fact, the wood of the tree is made into seals, which are used as charms by quacks and shamans in the treatment of disease.

The Gingko (Ginkgo biloba) is a deciduous tree and the only surviving member of the Ginkgoaceae. The genus Ginkgo is said to have thrived worldwide in the prehistoric period but now grows abundantly only in China, Japan and Korea. The Gingko was first introduced to Europe in an

18th century book by Engelberg Kaempfer, a German naturalist who had visited Japan. The Gingko tree, with fan-shaped leaves, grows fast and is resistant to cold weather, fire, diseases and urban atmospheric conditions. It is planted as a roadside tree or firebreak.

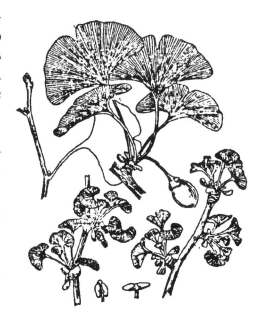

In the second month, the tree blooms with a greenish-white bud, which opens in the night and quickly drops off, so that the flowers are rarely seen. The fruits are borne prolifically on the branches and resemble lotus seeds. They ripen after frost and are pointed at the extremities and marked by 2 or 3 longitudinal ridges. The ripe fruit has a fleshy, foul-smelling brownish-white, smooth, hard-shelled outer covering. Its edible kernel is called Yin-kuo, pronounced Kinko in Japanese from which is derived the term, Gingko. However, in Chinese, it is more commonly called Pai-kuo. The kernel consists of two yellow, mealy cotyledons, covered with a beautiful, thin, reddish membrane. The Chinese consume Gingko nuts at weddings, the shell being dyed red. They are also frequently served at feasts and banquets and are a fair substitute for lotus seeds. They have a somewhat fishy taste and are supposed to

benefit asthma, coughs, irritability of the bladder, and uterine fluxes. Eaten raw, they were believed to destroy cancer and are counter-vinous. Cooked, they are said to be peptic and anthelmintic and thus are used to promote digestion.

In the Mid-Autumn Festival celebration, Gingko nuts are used in various dishes, soups and sweets, but usually not eaten alone.

Gingko Nuts and Chicken

Ingredients:

2 oz. fresh or canned Gingko nuts	1 whole Chicken breast
6 water chestnuts (diced)	4 stalks of Chinese broccoli
6 Chinese mushrooms (diced)	1/2 tsp. ginger (finely chopped)
1 clove garlic (minced)	1-1/2 Tbs. vegetable oil

Seasoning:

1/4 tsp. salt	1/4 tsp. sugar
1/2 tsp. cornstarch	pepper

Method:

1) Bone chicken and cut into small pieces (diced)

2) If using fresh gingko nuts, shell and blanch in hot water. If canned ones are used, wash and drain and set aside.

3) Cut water chestnuts and mushrooms into dices. Cut also into small dice sized pieces, the Chinese broccoli, using only the stems portions and not the leaves. Blanch in hot water.

4) Heat oil in a pan and add the ginger and garlic. When brown, add the chicken. Add all other ingredients. Stir-fry and add seasoning. Serve hot.

Gingko Nut Soup

Ingredients:

2 oz. dried bean curds (T'ien-chu)	3-4 oz. fresh Gingko nuts
8 fresh water chestnuts	1 oz. pearl barley
1/4 lb. lean pork	salt

Method:

1) Soak the pearl barley, dried bean curds sheets in water. Shell the Gingko nuts and place in a bowl of cold water.

2) Parboil the pork, then add it to a large pot of water. Bring to a boil and remove any surface scum.

3) Add fresh water chestnuts, dried bean curds, gingko nuts and pearl barley and bring to a second boil. Continue to boil for 2 or 3 minutes then lower heat and cover. Simmer for 1 hour. The dried bean curds would break up and should be stirred occasionally to help thicken the soup base. Before serving, add salt.

This soup is especially recommended to the elderly and children. It not only serves as a tonic but also helps improve the appetite. It is especially eaten during the late summer and autumn months.

Lysium Chinense

Hsüan-tsang is the religious designation of a man whose original name was Ch'ên I. A native of Honan province, he became a Buddhist priest when only 20 years of age and in the year 629 A.D., he set out for India, with a view to visit its holy places and to bring back copies of the sacred books of Buddhism. In 645 A.D., he returned and was received with public honors. The T'ang dynasty Emperor T'ai-tsung conferred upon him the honorary epithet of 'San-tsang' or 'Tripitaka.' He had with him 657 Buddhist books, besides many images and pictures, and 150 relics. He spent the rest of his life in translating these books with the assistance of several learned monks appointed by the Emperor. He wrote an account of his journey to India, entitled *Hsi-yu-chi* or *Record of Western Countries* and presented it to the Emperor in 646 A.D.

However, most people are familiar with the popular fiction with the same title, *Hsi-yu-chi*, written in 100 chapters by Wu Ch'êng-ên (ca. 1500-1582). This mythological account of the adventures of this Buddhist priest and his three famous disciples, Monkey, Pigsy and Sandy, is often told by storytellers and acted out in popular drama. In the popular story, Hsüan-tsang is referred to as either San-tsang (Tripitaka) or as T'ang-sêng, the T'ang dynasty Buddhist priest.

According to one of these popular stories, which is based on Chapter 65 of the popular fiction, as T'ang-sêng and his party were making their way along, without a care, they saw a long ridge in front of them over which the road led. T'ang-sêng reined in his horse to look. He saw that the ridge was overgrown with brambles and creepers. Although the line of the path could be made out, there were brambles and thorns all over it. "How are we going to manage through them?" he thought to himself, "Without a doubt, few travellers have taken this road."

It was already dusk and there was neither any inn or settlement nearby. Dismounting and in a very good mood, he said, "Disciples, I've put you to a lot of trouble. Let's stop here for the night and carry on at first light tomorrow."

It was in the middle of autumn and the foliage all around was dressed in golden hues and brilliant colors. There was a clear sky and a cool breeze, a beautiful and pleasant time of the year. Everyone rested comfortably and soon fell fast asleep. However, in the middle of the night, a cold frost descended accompanied by penetrating cold winds. Pigsy felt the cold so greatly that his entire body had the texture of chicken skin and he was awakened by the freezing cold. Grumbling and complaining, he muttered, "This is terrible! What is this god-forsaken place anyhow?"

Monkey who was also awakened said, "I'm not sure but I'll summon the T'u-ti-kung or local earth deity and ask him." Having said this, Monkey closed his eyes and chanted a sacred sutra. Immediately there was an old man with long white beard who emerged from the ground and bowed before him and said, "Great Sage, I am the local god of this area. With respect, I ask what instructions do you have for me?"

Monkey replied, "My Master, in journeying to the Western Paradise (India), has been stranded here. We do not even know what place we are in?"

The local earth deity replied, "Great Sage, you are in Ninghsia and it is the correct and necessary route to going to the Western Paradise for obtaining the Buddhist sutra."

Monkey again inquired, "These dense thorny brambles stretching across the road and blocking our path, what are they called?"

"This low-growing bush is called 'Kou-chi'," the local deity answered in response, "Originally, they grew in the open plains of the country called Chi. But the people there were cruel and greedy. They were so haughty that they tried to contradict the Laws of Nature which had been established in Heaven. They wanted the Kou-chi plant to grow tall and stately like trees to shade their open plains. This contemptuous act infuriated the Jade Emperor so he ordered all the Kou-chi plants to be removed to mountainous regions of the Northwest. He decreed that the Kou-chi plant was to remain a bush, disallowing them to grow tall. Therefore, they became low close-growing bushes only allowed to spread sideways."

The T'ang priest had been awakened and overheard everything. Folding his hands in prayer he said, "Namu omitofo. Mercy be with Amida Buddha. This is not difficult to understand. The roots of these plants being shallow, it has no strength to support much weight so it becomes necessary for it to spread sideways. Moreover, it could never have tall growth or look majestic like a tree."

There is a popular saying, "Words spoken along open roads will surely be heard." This is exactly what happened. The Kou-chi spirit heard the T'ang priest say,

"Shallow roots . . . no strength . . . not tall or majestic," and became angry and exasperated. Because of such an off-hand remark, the T'ang priest was made to suffer as an act of revenge.

T'ang-sêng and his disciples arose early next morning and packed their belongings in preparation for continuing their journey. At that moment, the T'ang priest felt a bit hungry and his stomach started to growl. He had not had any food for more than a day and a half and was hungry. Pigsy, who was always wanting to eat, started howling and crying out that he was extremely famished. Seeing this, Monkey said, "In these remote parts, although there are no settlements, I'm sure that there must be some wild fruits or berries. I'll go and find some and bring them back."

Monkey loved to eat fruits and peaches were his favorite. His knowledge of wild fruits was phenomenal. Looking at the dense growth of thorny bramble, he saw that they were covered with plump green berries. Picking some and sampling their taste, he found them to have a sweet-sour taste. He thought to himself, "Although these Kou-chi berries cannot be compared to the delicious peaches found in the Heavenly Orchards, nevertheless, they are edible and seemed to have no ill-effects when eaten. There being nothing else in sight, I think that they would suffice in satisfying our hunger." With such thoughts in mind, Monkey commenced to pick the wild berries and fetch them back for food.

Everyone took some and started to eat them. However, Pigsy, who had eaten his fill of some delicious sweet fruits the day before, found the taste to his disliking and he spat it out. He sat up with his hands folded, grumbling and complaining and refused to eat them.

After having eaten the Kou-chi berries, T'ang-sêng felt refreshed and it seemed that his eyes had brightened and he had clear vision. He felt strong in his muscles and bones and vigorous in strength and movement. Thinking back at what he had said of the Kou-chi plant the night before, he felt that his off-hand remark was unwarranted and mistaken. Nodding and pleased after having eaten the Kou-chi berries, he said, "Although this plant is not tall and majestic, nevertheless, it is a most beneficial and desirable herb."

After eating their fill and satisfying their hunger, they continued their journey, but the thorny bramble still blocked their path. T'ang-sêng openly asked, "What can we do?"

Boastfully Pigsy with a smirk on his face, laughingly said, "Pigs have always been good at removing thorns. I'll just clear up this road all the way to the West." With his rake in hand, Pigsy started attacking the thorny bramble, clearing a path ahead as the party followed behind.

Suddenly a long creeper stretched out from the thorny bramble and hooked onto the Kasa and robes of the T'ang priest. A mysterious voice said, "T'ang priest, you have eaten my fruit yet you have paid me nothing for it!"

T'ang-sêng looked closely at the direction of the sound and realized that it was the angry voice of the Kou-chi spirit. Respectfully and with utmost courtesy, he said, "I am only a poor pious priest. I wander throughout the land without any permanent residence. I have no money or any valuables. I pray that you will be gracious and understanding. Virtuous be you, virtuous be you."

These words did nothing to satisfy the anger of the Kou-chi spirit who shouted out, "Since you have no money, then I'll take a drop of your blood!"

As the T'ang priest was trying to untangle himself, a creeper whipped out and struck his finger bringing forth a drop of his blood. A strange phenomenon occurred. As soon as the drop of blood dripped on the Kou-chi fruit, immediately all the once-green fruit suddenly changed to a bright blood-red color.

Legend has it that if the flesh or blood of the most holy T'ang priest is consumed, it would accord longevity and immortality. The Kou-chi plant having had a drop of his blood began to contain the essence of these properties. Because of this legend, it became a popular belief for people to use Kou-chi as a most beneficial herb in their diet. In preparing soups or congee, it became a tonic to strengthen and invigorate the body and accord good health. Kou-chi is believed to nourish the liver and strengthen the eyes with brightness and clear vision. Moreover, the frequent consuming of Kou-chi would accord longevity and general good health.

Kou-chi (*Lycium chinense*) is a common shrub in the northern and western provinces of China. It has soft, thin leaves, which can be eaten and small reddish-purple flowers. The fruits are small red berries, having a sweet but rather rough taste. This plant is considered to be tonic, cooling, constructive, prolonging life, improving the complexion and brightening the eyes. The shoots or young leaves are recommended to be used in all forms of wasting disease. Used in the form of a tea, they are recommended to quench thirst and to remove the unpleasant symptoms of pulmonary consumption. The root is a light yellowish-brown and has very little taste or smell. It is supposed to have special action on the kidneys and sexual organs, as well as those virtues ascribed to the leaves and is used as a hemastatic in bleeding of the gums and wounds. The seeds are similarly used.

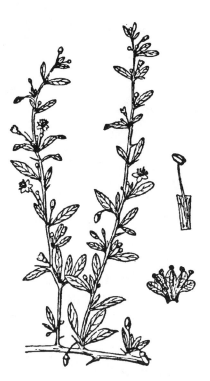

In the Mid-Autumn Festival celebration, Kou-chi is commonly used as a soup or even as a congee, however, it is sometimes served in other ways. In the Sung dynasty work, *T'ai-p'ing-ching hui-fang*, a 10th century book of remedies, there is an interesting recipe for strengthening the kidneys, sexual organs and back aches which calls for a soup made of Kou-chi leaves and pork kidneys, and flavored with some salt.

Kou-chi leaves could also be stir-fried with pork hearts and get the same medicinal results. It could even be made into an omelet. However, most popular among the Chinese are the following methods: one sweet and the other salted.

Sweetened Kou-chi Soup with Eggs

Ingredients:
1 bunch kou-chi   2 or 3 eggs
Rock sugar candy

Method:
1) Cut the young branches, tender shoots and leaves of the Kou-chi into 3-4 inch pieces and wash them thoroughly. Be careful as Kou-chi has thorns.
2) In a large pot, boil the Kou-chi with the unshelled eggs in water. After boiling for 30 minutes, remove the eggs and shell them.
3) Return the shelled eggs into the pot and add rock sugar. Boil for another 30 minutes.
4) With a pair of chopsticks, scrape off the kou-chi leaves from their hard stems and branches, discard these. Then with only leaves and tender shoots, boil for 5-10 minutes. Remove and serve hot.

Kou-chi Soup

Ingredients:
1 bunch kou-chi   1/2 lb. lean pork (sliced)
1 pair of chicken feet (optional)   3 Chinese red dates
salt

Method:
1) In a large pot of water, place pork and chicken feet. Remove the scum that is collected on the surface. Then to the clear liquid, add the Kou-chi along with the 3 Chinese red dates that have been scored with a knife. Bring to a second

boil. Cover and lower heat and simmer for 1-1/2 hours. Before serving, add salt.

Stewed Eel with Kou-chi berries

Ingredients:

2 eels

1/2 Tbs. Huang-ch'i

6 cups of chicken broth

1 tsp. salt

2 Tbs. Kou-chi berries

3 Tbs. salt

1 Tbs. wine

Method:

1) Clean eels by using 3 Tbs. of salt to scour the body in removing the sticky coating then rinse and wash with water. Cut the eels into 2 or 3 inch sections.

2) Place the eels into a large covered ceramic pot with the chicken broth. Add to it the Kuo-chi berries, Huang-ch'i, and wine. Place the ceramic covered pot into a pan of water and steam for 1 hour. Before serving, flavor with salt and adjust seasoning. Serve hot.

This dish is much favored by the Chinese during the autumn months when eels are eaten most. It is considered a tonic medicine which strengthens the body, sexual organs, bones and muscles, brightens the eyes, and alleviates weakness. Another very tasty dish that is frequently eaten by the Chinese uses the herb Jou-ts'ung-jung *(Orobanche ammophyla)*, which is a tonic in all of the wasting diseases and injuries. It is also considered as an aphrodisiac, promoting fertility in women and curing impotence in men. It is used in spermatorrhoea, menstrual difficulties, and all difficulties of the sexual organs.

Chicken and Jou-ts'ung-jung

Ingredients:

1/2 chicken or 1-1/2 chicken breast

3 large Chinese mushrooms

1/4 oz. Jou-ts'ung-jung

1 thick slice fresh ginger

3 Tbs. vegetable oil

2 Tbs. wine

1/2 cup water

1 scallion

5 cloves garlic

3 Tbs. soy sauce

1 Tbs. rock sugar

Method:

1) Soak mushrooms, remove stems and cut into small slices. Wash Jou-ts'ung-jung and cut into small slices.

2) Chop chicken into large pieces. Cut scallions into 2-3 inch sections.

3) Heat oil in pan and add ginger, scallions and garlic. Stir-fry until tender. Add water and bring to a boil. Add chicken, mushroom, soy sauce, wine and rock candy. Turn heat down and simmer for 5 minutes.

4) Add Jou-ts'ung-jung and boil for another 5 minutes. Pay strict attention that there should always be sufficient water so that it is not too dry. Add water when necessary. Remove and serve hot.

Chapter 6:
Mid-Autumn Festival Banquet

Formal dinners, banquets and feasts are quite different from the everyday meals both in service and the varieties of foods offered. Certain foods have special significance and must be served on specific occasions whether of celebration or sad commemoration. Definite courses are served at round tables seating 10 or 12 persons.

A first-class banquet may begin with dishes of pickles, peanuts and watermelon seeds served with spirits, wine or plain tea. These are not counted as a course since they are considered preliminaries.

Varieties of meats and cooked vegetables artistically arranged on a large platter are brought out first. This is called 'Ta-p'an-tzu', more commonly called 'P'ing-p'an'. This may be either hot or cold and may be served on one or two platters. Following this, are the 'Hsiao-tieh-ts'ai' or 'small dishes' of hot foods, which are usually stir-fried.

Next in order, there should be 7 or 9 hot 'big dishes' called 'Ta-ts'ai' or 'Ta-wan-êrh' served in turn. The main dish on the menu may be Shark's fin soup or another exquisite soup or chowder and at its appearance, toasts are drunk. Although this is translated as 'soup', it is really more of a thick chowder and is called 'Kêng' in Chinese rather than 'T'ang.'

According to Northern Chinese tradition, Peking Duck — its crisp skin garnished with green spring onions — would come next. Plates of thin small pancakes and special sauce accompany this dish.

The Cantonese-style banquet would here substitute Roast Suckling Pig with its succulent crackling skin skilfully cut into squares. Bird-nest soup (another kêng), duck, pigeon or other fowl and different kinds of foods such as abalone, prawns, snails or turtle would follow one after the other while a whole fish in its rich aromatic sauce is presented last. In Hawaii, the last dish in a 9-course dinner is 'K'ou-jou' or pot roast pork.

The guests help themselves from these common bowls, transferring what they need to the small plates in front of them by the dexterous use of their own chop-sticks or spoons. From time to time, they take wine with each other. With the appearance of each dish of food, toasts are made all around.

Following these 'big dishes' comes the tasty fried rice dish, 'Ch'ao-fan,' and noodles or vermicelli in soup. Sweet foods and tiny cakes on separate plates appear next. Sometimes plain rice is served with small dishes of salted eggs, pickled vegetables, sausages, roasted pork or salted fish in place of fried rice. In Hawaii, soup and plain rice is served at the end of the 9-course dinner.

The succession of dishes, follow an order similar to that of wine tasting, the delicate and mild-tasting dishes served first, progressing to the dishes with stronger seasoning to the sweet-sour fish towards the end. Between these dishes a pickled vegetable, mostly cucumbers or squash are eaten to 'clean' the palate before eating the next dish. The order of food served is somewhat at the discretion of the chef or at a restaurant, the *major-domo*.

Damp, hot towels which are handed round at the commencement of the meal, and after the Shark's fin soup, again make their appearance so everyone is freshened up by the time tea is served with fruit, sweetmeats and even cigarettes.

Less elaborate banquets will be comprised of 2 'small dishes' and 5 or 7 'big dishes.' The total number presented should be 5, 7 or 9 which are all 'Yang' numbers and considered lucky.

At every Chinese banquet, spirits and wine are served. The Chinese have a saying, "Wu-chiu pu-ch'êng-chia", literally: "It is not an auspicious event without wine" or the meaning, 'Food without wine is not considered a meal.' During the Mid-Autumn Festival celebration, a good grape wine, preferably a white wine is usually served. In the West, a good Sauterne, Beaujolais, or Riesling wine would be a good choice, although a white Zinfandel should be considered. Although wine and spirits are liberally used during celebrations, nevertheless, the Chinese are mindful that alcohol and vice are closely connected. The first wine-maker in China was disgraced for his discovery. He was Ti I who derived wine from fermented rice and wheat, a mixture with five different flavors. Overjoyed with his discovery, he presented the mixture through his daughter to the Emperor Yü, (2205 B.C.), the founder of the Hsia dynasty. After tasting the beverage, which gave him a stimulating sensation, Emperor Yü proscribed the mixture and ordered the discoverer to be exiled to a distant province. According to the *Shih-pên*, another discoverer of alcohol was Tu K'ang who made wine from rice. He is usually accepted as the first discoverer and as such is popularly known as the Patron Saint of wine dealers and restaurants. There are many stories of corruption and downfall of dynasties connected with alcohol. The last ruler of the Hsia dynasty, Chieh (1818 B.C.) was infatuated with his concubine Mei-hsi and revelled in debauchery and orgies until his downfall. The succeeding Shang dynasty's last ruler, Chou-hsin (1154 B.C.) created the most notorious case in wine-drinking history. To pander to the whims of his favorite Ta-chi, heavy taxes were levied to build the famous Deer Terrace. In this terrace was a 'wine pond' and a 'meat forest' with viands of every description hanging on the trees nearby. These outlandish excesses led to their downfall. With such reminders in popular stories and lore, the Chinese have become very temperate in their consumption of wine. However, it is always present in all rituals and celebrations.

A sumptuous Chinese dinner is incomplete without the traditional drinking games. One of these games is the 'Chiu-ling,' a poetry game in which any number of persons could participate. A leader is chosen, usually the host, who gives a number of 'key' words to be used as rhymes, or the first words of the lines. The leader commences by composing a line containing the first 'key' word in the stipulated place. The next person on his right composes another line containing the second 'key' word, keeping in rhyme with the first line — and so on, until all the 'key' words are used and the poem completed. If a line is well composed, all join in drinking to the author's health and good fortune. However, the author has to drink a cup alone if he commits a blunder. There are many patterns of forming the poetry, but the principles are the same. There is also a variation of this game using a set of dominos called 'P'ai-chiu-ling.'

A drinking game adapted from the 'Chi-ku chuan-mei' or 'Beating the drum to hasten the blooming of blossoms,' is another game in which any number of players may participate. A person sits behind a screen beating a drum while the guests at the table pass a filled cup of wine from one to another. The movement of passing the cup must quicken and then slow down as the beat of the drum indicates. If one spills the cup or happens to be holding the cup when the drum suddenly stops, he must drink the contents of the cup, and the game is again resumed. This is quite similar to the Western game of musical chairs.

There is a variation of this game played by the literati where instead of passing a cup of wine, a sheet of paper and pen were supplied. Taking a specific topic like the 'Mid-Autumn Festival celebration,' as the subject, the guests were to compose a poem word by word. After the leader wrote the first word, he would hand the paper and pen to the person to his right. The next person would write another word beneath it which had to make sense when joined with the first. The third man then took his turn, and so on. Meanwhile the drum kept on beating. If it beat loudly, the writing had to be done quickly. If it beat slowly, then the writer could take his time to think. Occasionally, the drum would stop and the one who had the paper and pen in hand had to drink a cup of wine. He was then excused from writing and passed the writing materials to the next person.

The most popular and commonly played drinking game is the finger-guessing game. This game is called 'Ts'ai-mei' or 'Ts'ai-ch'üan,' *Morra* in Italy, or the *Micare digitus* of the Old Romans. It is an amusing and witty drinking game played by two persons. This game consists of showing the fingers to each other across the table and calling out a number to indicate the sum of the combined fingers at the same moment. The loser has to take a drink of wine. This convivial game is common among all ranks and the boisterous merriment it creates is frequently heard at Chinese banquets.

To attempt to describe all the foods and events of Chinese banquets would necessitate a full study. However, it may be more feasible to discuss a sampling of the foods, in addition to what had been discussed in earlier Chapters, that are favored and eaten during the Mid-Autumn Festival celebration and some of the ways they are prepared. It must be remembered that the celebration of the Moon Festival is really two events, one as a formal dinner and the other as a later meal with Moon Cakes and other delicacies served. In earlier times, amongst the rich, this celebration may include a total of three complete meals, one at noon time, another in early evening and the third, late at night. However, many Chinese families nowadays celebrate it with a dinner and later eat Moon Cakes and other delicacies as desserts. Some additional special recipes follow.

Tossed Crab meat and Cucumbers

Ingredients:

2 cups peeled, seeded, and thinly sliced cucumbers

1 cup crab meat (small can)	1 Tbs. soy sauce
1-1/2 tsp. vinegar	1 tsp. sesame seed oil
1 tsp. sugar	1 tsp. ginger (finely minced)

Method:

Mix and toss all ingredients together in a bowl and chill in refrigerator. Remove and place in serving platter and serve chilled.

Tossed Jellyfish and Turnips

Ingredients:

1 lb. jellyfish	1 cup turnips [daikon] (shredded)
1/2 tsp. salt	1 Tbs. vinegar
1 Tbs. soy sauce	2 Tbs. sugar
1 Tbs. sesame seed oil	

Method:

1) Soak jellyfish in water overnight. Cut in thin strips, 2 inches in length. Rinse in boiling water. Drain and set aside.

2) Shred turnips and add salt and let stand for 1 hour. Drain all liquid from the turnips and set aside.

3) Combine and mix turnips and jellyfish. Add soy sauce, vinegar, sesame seed oil, and sugar. Chill in refrigerator and serve cold.

Pickled Mustard Cabbage

Ingredients:

3 lbs. of Chinese Mustard cabbage (chieh-ts'ai or Kaai-tsoi)

1 cup water	1 cup light brown sugar
1/2 cup vinegar	2 tsp. salt
1 tsp. wine	

Method:

1) Wash the mustard cabbage and allow to wilt and dry. Cut off most of the leafy parts. Then cut cross-grain into 1/2 inch pieces. 3 lbs. of mustard cabbage should yield about 6 cups. Set aside.

2) In a deep pan, boil water and add sugar and vinegar. When sugar has completely dissolved, add mustard cabbage and bring to a second boil. Stir occasionally. Remove from heat and add salt and wine. Set aside to cool. Place in a tightly sealed container and refrigerate overnight. Serve cold.

Cucumbers in Milk Sauce

Ingredients:

1 medium size cucumber	1 cup milk
1/2 cup water	1 tsp. cornstarch
1/2 tsp. salt	2-3 Tbs. oil
pinch of pepper	

Method:

1) Peel cucumbers, remove seeds and cut lengthwise into long 2-inch pieces.

2) Heat oil in pan and add cucumbers. Stir-fry until cooked. Add cornstarch, salt, pepper, water into milk. Pour milk mixture onto cucumbers and stir until sauce is slightly thickened. Serve hot.

Eels

Eels, called Shan-yü by the Chinese, belong to a large order of elongated cylindrical fish with long dorsal and anal fins. The Chinese and Japanese utilize as food, the fresh water fish of the class *Osteichthyes*, order *Anguilliformes*, family *Anguillidae.* It belongs to the same genus as, and bears close resemblance in appearance to the eels of North America.

Freshwater eels have long been a significant food in both China and Japan as well as in Europe, but they are not so popular in North America where most people find them too oily and rich. Smoked eels, on the other hand, are popular in North America even though they are so rich. Some saltwater eels, such as Morays *(Muraenidae)* and Congee *(Congridae)* eels, are eaten in various parts of the world, but to a far lesser extent than freshwater eels.

In China and Japan, eels seem to have been considered a nourishing and medicinal food since ancient times. The custom of eating eels at the height of summer and early autumn began in ancient times. During the 6th-8th lunar months, fried in oil or broiled with a teriyaki sauce, they have an excellent flavor. There is little waste and they contain much fish oil rich in vitamin A. The following are some recipes for preparing eels.

Stir-fried Eels

Ingredients:

2 lbs. eel	3 Tbs. soy sauce
2 cloves garlic (minced)	1 piece ginger (shredded)
1 scallion (chopped)	1 tsp. sugar
1/2 tsp. red pepper (shredded)	1 tsp. cornstarch
1 Tbs. wine	MSG
oil for deep frying	Chinese parsley for garnishing

Method:
1) Bone and cut eel into long pieces.
2) Heat oil and nearing the boil, add eels and fry for 30-40 seconds. Remove, drain and set aside.
3) Pour out oil, leaving about 2 Tbs. remaining. Stir-fry ginger and add wine, soy sauce, sugar, MSG and eels. Stir-fry quickly over high heat. Mix cornstarch with 2 tsp. water and 1 Tbs. oil. Add mixture and stir-fry quickly. Remove and place in serving plate. Sprinkle chopped garlic, shredded ginger and red pepper.
4) Heat 2 Tbs. oil. When very hot, pour it over the eels and garnish with parsley.

Eels with Celery

Ingredients:

1 lb. eels	1-1/4 cup celery (shredded)
1/4 tsp. salt	1 slice ginger (shredded)

1/4 tsp. sugar
1 Tbs. soy sauce
1 Tbs. sesame seed oil
1/4 tsp. MSG
vegetable oil for deep frying

1/4 tsp. cornstarch
1 tsp. vinegar
2 red peppers (shredded)
1/2 Tbs. hot bean paste (Tou-pan-chiang)

Method:

1) Cut eel into 3-inch strips (1/2 inch wide)
2) Cut celery lengthwise into 3-4 inch strips (1/2 inch wide).
3) Remove seeds from red peppers and julienne.
4) Combine the seasoning by mixing salt, MSG, sugar, cornstarch, soy sauce, vinegar, sesame seed oil and 1 Tbs. water in a bowl. Blend thoroughly and set aside.
5) Heat oil in pan. When hot, place eel into pan and deep fry for 30-40 seconds. Remove, drain and set aside.
6) Pour out oil, leaving only 2 Tbs. of oil remaining. Add ginger, red pepper and hot bean paste. Stir-fry.
7) Add celery and stir-fry until celery is soft. Add eel and seasoning mixture. Stir-fry rapidly and remove. Serve hot.

Carp

Carp is commonly eaten by the Chinese throughout the year. On festivals and happy occasions, Carp is always served. The carp (*Cyprinus carpio*) is a freshwater fish of the class *Osteichthyes*, order *Cypriniformes*, family *Cyprinidae*. It is distributed in the temperate and subtropical zones in Asia and Europe and lives in lakes, marshes, ponds and rivers. It grows to over 1 meter (39 inches) in length. It is an important food fish in China and Japan. The carp called Li-yü in Chinese is a homonym for 'an abundance of profit or success.' In addition, it serves as a symbol for strength and perseverance. This concept originated from a Chinese legend of a carp that was transformed into a dragon after it had jumped up a waterfall in the upper reaches of the Yellow River. In all celebrations of promotions and literary accomplishment, Carp is always served. The following are some recipes.

Sweet-sour Carp

Ingredients:

1 large carp
3 Tbs. soy sauce
1 Tbs. wine
4 Tbs. oil
1 clove garlic

2 scallions (shredded)
1 small piece ginger
3 Chinese mushrooms (julienne)
4 Tbs. carrot (julienne)
4 Tbs. bamboo shoots (julienne)

Seasoning:

1 Tbs. soy sauce
1 tsp. salt
4 Tbs. vinegar
MSG

6 Tbs. sugar
3/4 cup chicken stock
2 Tbs. ketchup

Method:

1) After cleaning fish, score on both sides with slanting deep diagonal cuts about 1 to 1-1/2 inches apart. Coat fish with cornstarch. Deep-fry fish in oil until crispy. Remove and set aside.

2) In a pan with 2 Tbs. of oil, stir-fry mushrooms, carrots, garlic, scallions, ginger, bamboo shoots. Add seasoning and continue to stir-fry. Thicken with mixture of cornstarch and water.

3) Pour thickened mixture over fried fish. Serve hot.

Braised Carp in Spicy Sauce

Ingredients:

1 large carp	1/2 cup celery (cut in strips)
1/4 cup scallions (chopped)	1 Tbs. ginger (finely chopped)
1 Tbs. garlic (finely chopped)	2 cups chicken stock
1/4 tsp. pepper	2 Tbs. wine
1/4 tsp. MSG	1 tsp. soy sauce
1/2 tsp. sugar	1/2 tsp. vinegar
1-1/2 Tbs. cornstarch	oil for deep frying
1 Tbs. hot bean paste (tou-pan-chiang)	
1/2 tsp. salt	

Method:

1) After cleaning fish, score on both sides with slanting deep diagonal cuts about 1 to 1-1/2 inches apart. Coat fish with cornstarch. Deep-fry in oil until crispy. Remove and set aside.

2) Heat 2 Tbs. oil in a pan. Add the hot bean paste, ginger and garlic and stir-fry over moderate heat. When the aroma is released, pour in the chicken stock. Season with salt, wine, soy sauce, sugar, pepper and MSG. Add fish, cover and simmer for 15 minutes. Shake the pan occasionally so that the fish does not burn.

3) When the fish is cooked through, remove and place on a serving platter. Add the celery and scallions to the remaining liquid and thicken with a mixture of cornstarch and water. Add vinegar and 1 Tbs. of oil. Pour the sauce over the fish and serve hot.

Duck

Although there are some Chicken recipes included, chicken is not usually served in Mid-Autumn Festival dinners. Duck is the favored dish along with lamb or mutton. Other dishes would be frog, crabs and other fish dishes. The following are some representative recipes.

Eight-precious Stuffed Duck — I

Ingredients:

1 4-lbs. duck (boned and cleaned)

1/4 cup Chinese mushrooms (diced)	1/4 pearl barley
1/4 cup water chestnuts (diced)	2 tsp. wine
1/4 cup gingko nuts (canned)	2 cups chicken stock
1/4 cup lotus seeds	1 tsp. salt
1/2 tsp. MSG	

Method:
1) Boil barley in water until soft. Remove, rinse and soak in cold water. Soak mushrooms, lotus seeds, gingko nuts and water chestnuts in water. Drain and set aside.
2) Drain barley and mix with mushrooms, lotus seeds, gingko nuts and water chestnuts. Season with salt, wine and MSG. Combine and mix thoroughly.
3) Stuff duck with mixture and sew up opening.
4) Place duck in a large pan with chicken stock. Place in a steamer. Cover and steam for 3-4 hours. Reserve any liquid and thicken with a mixture of cornstarch and water. Pour over duck. Serve hot.

Eight-precious Stuffed Duck — II

Ingredients:

1 4-lbs. duck (boned and cleaned)
1 cup glutinous rice
3 pts. water
2 Tbs. dried shrimp
3 Tbs. wine
1 Tbs. Chinese mushrooms (diced)
3 Tbs. soy sauce
1/4 cup sugar
3 cups chicken stock

1 Tbs. pork (diced)
1 Tbs. chestnuts (diced)
1 Tbs. gingko nuts (canned)
1 Tbs. lotus seeds
1 Tbs. bamboo shoots (diced)
2 Tbs. cooked ham (diced)
1 scallion (chopped)
1 small piece ginger

Method:
1) Soak dried mushrooms, dried shrimp, lotus seeds, all in separate bowls and set aside.
2) Into boiling water, place the glutinous rice and allow to boil for 5 minutes. Remove, drain and allow to soak in cold water for 3-5 minutes. Drain and set aside.
3) In a large bowl, place glutinous rice and add pork, chestnuts, dried shrimp, ham, gingko nuts, lotus seeds, mushrooms, bamboo shoots, 1 Tbs. each of wine and soy sauce. Mix thoroughly.
4) Stuff mixture into the duck and sew up the opening.
5) Place the stuffed duck in a large pan. Add 2 Tbs. each of wine and soy sauce, scallions, ginger and chicken stock. Bring to a boil. Lower heat, cover and simmer for 2 hours. Remove and serve hot.

Eight-precious Stuffed Duck — III

Ingredients:

1 4-lbs. duck (boned and cleaned)
1/2 cup taro (diced)
1/2 cup lotus seeds
1/2 cup bamboo shoots (diced)
3 Chinese mushrooms (diced)
2 Tbs. carrot (diced)
1 tsp. sesame seed oil
1 slice ginger
1/4 cup lean pork (diced)

4 scallions (chopped)
1/4 tsp. black pepper
2 Tbs. soy sauce
1/2 tsp. MSG
1/2 tsp. salt
1/2 Tbs. flour
1/2 tsp. cornstarch
oil for deep-frying

Method:

1) Deep-fry taro. Remove, drain and set aside.

2) Heat 3 Tbs. of oil in a pan and stir-fry the taro, pork, lotus seeds, bamboo shoots, mushrooms, carrot and scallions. Add black pepper, MSG, salt, wine, sesame seed oil and flour. Mix thoroughly and continue to stir-fry until cooked. Remove and set aside.

3) Stuff mixture into duck and sew up opening. Rub the outside of the duck with 2 Tbs. of soy sauce.

4) Deep-fry duck until golden brown. Remove and allow to cool. Brush 1 Tbs. wine over the duck. Place duck in a pan and steam over high heat for 2 hours.

5) Remove the duck and place on a serving platter. Drain the pan of the juices from steaming the duck and thicken with a mixture of cornstarch and water in a sauce pan. Pour over duck. Serve hot.

Stewed Duck with Chestnuts

Ingredients:

1 4-lbs. duck	6 Chinese mushrooms (quartered)
2 cups chestnuts (shelled)	1 Tbs. ginger (minced)
1 tsp. light soy sauce	1 tsp. sesame seed oil
1 clove garlic (minced)	1 sm. piece dried orange peel
1 tsp. wine	1 tsp. salt
1 scallion (chopped)	1 tsp. cornstarch

Method:

1) Chop duck into bite-sized pieces. Marinate duck with light soy sauce, sugar and cornstarch. Allow to stand for 20 minutes.

2) Heat a pan with oil and brown the duck pieces. Remove and set aside.

3) Boil chestnuts in water until soft. If there are any skins, remove them.

4) Heat pan with 1 Tbs. oil. Add scallions, ginger, mushrooms, chestnuts and salt. Add duck pieces and stir-fry. Add enough water to cover. Stew duck for 45 minutes. Serve hot.

Lamb

Lamb in Aspic

Ingredients:

1 lb. lamb shoulder (boned)	4 cups water
2 Tbs. soy sauce	2 strips agar-agar
2 Tbs. sugar	1 carrot (cut into large pieces)
1 clove garlic	1 star anise (Pa-chiao)
1 scallion	1 piece ginger
1 Tbs. wine	MSG

Method:

1) Cut lamb into 2-inch pieces. Place lamb into pan with water to cover. Bring to a boil and cook for 3-4 minutes. Pour off all water. Add to the lamb, garlic, star anise, scallion, ginger, wine, soy sauce and carrot and 4 cups of water. Bring to a boil, reduce heat and simmer 1-1/2 hours.

2) Remove and discard garlic, star anise, scallion, ginger and carrot. Add sugar and agar-agar and simmer for 1/2 hour. Pour into a flat bottom pan. Cool and refrigerate. Cut and serve cold.

Stewed Mutton

Ingredients:

2 lbs. mutton

1 turnip

4 cloves garlic

1 small head of lettuce

2 sprigs Chinese parsley for garnish

10 water chestnuts

1/2 cup ginger (thinly sliced)

1 small piece orange peel (Kuo-p'i)

4 cups chicken stock

Seasoning:

1/4 tsp. salt

1 Tbs. wine

2 Tbs. fermented bean curd (Nan-ju)

1 block Chinese brown sugar (huang-t'ang)

1 Tbs. ground bean sauce (yüan-sai-chiang)

Method:

1) Cut mutton into pieces and dry fry in hot pan until dry. Remove and set aside.

2) Cut turnip and lettuce into thick pieces. Chop parsley. Soak and shred orange peel. Place all aside.

3) In a deep pan, heat 2 Tbs. oil and add ginger, garlic, fermented bean curd and bean paste. Stir-fry and add mutton. Sprinkle wine, and add 4 cups chicken stock and bring to a boil. Add water chestnuts and orange peel. Lower heat and stew for 40 minutes. Add brown sugar and turnips and stew for another 30 minutes. Adjust seasonings to taste. Add parsley and lettuce and cook for 2-3 minutes. Serve hot.

Soups and Other Dishes

Sauteed Frog Legs with Vegetables

Ingredients:

1-1/2 lbs. frog legs (chopped)

1/2 medium size carrot (sliced)

1 green pepper (seeded & sliced)

1 piece ginger (minced)

2 cloves garlic (minced)

1 Tbs. wine

1/2 cup bamboo shoots (sliced)

1 Tbs. soy sauce

1 scallion (cut)

1 Tbs. cornstarch

1/2 tsp. salt

1/2 tsp. sugar

1/2 tsp. MSG

1 tsp. sesame seed oil

1/4 tsp. black pepper

1 tsp. oyster sauce

Method:

1) Cut frog legs into bite size pieces. Coat with 1/2 Tbs. cornstarch and set aside.

2) Combine salt, sugar, oyster sauce, black pepper, soy sauce, MSG, sesame seed oil, 1 tsp. cornstarch and 1 Tbs. water in a bowl. Blend and mix evenly. Set aside.

3) In a pan, heat some oil and deep fry frog legs pieces until the cornstarch coating is cooked. Remove and set aside.

4) Stir-fry scallion, ginger, garlic with 1 Tbs. of oil. Add green peppers, bamboo shoots, carrots. Stir rapidly. Add 1 Tbs. wine, frog legs and seasoning mixture. Stir-fry over high heat and remove. Serve hot.

Frog Legs and Chicken

Ingredients:

1/2 chicken breast (boned and diced)	1 tsp. salt
1/2 lb. frog legs (cut in bite size pieces)	1/2 cup chicken stock
1/4 cup fresh mushrooms (cut in pieces)	1 tsp. sugar
2 Tbs. ginger (sliced)	2 tsp. wine
2 Tbs. scallions (chopped)	4 Tbs. vegetable oil
1/2 tsp. MSG	2 Tbs. cornstarch
1 tsp. light soy sauce	

Method:

1) In a large bowl, place chicken and frog legs. Season with wine, salt, cornstarch and MSG. Set aside.

2) Heat 4 Tbs. oil in a pan. Add ginger and scallions. Stir-fry. Add chicken and frog legs, mushrooms and continue to stir-fry. When meat is nearly cooked, add chicken stock. Adjust seasonings and thicken with mixture of cornstarch and water. Serve hot.

Sauteed Frog Legs and Chicken Livers

Ingredients:

1-1/2 lbs. frog legs (cut in bite size pieces)	
1/2 cup chicken livers	1 tsp. wine
6 Chinese mushrooms (Quartered)	1 Tbs. oil
1 Tbs. light soy sauce	1 tsp. sugar
1 scallion (cut in 2 inch lengths)	1 Tbs. ginger (minced)
1 cup Chinese broccoli (cut in 2 in. lengths)	1 tsp. cornstarch
1/2 tsp. MSG	

Method:

1) Place frog legs in a bowl and season with salt, sugar, MSG, light soy sauce, wine and cornstarch. Set aside.

2) Heat 1 Tbs. oil in pan. Add ginger, scallions, and frog legs. Stir-fry. Add chicken liver, mushrooms, and broccoli and cook for a few minutes until meat is tender. Serve hot.

Sausages and Cabbage

Ingredients:

1 Chinese sausage (La-ch'ang)	1 slice ginger (minced)
1 duck liver sausage (Ya-jun-ch'ang)	3/4 cup Napa cabbage

Seasoning:

1/2 tsp. salt	1/2 tsp. sugar
1 tsp. light soy sauce	

Method:

1) Pour hot water over the sausages and allow to soak for 5 minutes. Remove, pat dry and cut in slices. Set aside.

2) Coarse cut the Napa Cabbage into 3/4 inch strips.

3) Heat 1 Tbs. oil in pan. Add sausages and lightly stir-fry. Remove and set aside.

4) Heat pan with 2 Tbs. oil. Add ginger and Napa cabbage. Stir-fry. Add 2 Tbs. water and all the seasoning. When the cabbage is limp, add sausages. Stir-fry. Serve hot.

Taro, Fish and Roast Pork Casserole

Ingredients:

1 cup taro (sliced)	1/2 lb. fish fillet (cut in large slices)
2 stalks scallions	1/2 lb. roast belly pork (huo-nan)
1/4 tsp. sugar	2 cups water

Marinade:

1-1/2 tsp. light soy sauce	2 tsp. cornstarch
Pinch of white pepper	

Method:

1) Peel and slice taro. Pour hot water over the taro and then pat dry. Heat a small amount of oil in a pan and fry the taro. Remove and drain. Set aside.

2) Cut Roast pork into bite sized pieces and set aside. Cut the fish fillets into large slices and place in bowl with marinade. Allow to stand for 10-15 minutes. After marinated, quickly fry fish in oil, remove, drain and set aside.

3) In a casserole pan, heat 1 Tbs. oil. Add ginger, taro, roast pork, sugar and 2 cups of water. Bring to a boil. Lower heat and simmer for 5-10 minutes. Add fish and scallions (white parts only) and cook for another 3 minutes. Sprinkle some sesame seed oil over it and serve hot.

Pineapple Fried Rice

Ingredients:

1/2 fresh pineapple	2 large fresh mushrooms (diced)
2 Tbs. shredded dried pork (jou-sung)	
2 Chinese mushrooms (diced)	
1 Tbs. green peas	1 egg (beaten)
2-1/2 cups cooked rice	1/2 tsp. salt

Method:

1) Hollow out the pineapple and mince the pineapple scooped out. Set aside.

2) Heat a pan with a small amount of oil. Add mushrooms, minced pineapple and green peas. Stir-fry. Remove from pan and set aside.

3) Heat 2 Tbs. oil in pan. Add cooked rice, 1/2 tsp. salt. Stir-fry until rice is a bit dry and slightly toasted. Add mushrooms, pineapple and green peas. Mix and stir-fry. Slowly dribble in the beaten egg while stir-frying. When everything is cooked, remove and place in hollow of pineapple. Sprinkle shredded dried pork over fried rice. Serve hot.

Sandwiched Winter Melon and Ham in Broth

Ingredients:

2 lbs. winter melon	1/2 ham
3 Chinese mushrooms	1 tsp. salt
1-1/2 Tbs. wine	1 scallion
6 Cups chicken stock	MSG

Method:

1) Remove winter melon rind. Cut into 12-14 thick slices. Make an incision into the middle of each piece, but do not cut through.

2) Cut ham into as many slices as slices of winter melon. Place ham on a plate and steam with scallions and 1 Tbs. wine, 2 Tbs. sugar. Remove and set aside.

3) Place a piece of ham inside each slice of winter melon. Arrange in a deep dish. Add mushrooms, 1 tsp. salt, MSG, 1/2 tsp. wine and 6 cups of chicken stock. Place in steamer and steam for 1 hour. Remove and serve hot.

Laver Soup

Ingredients:

4 cups chicken stock	1 Tbs. dried shrimp (minced)
1 tbs. soy sauce	1 tsp. scallions (chopped)
1 tsp. sesame seed oil	4 sheets laver (tzu-ts'ai)

Method:

In a pot, bring chicken stock to a boil. Add minced dried shrimp, soy sauce, scallions and sesame seed oil. Add laver and remove from heat. Serve hot.

Seaweed and Fish ball Soup

Ingredients:

1/2 lb. fish cake	1/2 cup lean pork (julienne)
6 cups chicken stock	1 Tbs. soy sauce
1/2 tsp. salt	1/2 tsp. MSG
1 tsp. scallion (minced)	1 8-inch strip of kelp (hai-tai)
1/2 cup seaweed (hai-ts'ao)	1 tsp. cornstarch
2 Tbs. water chestnut (minced)	1 tsp. wine

Method:

1) Pour hot water over both the kelp and the seaweed and allow to soak in water. When ready to use, drain and set aside.

2) In a bowl, mix fish cake with minced water chestnut and scallions. Set aside. In another bowl, mix the pork strips with wine and cornstarch. Set aside.

3) Bring the chicken stock to a boil. Add the pork strips, kelp and seaweed. Boil for 10 minutes.

4) Taking a spoon, scoop and form small fish balls and drop into the boiling soup. Add all other seasonings. Lower heat and simmer for 5-10 minutes. Adjust seasoning and serve hot.

Fish Cake Spinach Soup

Ingredients:

1/2 lb. fish cake	1 egg white
1/4 tsp. ginger	1 tsp. salt
1 tsp. wine	1/4 tsp. MSG
1 Tbs. cornstarch	5 cups chicken broth
1/2 lb. spinach leaves	

Seasoning:

1 tsp. salt	1 Tbs. wine
1/2 tsp. MSG	

Method:

1) Wash and cut spinach leaves. Drain and set aside.

2) Place chicken stock in a pan and bring to a boil.

3) Beat egg white slightly. Add to fish cake and blend well. Add ginger, salt, wine, MSG and a mixture of 1 Tbs. cornstarch in 5 Tbs. water. Mix well. Form balls and drop into boiling soup.

4) Into the boiling soup, add spinach leaves and bring to a second boil. Add seasoning. Boil for another 2-3 minutes. Remove and serve hot.

Coconut Snow Balls

Ingredients:

2 cups glutinous rice flour	1/4 cup water
3 Tbs. sugar	4 Tbs. vegetable shortening
1/2 cup wheat starch (têng-mien-fên)	
1/4 cup boiling water	

Filling:

1-1/4 cups shredded coconut or flakes	1 cup sugar
1/2 cup unsalted peanuts	

Method:

1) Sift glutinous rice flour on table or pastry board. Make a depression in the center and slowly pour in water. Knead into a soft dough. Set aside.

2) Sift wheat starch in a mixing bowl. Pour in boiling water. Mix and stir until completely blended and smooth. Set aside.

3) Mix the chopped nuts, sugar and 1 cup of coconut together for a filling and set aside.

4) Knead both doughs together, adding sugar and vegetable shortening. Mix thoroughly.

5) Steam 2/3 of the dough for 15 minutes. Take out and knead together with the remaining 1/3 dough.

6) Roll out dough into a long sausage shape and cut into 36-40 pieces. Roll out each piece into a ball and shape into a small nest. Spoon some filling into the center. Draw edges together to enclose and lightly roll into a ball.

7) Place into steamer and steam for 3-4 minutes. Remove and roll in 1/4 cup shredded coconut or flakes. Decorate with a piece of cut cherry. Serve either hot or cold.

GLOSSARY OF CHINESE TERMS

Ah-nan
阿南

An
安

An P'ing
安平

Ch'a-shao
义燒

Ch'a-shao-su
义燒酥

Chang Hsiao-kuei
張小貴

Chang Lao-kuei
張老貴

Ch'ang-O
嫦娥

Ch'ang-O pên-yüeh
嫦娥奔月

Ch'ang-shêng-kuo
長生菓

Chang Shih-ch'êng
張世誠

Chao
趙

Ch'ao-fan
炒飯

Chao-hun
招魂

Ch'ao-mi-fên
炒米粉

Chê-tung
浙東

Ch'ên
辰

Ch'ên I
陳禕

Chên-p'ing
鎮平

Ch'ên Yu-liang
陳有諒

Chêng
政

Chêng-ping
丞餅

Ch'i
齊

Ch'i Chi-kuang
戚繼光

Chi-ku chuan-mei
擊鼓傳梅

Ch'i-lin
麒麟

Ch'i-min yao-shu
齊民要術

Ch'i-nan
齊南

Ch'i-pao-chou
七寶粥

chia
甲

Chia (surname)
賈

Chia Ssu-hsieh
賈思勰

Chiao
蕉

Chiao-ch'i
脚氣

Chiao-ch'i chih-fa tsung-yao
脚氣治法總要

Chiao-ku
蕉姑

Chiao-yen
椒鹽

Chieh-ts'ai
芥菜

Chieh-yüan
解元

Ch'ien-lung
乾隆

Chien-shui
鹼水

Chih-hsien
知縣

Chih-nü
織女

Ch'in
秦

Chin-hua
金華

Ch'in I
秦怡

Chin-tui
金推

Chin-t'ui
金腿

Chin-kuei yao-lüeh
金匱要略

Chin-shih
進士

Ch'ing
清

Ch'ing-pai lei-ch'ao
清稗類鈔

Ch'ing-shui mei-kuei yüeh-ping
清水玫瑰月餅

Ch'ing-sung
青松

Ch'ing-t'ien
青田

Ch'iu-ch'ü
秋菊

Chiu-huang
韮黃

Chiu-ling
酒令

Cho-chung-chih
酌中志

Chou (Congee)
粥

Chou
周

Chou-hsin
紂辛

Chou-i
周易

Chou Mi
周密

Ch'u
楚

Ch'u-chou
處州

Chu-sha-ping
朱砂餅

Chü-ju
粔籹

Ch'u-tz'u
楚辭

Ch'ü Yüan
屈原

Chu Yüan-chang
朱元璋

Ch'üeh-tê
缺德

Chung-ch'iu
中秋

Chung-ch'iu-chieh
中秋節

Chuseok
추석 (秋夕)

Daikon
だいこん (大根)

Dango
だんご (團子)

Erh
餌

Erh-hsien-chü
二仙居

Fan-mao
翻毛

Fang Kuo-chên
方國珍

Fang-shih
方士

Fu-ling
茯苓

Fu-ling chia-ping
茯苓夾餅

Fu-sang
扶桑

Fu-shu
福鼠

Hai-chê-p'i
海哲皮

Hai-tai
海苔

Hai-ts'ao
海藻

Han
韓

Han-jên
漢人

Han Yü
韓瑜

Ho-shên
和珅

Hsi-kua
西瓜

Hsi-kua-shuang
西瓜霜

Hsi-yu-chi
西遊記

Hsia
夏

Hsia Chi-kang
夏紀綱

Hsiao-mu-wa
小木娃

Hsiao-tieh-ts'ai
小碟菜

Hsieh-p'ing-an
謝平安

Hsien
縣

Hsiu-ts'ai
秀才

Hsin
辛

Hsing
餳

Hsing (Smell or taste)
腥

Hsing (Sweet meats)
餳

Hsing-hua
興化

Hsing-hua (shan)
杏花山

Hsü K'o
徐珂

Hsü Shou-hui
徐壽輝

Hsüan-tsang
玄奘

Hsüeh-li
雪梨

Hsüeh Tê
薛德

Hu-kuang
湖廣

Hu-ssu-hui
忽思慧

Hua-shêng
花生

Huai
淮

Huan
桓

Huan-ping
環餅

Huang-ch'i
黃耆

Huang-ling tou-sha su
黃菱豆砂酥

Huang-t'ang
黃糖

Hung-ling
紅菱 (洪靈)

Hung-ling lien-jung su
紅菱蓮蓉酥

Hung-lou-mêng
紅樓夢

Hung-shih
紅柿

Huo-nan
火腩

Huo-t'ui yüeh-ping
火腿月餅

I-ching
易經

I-t'ang
餳餹

Imo
いも(芋)

Imo meigetsu
芋美月

Jên Han
任漢

Jo-jou ch'iang-shih
弱肉強食

Jou-sung
肉鬆

Jou-ts'ung-jung
肉蓯蓉

Jugoya
十五夜

Jung
容

Jung-chou
容州

Kaai-tsoi
芥菜

Kan-ch'êng
干乘

K'ang-hsi
康熙

Kao
糕

Kao-an
高安

Kao-huan
膏環

Kao-ping
糕餅

Kawi
가위(嘉俳)

Kêng
羹

Kou-chi
枸杞

Kou-jou
㧓肉

Kua-tzu
瓜子

Kuan-chia-kung
管家公

Kuan-tung
關東

Kuang-han yüeh-kung
廣寒月宮

Kung-p'in
貢品

Kuo-kua
菓瓜

Kuo-niu
蝸牛

Kuo-p'i
菓皮

Kuo Tzu-hsing
郭子興

La-ch'ang
臘腸

La-pa
臘八

La-pa-chou
臘八粥

La-ya
臘鴨

Lao-p'o yüeh-ping
老婆月餅

Lao-t'ou-lo
老頭樂

Li (surname)
李

li
里

Li-chi
禮記

Li-chia-chuang
李家庄

Li Shih-chên
李時珍

Li-yü
鯉魚

Lien-jung
蓮蓉

Lien-jung (Happy union)
聯容

Lin I
林邑

Ling
靈

Ling (Water Caltrop)
菱

Ling-fên
菱粉

Ling-hua
菱花

Liu Chi
劉基

Liu Fang-po
劉方伯

Liu Fu-t'ung
劉福通

Liu Jo-yü
劉若遇

Liu Kuang-ch'i
劉廣濟

Liu Po-wên
劉伯溫

Liu Tsu-wang
劉祖望

Liu-tu
六都

Lo
駱

Lo Hua-shêng
駱花生

Lo-hua-shêng (Peanut)
落花生

Lo Pin-wang
駱賓王

Lo-ti shêng-kên
落地生根

Loh-shai-kaai
撈世界

lü
閭

Lu-i-hsiang
綠衣香

Lu-i ku-niang
綠衣姑娘

Lu Ming-shang
魯明善

Lu-yu
碌柚

Ma-ch'ih-ts'ao
馬齒草

Man-fu
滿福

Mao
卯

Mei-hsi
妹喜

Mi-kuan-êrh
蜜罐兒

Min-ch'ing
閩清

Ming
明

Ming-ching kao-hsüan
明鏡高懸

Ming-fu
明府

Mou
畝

Mu
木

Nan-hsün
南巡

Nan-jên
南人

Nan-ju
南乳

Nien-kao
年糕

Nien-t'ou
捻頭

No-mi-fên
糯米粉

Nung-sang-i-shih tso-yao
農桑衣食撮要

Pa-chiao
八角

P'ai-chiu-ling
牌酒令

Pai-kuo hsien-i
白菓仙醫

Pai-ling wu-jên su
白菱五仁酥

Pai-shih
白柿

P'an (shan)
盤山

P'an-ku
盤古

Pao-ping
包餅

Pao-tzu
飽子

Pên-ts'ao
本草

Pên-ts'ao kang-mu
本草綱目

P'êng-lai
蓬萊

P'êng Yün-chang
彭蘊章

Pi-fêng-mên
碧逢門

P'i-p'a
琵琶

Pi-shu-shan-chuang
避暑山庄

P'i-tan
皮蛋

Pien-fu
蝙蝠

Pin-lang
檳榔

Ping
餅

P'ing-hai
平海

P'ing-p'an
拼盤

Ping-p'i
冰皮

P'ing-wang
平王

Po-ping
薄餅

Po-po
餑餑

Pu
補

Pu-lu
補碌

P'u-t'i-ssu
菩提寺

San-ts'ai
三才

San-tsang
三藏

San-tzu
饊子

Sashimi
さしみ (刺身)

Satsuma-imo
薩摩いも

Sê-mu
色目

Sha-t'ien
沙田

Sha-t'ien-yu
沙田柚

Shan-cha
山楂

Shan-yü
山芋

Shan-yü (eels)
鱔魚

Shang
商

Shao-hsing
紹興

Shih 豉 or (tou) shih
豆豉

Shih-huang-ti
始皇帝

Shih-kao
柿糕

Shih-liao chih-ping
食料治病

Shih-lo
石螺

Shih-mo I-sun
石抹宜孫

Shih-pên
世本

Shih-ping
柿餅

Shih-shuang
柿霜

Shik-ye-chuk
食夜粥

Shiso
紫蘇

Shuang-huang
雙黃

Shuang-huang (tune)
雙簧

Shun
舜

Shun-ti
順帝

Ssu-ku ch'üan-shu
四庫全書

Su Tung-po
蘇東坡

Sui-yüan shih-tan
隨園食單

Sung
宋

Sung-nan
淞南

Sung-nan yüeh-fu
淞南樂府

Sung Yü
宋玉

Susuki
すすき (薄)

Ta-chi
妲己

Ta-p'an-tzu
大盤子

Ta-ti
大地

Ta-ts'ai
大菜

Ta-tu
大都

Ta-tzu
撻子

Ta-wan-ts'ai
大碗菜

T'ai-chou
臺州

T'ai-hu
太湖

T'ai-ts'ai yüeh-ping
苔菜月餅

T'ai-tsung
太宗

T'ang (dynasty)
唐

T'ang
湯

T'ang-kuo
糖菓

T'ang-sêng
唐僧

T'ang-yüan
湯圓

T'êng-lo-hua
藤蘿花

Têng-mien-fên
澄麵粉

Têng-yün
登雲

Teriyaki
でりやき

T'i-chiang
提漿

Ti I
狄儀

T'ien-chu
甜竹

T'ien-lo
田螺

Ting-yüan
定遠

T'o
酡

Tou-pan-chiang
豆瓣醬

Tou-sha
豆砂

Ts'ai-ch'üan
猜拳

Ts'ai-kua
菜瓜

Ts'ai-ling-tu
揉菱渡

Ts'ai-mei
猜枚

Ts'ao-kuo
草菓

Tsuei-ma-faar
脆麻花

Ts'ui-lien
翠蓮

Tsung-tzu
粽子

T'u-chih
土芝

T'u-êrh-yeh
兔兒爺

Tu K'ang
杜康

T'u-ti-kung
土地公

t'u-t'ou
土豆

T'u-tzu-wang
兔子王

T'uan-yüan-ping
團圓餅

Tung Chi
董汲

Tung Yung
董永

tzu
子

Tzu (Cakes)
餈

Tzu-lai-hung
自來紅

Tzu-lai-pai
自來白

Tzu-su
紫蘇

Ue-shaang
魚生

Ue-waat
魚滑

Wang
王

Wei
魏

Wên-ch'ang-hsien
文昌縣

Wên-chou
溫州

Wo-k'ou
倭寇

Wu Ch'êng-ên
吳承恩

Wu-chiu pu ch'êng-chia
無酒不成佳

Wu-jên
五仁

Wu-kang
吳綱

Wu-lin chiu-shih
武林舊事

Wu-wang
武王

Ya-jun-ch'ang
鴨閏腸

yang
陽

Yang-k'o
楊核

Yang-k'o-tzu
楊核子

Yang Kuang-fu
楊光輔

Yao
堯

Yeh
椰

Yeh-tzu
椰子

Yeh-tzu-kao
椰子糕

Yeh-yüeh
夜月

Yen
燕

Yin
殷

yin (negative)
陰

Yin-shan chêng-yao
飲膳正要

Yin-ho
銀河

Yin-ho yeh-yüeh
銀河夜月

Ying-chou
潁州

Yu
由

Yu (Pomelo)
柚

Yü
虞

Yü (Taro)
芋

Yü-chieh
芋莢

Yu-chou t'u-fêng yin
幽州土風吟

Yü-nai
芋艿

Yü-nan
遇難

Yü-shêng
魚生

Yü-shêng-chou
魚生粥

Yü-t'ou
芋頭

Yu-wang
幽王

Yüan
元

Yüan Mei
袁枚

Yüan-hsiao
元宵

Yüan-sai-chiang
原晒醬

Yüan-sui-ping
芫荽餅

Yüan-yang-chên
鴛鴦陣

Yüeh
月

Yüeh-hua
月華

Yüeh-ling
月令

Yüeh-ping
越病

Yüeh-ping (Moon Cake)
月餅

Yüeh-sê chiang-shêng
月色江聲

Yüeh-wang-t'ou
越王頭